Pets for Legion

Shawn David Brink

Pets for Legion

Pets for Legion ©2021, Shawn David Brink

Tell-Tale Publishing Group, LLC

Swartz Creek, MI 48473

Printed in the United States of America

And he asked him, *What is thy name?* And he answered, saying, *My name is Legion: for we are many.* – Mark 5:9 – *The Bible (KJV)*

Chapter 1

Sasha James sat at the teacher's lounge table and stared at her calorie-heavy lunch. The longer she stared, the deeper she frowned. The school year was only three weeks in and she was already five pounds heavier. It was sad to see the regression after last year's weight-loss. Her diet had been due to emotional baggage and stress. Added to that was the societal belief that skinniness was a virtue.

Getreide, Iowa, had been founded back in the late nineteenth century by German immigrants and not much had changed in its ethnic makeup since then. So, of course it stood to reason that the lunch ladies at Getreide Lutheran Parochial Elementary would be of old-world traditions using only full-calorie ingredients.

She stared at the pile of kraut flanked with brats. Then she looked at the carton of milk sitting beside it. That milk just didn't fit. A stein of beer seemed more appropriate.

Sasha laughed as she imagined the ridiculousness of the students hoisting oversized mugs of beer in the air as they licked their trays clean. In her mind's eye, all the boys wore lederhosen while every girl had on a dirndl.

"What's so funny?"

The polka music blaring in her head faded as the voice spoke to her. "Hmm?"

"What's so funny? I heard you laugh just now," said Mr. Kahler, the only other teacher in the room.

"Oh, it's just something I was thinking," she said hoping to avoid an awkward situation.

Mr. Kahler nodded, regarding her for a moment through wire-rimmed glasses before returning focus to his newspaper.

Smooth, she thought to herself. Sasha was not good in new situations even though she had experienced many lately with her divorce, having to find a new place to live, and obtaining a job as an elementary school paraprofessional.

She felt the need to amend her previous statement in an attempt to minimize the weirdness factor. "It's just that sometimes things are hilarious in your mind, but if you said them out loud, people would think you were a bit unbalanced."

Mr. Kahler lowered his paper just enough to peek out at her. Those eyes told her the truth. He already saw her as a bit unbalanced. Much to her relief, he broke the stare after only a second and went back to his reading.

"I trust you got yourself all settled into your new place," he spoke without removing the newspaper barrier that stood between them.

"Yes. Thanks for asking." She knew that the school's principal had asked Mr. Kahler to help move her things in, but he had declined at the last moment citing illness. "I hope you're feeling better."

"What?"

"You were ill on the day when I moved in, remember?"

"Oh, yes. I am feeling better. Thanks for asking." The silence that followed his statement was uncomfortable. Luckily, Mr. Kahler continued. "I'm sorry I couldn't help you more. I trust that others showed up to assist?"

Nobody else came, but Sasha was not about to let that come out. "I got most everything moved in. I still have some things at a storage facility which I'll need to move at a later date."

"Well," Mr. Kahler responded. "I still have your address. Do let me know when you need help with the remainder and I will see what can be done."

Feeling sufficiently patronized, she decided to resume eating her million-calorie lunch. Her first bite was halfway from the tray to her mouth, when shouting sounded from outside followed by screams.

Sasha jumped to her feet just as the room's window shattered. "What in the world...?"

Mr. Kahler dropped his paper and stared at her with a dazed look before slumping into a pile on the floor. Beside Mr. Kahler's body was the rock which presumably broke the glass.

"Oh my gosh! Oh my gosh! Oh my gosh!" she repeated as she ran to him.

The stone didn't break the skin, but a lump was already visible on his head. She checked his pulse. He had one. She checked to see if he was breathing. He was.

The screaming from beyond the window continued. She ran to it and looked out.

There she saw a child being chased by a man with a knife. The assailant wore a hooded sweatshirt with the hood pulled up, hiding his identity.

On instinct, she knocked out the remaining glass with her food tray and jumped out the window. Shrubs and soft ground broke the six foot drop.

She scrambled out of the shrubbery, winced at her many scratches and stood up.

Now on ground level, she realized a group of students and teachers were crowded around the fight. A few were strangers, people who she assumed were passing by and stopped to either help or gawk.

Sasha couldn't see what was going on. A big man stood in front of her. He was wearing a red baseball cap, dressed in jeans and a denim shirt. He reminded her of her ex-husband, built like a football linebacker. Unlike her ex, however, this man had long reddish hair that went half-way down his back.

The screaming continued. Why wasn't anyone doing anything? She gripped the bystander in front of her. Grabbing fistfuls of that denim shirt, she braced her feet against the backs of his heels and flung him behind.

Under other circumstances, she doubted that she could have performed this act, but she was overdosed on adrenaline and he had obviously been caught off guard.

He cussed as he fell. Maybe later, she would have the opportunity to apologize, but not now.

With Mr. Linebacker out of her path, she could see. What she saw, however, drew the blood from her veins.

The hooded man with the knife had taken down the student. Straddling the child, he raised the knife above his head, the blade pointed downward.

She held her breath in terror, waiting for the sacrifice to commence, but for some reason the knife did not come down. Taking advantage of the delay, she ran up to the attacker and kicked the weapon out of his grasp.

"What are you doing?" she screamed.

The man said nothing. He simply looked up at her out of the darkness of his drawn hood. Underneath the assailant, the child's screams became sobs.

"Get off him!" she shrieked.

The man seemed slow to respond. It was an unsettling slowness.

In the distance, sirens blared.

The sirens seemed to draw Mr. Hoodie out of his stupor. He looked around with jittery movements.

"You heard the lady, get off him!" A nearby spectator shouted.

"Get off him now!" Sasha shouted.

"You tell him Ms. James," one of the other students chimed in.

Now that the man was unarmed, the crowd suddenly seemed braver, tightening the circle around him. Someone grabbed Mr. Hoodie by the shirt and pulled him off the student.

It was the man with the red cap and long hair. Sasha was glad that he seemed uninjured by his fall.

Together, they rolled off the student. Mr. Hoodie squirmed free of the other man's grip and then took off through the stunned crowd.

In a rage, Mr. Linebacker took off after him. The duo rounded the corner and were gone.

For Mr. Hoodie's sake, Sasha hoped that the police would get to him before Mr. Linebacker. She knew from experience that you just don't upset people of that size.

She looked down at the child. He was shaking and crying. Her heart went to him.

The crowd parted as the police arrived.

***

He ran, his cold eyes glaring from under the darkness of his drawn hood. He looked back only once, just to see if the big man still followed.

He failed. The chief would be disappointed.

Having outdistanced the larger man, he darted down an alley and hopped a fence. He entered the house, taking two steps past the threshold before hearing the door slam shut behind him. Spinning around, he saw the one he feared.

"Hello, Clay. How did things go today?" the chief wanted to know.

Clay looked down so that the fringe of his hood hid the man from his view.

"You failed me didn't you?"

Clay fidgeted with his hood. "I tried my best, Chief."

"Your job was simple. Kill Daniel. That was all you had to do."

"Yes, but some woman showed up. It was her fault that I failed, not mine. She ruined everything."

The chief stared hard at Clay before nodding and drawing close. He put his arm around him, directing him deeper into the house. Together, they moved away from the entry through the kitchen and then the dining room where the doorway to the basement existed.

He was so close Clay could feel the fabric of the hood shift with every syllable the chief spoke. "This woman has become an obstacle to us."

"Yes, Chief."

"Well, we can't have obstacles now can we?"

"No, Chief."

"All obstacles to our plan must be eliminated."

"Yes, Chief."

"Then the answer is clear. We must remove this woman from the equation. Her sacrifice in lieu of Daniel's."

Clay nodded.

"Do you know who this woman is?"

"Her name is Ms. James," he answered, remembering what he'd heard one of the children shout. "She must work at the school. I saw her drop out of the window that Daniel broke with the rock he meant for me."

The chief opened the door do the basement. "Come. You need rest before tearing down this obstacle. You must rest."

"Yes, Chief."

Sounds drifted up through that open basement door, faint but audible. Somebody down there was crying. This was nothing new. There were often wailings of one sort or another drifting up those basement steps, but Clay would be able to rest despite the din. He always did.

"Rest for a few hours. Be refreshed. Then you can go after this woman, this Ms. James."

He nodded.

Together they descended the stairs.

Chapter 2

Getreide was a small town with limited resources. The volunteer officer who questioned her mumbled when he spoke. She judged him to be about seventy years old, yet his demeanor showed a total lack of experience.

Despite his amateur skills, or perhaps because of it, she gleaned some information regarding the situation. The child's name was Daniel Owens. He was a twin, but his brother had disappeared earlier that year. Unfortunately, the case had grown cold. No leads and no tips.

Regarding today's incident, Daniel claimed that he didn't know his attacker. They had confiscated the stranger's knife and hoped the forensic lab could pull some readable prints, but of course that would take time.

It was 5:30 in the afternoon before Sasha James left Getreide Lutheran Parochial Elementary. The school had been on lock-down status until the police verified that no other threat existed. Then, and only then, were parents allowed to come and claim their children.

With a lot on her mind, she left the school in her Ford Focus Hatchback, which until recently, had served both as her transportation and residence. The divorce had left her destitute and she had only begun to rebuild her life.

She drove home to her newly acquired studio apartment, a place that seemed like a mansion compared to her previous living arrangement. She felt grateful.

***

The chief ascended the basement stairs, making sure Clay was sleeping soundly before leaving. Given the task at hand, he wanted him fully rested and at peak performance.

Without a sound, the chief locked up the house and backed his white Chevy S-10 out of the garage, turned it around and began the slow drive down his long gravel driveway.

He lived in the middle of town, yet, he enjoyed the privacy of a big lot. The old house could not be seen from the street due to the mature pines that dominated the property. The rear of the lot backed up against Getreide Creek. To the east were railroad tracks and to the west was his only neighbor, a lot owned by a trucking company who used it for parking trailers.

He liked the seclusion. It allowed him to explore the darker places in life.

Most people would not appreciate these darker places. Then again, most people did not share his history.

Unlike the rest of the world, the darkness took him for what he was. It never judged him or pushed him around but simply accepted him for who he was.

He came to a stop at the end of the drive and watched the cars pass by. He grinned as he watched. Those who drove by were all like rats in a lab - all of them running as fast as they could through the daily grind of a maze in order to get their chunk of cheese and waste away in the perpetual motion machine of life.

None of them understood that he was the scientist running the lab. He was the one controlling the rats and changing up the maze. He decided who got the cheese and who went without, who lived and who died.

He turned out onto the street, motivated to embark on this little mission of discovery. He was eager to learn more about the mysterious Ms. James that worked at Getreide Lutheran Parochial Elementary, the one who dared delay the execution of his planned itinerary.

He thought about this as he drove on and smiled, because he had an acquaintance at the school who he was sure could be persuaded to help him.

Chapter 3

The only light in the room came from a small reading lamp. He draped an old, red t-shirt over it to dampen the harshness.

He sat alone in the macabre, crimson glow and tried to relax, reclining in his easy chair with a damp washcloth over his eyes.

In one hand, he held a glass that had once contained bourbon on the rocks. Now only the rocks remained.

Mr. Kahler removed the damp washcloth and pressed the bottom of the glass against the throbbing bruise on his forehead, wincing as the coldness shocked his injury.

He couldn't believe his horrible luck. That rock could have sailed anywhere. It could have landed harmlessly on the floor. It could have even struck the one who had been rudely yammering while he was trying to read the newspaper, but no, it landed right on his noggin.

The paramedics told him he was lucky to have sustained nothing more than a bruise. Given the size of that rock, they said it could have been much worse, even fatal.

Mr. Kahler scoffed. He certainly didn't feel lucky.

Given recent events, he wouldn't have minded a fatal blow, but apparently, that just wasn't in the cards. What he did have was one massive headache.

He needed to grade some papers, but he lacked the desire to do so. Besides, having just consumed his second bourbon, he was in no condition for such work.

He decided to have a third drink and call in sick tomorrow when the doorbell rang. He looked at his clock. It was almost seven in the evening, not too late for company. Still it was an unusual thing for his doorbell to ring. A lifelong loner, he rarely entertained visitors.

The doorbell rang again and he struggled to get himself out of the recliner. "Just a second!"

The bourbon in his system slowed down his progress, but after wiggling like the worm he was, he managed to get to his feet.

Ding dong!

"I said just a second!"

Ding dong! Ding dong! Ding dong!

Mr. Kahler pulled the door open with all of his might. He was in no mood for this. "What in the blazes do you want?!"

His shout died as he recognized the white Chevy S-10 in his driveway. His eyes traveled from that truck to the one on his porch just as his body went numb with fear.

The empty bourbon glass fell from his hands. He heard it shatter upon the threshold, but he did not look down because the one who stood before him commanded his complete attention.

***

Shards of glass and half-melted ice cubes skidded along the hardwood entryway, but the chief took no notice. He was having too much fun staring down the one who answered the door.

He enjoyed watching this one squirm. Mr. Kahler had always been a timid man, but now as he stared him straight in the eye, he could tell that the man was 100% spineless.

After a moment, the chief spoke. "That's quite a nasty lump you got there, Andrew," he said, using Mr. Kahler's first name. "What on Earth happened to you?"

"I'm sure you already know," came a sour response.

The chief was surprised. Perhaps there was a little spark in this one's belly after all. He didn't appreciate this newly found courage but decided to overlook it for the time being. "Oh, yes, Clay told me about a stray rock. So it found your head." He chuckled. "What bad luck that you were there. Talk about being in the wrong place at the wrong time."

Mr. Kahler responded with a huff. The chief could smell bourbon on Andrew's breath and his uncharacteristic burst of courage suddenly made sense. "May I enter?"

Despite the inebriation, the chief could see the courage dissolve at his request. Still, Mr. Kahler did not move.

"Can I come in, Andrew?"

After a brief hesitation, Andrew stepped aside. The chief walked in, carefully stepping over the shattered glass and melting ice.

"You had better clean up that broken glass. Don't you think?" the chief said knowing that he now had his puppet by the strings.

Andrew knelt down and began picking up the shards. "Ouch!"

The chief's satisfaction level increased exponentially as he watched Andrew put his pricked finger into his mouth. "Careful. We don't want you to get hurt now do we?"

Andrew looked up with his finger still in his mouth. By the expression on his face, the chief could tell that his insinuation had hit home.

"Shut the door, Andrew."

Andrew shut the door.

"So, as you know, Clay stopped by the school today."

Andrew Kahler remained silent.

"He came for Daniel."

Still no response.

"Of course, you know that Daniel was next on the list, so that shouldn't really surprise you."

He saw Andrew cringe at this statement. He always had responded that way when hearing mention of "the list."

"But, unfortunately, we can't cross Daniel off just yet."

Mr. Kahler let out something resembling a whimper.

"A woman got in the way." He drew nearer to poor, old Andrew and continued with little more than a whisper. "Can you believe it, Andrew? There was a whole crowd around the scene, but no one had the guts to intervene. They were all spellbound except for this little lady."

"I don't understand," Andrew spoke around his injured finger. "What does this have to do with me?"

"Oh, it has much to do with you. You see, I believe she works at the school. I'm sure that you know who she is. I need information about her. We can't have people like this running around. She is an impediment to the agenda. Don't you agree?"

Andrew's removed the injured finger from his mouth and the chief could see that the man's lip was trembling. After a moment, Andrew nodded.

"I am glad we're on the same page. Now, what do you know about this woman who is resistant to our spells? Who exactly is this Ms. James?"

The look in his little puppet's eyes told the chief that Andrew knew the woman in question. And yet he chose to lie. "I don't know her." he paused before adding, "I only know of her."

"I see," the chief responded as he sat Andrew down in the recliner next to a red-draped lamp. "Well, I hope for your sake that you know enough of her to satisfy my curiosity."

Andrew grew visibly paler before the chief's eyes, and the chief did not have the luxury of patience. For Andrew's sake, he hoped that a dialog would soon commence.

"Like I said before, Andrew, I don't want you to get hurt."

Chapter 4

Sasha entered her apartment and went straight to the fridge. The day's events certainly burned some extra calories. Plus, she hadn't had the chance to eat her lunch after all that occurred.

She opened the refrigerator. Inside, there were only two items, a half-eaten package of sliced bologna and a small squeeze-bottle of off-brand mustard. Little could be done to improve her situation until she received the next paycheck. With a sigh, she took a slice of the pink meat, squirted on some mustard, and with a prayer of thanks, began to eat.

Cellphones weren't exactly a luxury to most people, but they were to her, as least for now. Luckily, her landlord included a no frills or long distance landline with her rent.

She looked at her answering machine, which was as obsolete as the landline, but it was free and free was good.

Two messages. She hit the playback. The first message was from Gary Fitzpatrick Esquire, her divorce attorney. He said he was calling just to make sure she was okay. He had heard about some sort of disturbance at the school and wanted to make sure it had nothing to do with her ex-husband. Her ex was under court order to stay away from her. So far, he had obeyed that order and had probably been too drunk ever since to go after her even if he had wanted to. She suspected that her attorney was more interested in getting paid than about her safety. The man had a wardrobe of thousand dollar suits and a new BMW to make payments on, after all.

She had no intention of calling him back that evening, not after the day she had experienced. Maybe tomorrow, she would call him back and let him know that his portion of her paycheck would be arriving in his bank account on-time and uninterrupted.

The message ended. She hit delete. The next message was a tear-jerker. It was from Daniel's mother. The message of praise and thanks and weeping went on until her machine cut it off.

Sasha's heart went out to Daniel's mother. That woman had been through so much. In fact, that whole family had. She jumped from her thoughts as the phone rang. Of course, the landline had no caller ID.

She picked up on the second ring. "Hello?"

No answer.

"Hello?"

Just breathing.

"Richard?" Her voice trembled as she said her ex-husband's name. "Richard, if this is you, then, you had better hang up right now!" She said attempting an air of authority.

Click. Whoever it was hung up.

She told herself that the caller had probably just misdialed. Still, she got up and locked the door with trembling hands.

***

The chief hung up the phone and stared at the lamp with the red t-shirt over the shade. She was home. "Sasha," he said out loud. The name rolled off his tongue like honey.

It felt good to call her by her first name, the name Mr. Kahler had divulged out of the goodness of his little heart. That name had not come easily but through a smidgeon of coercion.

At the conversation's beginning, Andrew acted as if he barely knew this woman. Luckily, he came to his senses and throughout the course of their little heart-to-heart, gave him everything he wished to know including her phone number and address.

The chief shook his head as he thought about how Andrew had been so reluctant to give him what he needed. "You always were a stubborn one, stubborn as a mule."

Andrew did not respond. He simply sat there, lounging in the recliner.

"You know, we're in this together, old chum," he continued. "As such, we need to work as a team for self-preservation, if for no other reason."

Andrew remained quiet and unmoving.

"This Sasha James has become an irritation. She would have done well to stay out of our affairs. Now, I really feel the need to remove her. She is an obstacle and as we both know obstacles are not permissible."

Andrew said nothing.

The chief flung gasoline all around the place and lit a match. The flames flashed to life. Still, Andrew did not get up or even stir.

"Well, the evening is fast waning. So, I think I will be going. No need to get up. I can see myself out."

***

The chief drove away from Andrew Kahler's place, glancing once or twice in the rearview mirror as it grew distant. Already, the windows of the house were flickering orange from the growing flames. Soon, the place would be engulfed and so would its lone occupant.

The chief wasn't remorseful about what he had done to Andrew. He had no room for remorse in his life. Anyway, everything that had occurred, although unfortunate, had been necessary. If he had not used less than conventional interrogation techniques, then no doubt, Andrew would have remained tight-lipped about Sasha.

He was a bit disappointed, though, that he had to eliminate poor, old Andrew. That man had been a great asset to the cause. Tonight, however, he realized how much of a liability that asset had become. The unavoidable fact was Andrew had to die.

He looked down at the paper which contained Sasha James' address. He would need to pay her a visit, but not alone.

Incinerating a house was one thing. After all, fire worked well as an evidence-destroyer. It was quite another thing, however, to murder a woman who lived in an apartment complex filled with residents. There would be too many potential witnesses.

Discretion was the key in the next phase in his mission. He would go back to his own home first and wake up Clay. Hopefully, his henchman would do better this time than he had before in the Daniel scenario.

Yes. For everyone's sake, he had better be more successful this time.

***

Andrew Kahler had grown to hate the chief. That man had weaseled his way into his life acting like a friend, when all along, he had been a snake waiting for the right moment to strike.

At first, it all seemed so innocent, just a man wanting a friend. This appealed to Andrew. He was a loner with so few friends. But, oh, how things escalated over time.

On a certain level, he blamed Getreide Lutheran Parochial Elementary. If they only paid their teachers what they were worth and kept their confidential student records more secure, then he would never have given in to the temptation that the chief offered.

Deep down, he knew that the blame rested on him, but if he ever truly admitted that to himself, then he would also have to admit that he was a murderer, and that was something that he could not live with.

He felt strangely warm but could not recall turning up the thermostat. He tried to remember the events of the day, but it was all quite blurry.

Bits and pieces flashed into his memory. He remembered, for example enjoying a good glass of bourbon. Or was it a few glasses? Was that why his mind seemed so off kilter?

He wasn't by nature a big drinker. So, why had he felt the need to drink today? The answer flashed before him. *Daniel was almost murdered.*

Andrew Kahler cringed, because he was the snitch who led to this murder attempt just as he was the snitch responsible for the demise of Daniel's brother and many others. He had never wanted anything like that to happen to anyone, but he was in too deep now. Coming clean would mean jail time for Andrew the snitch. He knew the saying about snitches in prison: snitches get stitches. He didn't want stitches.

Until today, he went with the flow. But, today, he made a decision. He would not be an accomplice to murder anymore.

My gosh, it is warm in here, he thought as further memories invaded his mind.

Despite the consequences, he was proud of his actions today. He had not taken pride in himself for quite some time, but today he finally acted like a man. Today, he could stand tall.

He told the chief face-to-face that he was dropping out.

Things spiraled down from there as Andrew suspected that they would. He took the beating like a man feeling the punishment was well-deserved for his many sins; his only regret was he had not been killed. He had wanted death, in fact, he had begged for it, but the chief denied mercy in his standard, sadistic fashion.

Under the chief's thumb, he may have given away Sasha James' information. He wasn't sure though. What he endured left his mind hazy.

He tried to open his eyes. One wouldn't open at all, too swollen. The other eye was better off since the bruise had burst and drained. That eye stung from heat and smoke.

What he saw terrified him. Flames were everywhere. He was either in a fire, or he had arrived in Hell.

He tried to move but found it difficult to get out of that recliner. On the third attempt, he succeeded, rolling off the chair and onto the floor.

Andrew moaned. He hurt from head to toe.

He bumped his hand against the recliner and howled. That's when he remembered one of his fingers being broken. The chief had used a meat tenderizer from the kitchen to do that job.

He tried to stand up but quickly fell back to the ground as a few of his toes were like that finger. Plus, the air was clearer near the floor.

For a moment, he thought about just letting the flames consume him. It would be an excruciating way to go, but perhaps going out this way would serve as penance for his evil deeds.

Then, he thought of the chief. The man was alive and well, certainly not roasting to death. Such thoughts brought a rage that motivated him to live.

He began to crawl in the direction that, he hoped, would lead him out of the thicket of fire. The smoke and blaze was disorienting. The heat was unbearable.

He heard a crash. The ceiling gave way in front of him. A wall of burning debris now blocked his way.

There would be no escape in that direction. He turned back, but the flames had risen there as well, caging him.

He wailed like a baby, his tears evaporating before they made it more than an inch down his cheeks.

The heat was intense. He put his hands over his face as a shield. When he pulled them away, the skin on his face came with them.

He only had two choices. He could sit there and die, or he could push through the flames, and probably still die.

He stood up. He rushed the fire. Agony assaulted him as his flesh roasted.

Chapter 5

The chief went home and entered his house. Without pause, he went into the basement. It was time to wake up his little sleeping beauty.

The basement was average for the house's style and age. It had a concrete floor, mason-block walls, and a ceiling with exposed rafters that supported the level above. In more recent years, a previous owner had divided the basement up into a series of rooms using simple frames and drywall. The chief stood in the first room and turned on the light.

This room was the largest of the basement. It ran the length of the house just slightly wider than what would be considered a hallway with separate rooms off to one side. He saw Clay resting just where he knew he would be at the opposite end of the basement.

Clay needed no blanket and so the chief had never supplied him one. He was curled up like an oversized fetus upon the cold concrete. He had removed his hoodie and was using it as a pillow.

The chief neared his henchman and nudged him with his foot. "Get up, Clay. We have work to do."

Clay's eyes opened and stared up at his chief. He sat up and stretched his arms.

"Are you rested?" he asked Clay.

"Yes, Chief."

"Tonight we must eliminate that which has gotten in our way."

"Yes, Chief."

"You will need additional power for this job, not that I expect this Sasha James to be a particularly hard challenge but better safe than sorry as people like to say."

"Yes, Chief."

"Come with me below."

The chief looked down at the hole which had been dug near where Clay liked to sleep. He remembered the day when the digging first commenced, the day those voices first called his name. He'd only had an old miner's pick to chip away at the concrete, but it was all he needed.

Together, he and Clay descended into the hole. It was dug at an angle and went about 20 feet below the basement. It was not a difficult descent. He had retrofitted railing along the side, strung multiple strings of old Christmas lights along the ceiling and cut out simple stairs from the hardened dirt in the places where the descent became particularly steep.

Standing side by side at the bottom, the chief turned on a flashlight. Here was where the tunnel connected to the cavern.

"The doorstep to the underworld," Clay whispered.

"Yes, Clay," the chief answered.

"This is a where I was born."

"Yes, Clay. This is your home."

Clay smiled proudly, but his smile disappeared as a sorrowful noise traveled up from the cavern's unseen reaches. It was a sad moaning, sad.

"Don't be afraid," the chief coaxed his henchman. "You know that we need more power within you.

Clay hesitated. Then nodded.

"You know what we need to do in order to get that power."

Clay nodded again.

"We must go see the pet."

The chief nudged Clay, and together they began to walk. With every step, the moaning grew louder and the chief grew more covetous for the power that would soon pour into his servant's body. As they progressed through the cavern, the smell of the air changed to the smell of rotten eggs forgotten in an unplugged refrigerator.

Beyond the range of the flashlight, water trickled. The chief heard it but could not tell if it was nearby or far off. The cavern was very mysterious in that way; sometimes making him feel claustrophobic and other times hinting at infinity.

The moaning one was near now. Along with that forlorn sound, the chief heard chains rattling. In the distance, he saw the red glowing and knew he was near his destination. The glowing marked the doorway to the underworld. Still, the chief kept the flashlight on.

They rounded a speleothem corner and there it was. Calling it a doorway was gracious. It was nothing but a crack in the cavern floor, perhaps five feet wide and 30 feet long and glowing with a deep, red light, the color of coagulating blood.

Here the air was so stench-filled it felt thick as the chief inhaled it into his lungs. He could feel the hairs on his head wave slightly as he approached. Hot air currents commanded them.

He heard the chains again as they dragged somewhere in the unseen gloom. There was only one way to locate the one shackled to those chains. He went to the column which the chain had been fastened around.

This column was ancient and scared from the chains that had rubbed against it for so long. Eons ago, it had been a stalactite dripping onto a stalagmite base, but over the generations the two had merged somewhere in the middle. It was now one massive entity, solid and imposing.

The chain was intentionally long. He wanted his guest to have freedom to move about within the confines of his prison.

The chain zigged and zagged out into darkness away from the light of the crack. The chief pointed his flashlight in that direction, but the beam was insufficient to illuminate the one on the end of the chain.

He took one step and hesitated. Even with the flashlight, he did not like the idea of venturing into the darkness to fish out such a desperate prisoner. Desperation bred unpredictability and unpredictability spelled danger. Only a fool took such an unnecessary risk, and he was no fool.

Instead, he picked up the chain. He would pull the prisoner to him in lieu of hunting him out of the darkness.

He was about to start pulling when it happened. First, shock. Then, pressure becoming pain, followed by frustration. The chain wrapped tightly around his neck as the pet clung to his back, leveraging the chief's own body against him. He leaned forward, trying to buck the pet off but to no avail.

This act reeked of desperation. This was not the child who had been brought here a month ago. This being at the end of his rope was willing to do anything to survive.

He looked at Clay, but poor, old Clay remained the same as always: slow and dim. The chief was indeed Clay's master only reacting when commanded. Taking the initiative simply wasn't in Clay's wiring.

He tried to command Clay, but the chain was wrapped tight. Speech failed him. Instead, only a rattling gasp escaped his lips.

Time for another tactic. As hard as he could, he slammed back against the column, smashing the child with all his strength.

The one on his back shrieked a pain-ridden shriek, but the chains around his neck did not loosen. He slammed him again and again.

He lost count of how many times he slammed the pet into the column. The chief's vision became spotty, evidence that his oxygen levels were dropping. If he lost consciousness, then the pet would no doubt have his revenge. He could not allow that to happen.

Rallying his strength, he slammed the pet into the column with all he had left. Finally, the chains around his neck loosened.

Those steel links slacked only minutely and only for a moment, but that was all the chief needed to command his dim-witted henchman. "Clay, get him off me!"

Clay jolted as if being startled from a daydream. Instantly, he grabbed the pet and peeled him off the chief's back, holding him in mid-air as if he were no more of a threat than a newborn kitten.

Doubled over and coughing, the chief was grateful for Clay's strength. Being both loyal and strong, Clay's only flaw was a general lack of intellect.

After a moment, he turned and looked at the chained imp that still dangled from the end of Clay's tree-branch limbs. The kid was kicking and punching, but Clay didn't seem to care.

The prisoner began to scream. They were not the screams of a human, but something that had devolved into something less.

"Shut him up!" the chief commanded.

Immediately, Clay took one of his spade-shovel sized hands and pressed it over the little wraith's face. The silence that ensued was most satisfying.

Chapter 6

The lights from numerous Fire and Rescue vehicles illuminated a scape of blackened ash and destruction. This was all that remained after the flames had taken their share.

The firemen did what they could, which was little more than ensure that the blaze didn't spread to neighboring houses. There was no point in doing more as the home was a total loss.

Now that the flames were gone and only smoldering ashes remained, fire hoses doused the wreckage to eliminate flare-ups. As the water steamed over any remaining hotspots, the Captain looked over the ruins, hoping that the home had been vacant; knowing that if anyone had been inside, dental records would be needed for identification.

As he gazed over the carnage, a shiver escaped him.

***

The digital alarm clock on Sasha James' nightstand said it was 9:15 at night. She had been trying to sleep for over an hour. She usually didn't go to bed this early, but with all of the stress the day had brought, she felt the need for recuperation. No such luck.

Sleep eluded her. Images of the past day's events flashed before her every time she closed her eyes. More than once, sleep drew near only to flee as she jolted in her bed, thinking her phone was ringing and terrified that Richard was on the other end of the line. At those moments, she would pick up the receiver only to hear the dial tone and nothing more.

Her thoughts also drifted to memories of Mr. Hoodie, the mysterious would-be murderer.

She finally gave up when sirens screamed to her from somewhere beyond the walls of her apartment. With the sirens came the booming of a fire engine horn somewhere outside.

She wondered where the fire was. The sirens grew progressively weaker as the engine traveled further away from her. Then it was gone, leaving her in silence.

Kicking her covers from her, Sasha got up and turned on the light. She was thankful that she lived in a studio apartment. There were few places unseen at a glance.

She took the five feet journey from her bed to her kitchen table and sat down at the single chair. "Breath in – breath out. Breath in – breath out." She chanted her mantra focusing on a steady flow of air in hopes of calming herself. After a few minutes, she attained a state akin to relaxation.

Then, in the silence, she heard a noise.

Immediately, she tensed. She heard the noise again. It was coming from her bathroom.

The noise wasn't particularly loud. In fact, she would not have noticed it at all if she had not engulfed herself in such absolute silence.

She looked at her phone. Suddenly, it seemed so far away from her, sitting on the little end-table beside her bed. Who would she call, the police? And what would she say? *There's a noise coming from my bathroom.* It sounded so weak in her head.

She stood up and grabbed her only weapon. The softball bat had been Richard's but she had requisitioned it.

The noise continued, a light ticking, tapping sound. Could it be a dripping faucet? No. It was not rhythmic enough to be a drip. *Tick, tap, tap, tick.* It continued its non-steady beat.

She thought of simply turning and fleeing the apartment. Then what? Fear ruled her past, but she pledged it would do so no more. Keeping her old habits at bay, she stood her ground.

Slowly, she approached the bathroom. *Tick, tap, tap, tick, tap.*

Looking down, she glanced at the shaft of light emanating from under the door. She liked to keep that light on so that she could find her way to the toilet during the night.

She detected no shadow. Yet, she could not conclude definitively that nothing was standing on the far side of that door waiting for her. The noise continued.

She grabbed the door's knob in one hand while preparing to swing the bat with the other, but she did not turn the knob. Nor did she open the door. Her situation was far from optimal, preferring to have both hands on the bat, but unable to do so if she was to open the door. She stood there mid-pose deciding what to do.

"I know you're in there," she said as she let go of the doorknob in lieu of a two-handed grip on her weapon. "Come out and nobody gets hurt."

She hated the sound of her voice at that moment. It certainly did not make her sound like a woman who had left her fears behind.

"I said come out!"

She waited. Nothing happened. The sound continued. *Tick, tap, tick.*

She reached for the knob once again. Her hand was trembling and it took all of her concentration to grab it.

When she finally succeeded, the vibrations from her shivering body rattled the door. *So much for the element of surprise.*

She couldn't back down, not now. Committed to her strategy and without other options, she opened the door and swung the bat with all of her ability.

Her apartment was small. So was her bathroom. She knew that if she swung the bat, it would likely strike the intruder unless he or she was in the shower.

The bat met only air and stopped when it met the wall. The impact broke two bathroom tiles loose. They fell to the ground in pieces.

The shower curtain was open. The shower was empty.

She kept the bat at the ready, perplexed. As a rule, she didn't believe in ghosts. Yet, no other explanation presented itself.

Tick, tap, tick. The noise continued. She followed that sound and discovered a moth banging into the bathroom light. *Tap, tick, tick, tap.*

Suddenly, the bat felt heavy. She let it dangle from the end of her arm as she tried to catch her breath and slow her heartrate. Her nervous energy released in an uncontrolled laugh. She was glad to laugh. It was either that or cry. The moth, seeing its opportunity, exited the bathroom.

"You have got to get some sleep," she said to herself as she watched the big bad intruder flutter off in a storm of lepidopteran fury.

She opened the medicine cabinet in her bathroom and grabbed a bottle of sleeping pills. The doctor prescribed them to her shortly after she left Richard.

She always avoided taking those pills if she could help it. In fact, she took them only once before and slept a little too deep for comfort. After that, she swore she would never take them again. Yet, Sasha kept them and now was reconsidering her stand.

She popped the cap and put one of the pills in her mouth. Using a bit of water from her bathroom faucet, she washed the pill down her throat.

By the time she turned off the faucet and dragged the bat with her back to bed, the effects of the drug took hold. *Good,* she thought. *A good night's sleep will make everything feel better.*

She hugged her bat as if it were a cuddly teddy bear. Closing her eyes, she let the drug take her away. In the distance she could still hear the moth ticking and tapping, but she no longer cared and after a moment, even that sound evaporated into silence.

Chapter 7

The chief felt relieved. Clay didn't kill the pet. He only suffocated him to the point of losing consciousness. Good. He needed the boy alive. He needed his soul to appease those that resided in the nearby abyss.

Clay set the child down near the edge of the crevasse, illuminating the unconscious figure with devilish light from the hellfire within. The chief began the ritual of summoning those from within the abyss. He dropped to his knees while raising his hands above him. He closed his eyes not daring to look Legion in the face and breathed in the sulfuric, rotten egg scent of those who dwelled deep in that crack. "Legion!" he called out in a guttural tone. "Arise! Come to me!"

There was no response, but this was no surprise. Legion was often less than punctual but always came eventually. He thought back to when he had first heard Legion calling him. He was so lonely back then. In fact, it was his loneliness that drove him to spend hours with the Ouija board and even more hours digging from the basement to the cavern. His time and toil was not wasted. For here in the spirit world, he found friends, powerful friends, and they were many.

According to the Bible, Legion was such a powerful group that even Jesus had trouble defeating them. In fact, he banished them to this abyss. The chief didn't know what to think of Jesus, but he knew one thing - that man had died on the cross 2,000 years ago. Legion, on the other hand, was, is and would be always. Legion was tangible and Chief could see him, literally. Not so with Jesus.

Voices brought him out from his inner monolog. He dared not open his eyes but could feel the power of demons nearing him. Legion arrived.

"We are here," the voices called out to him in breathy whispers. "What is your desire?"

The chief found it difficult to speak as the power caressed his body. It was overwhelming, but he pushed passed it. "Clay has been stopped from killing the boy's twin."

"Who has stopped the killing?" Legion wanted to know.

The chief shivered. "It was a woman."

"What woman?"

"Her name is Sasha James. We know where she lives. I simply implore you to give power to us so as to ensure her elimination."

"No," came Legion's reply.

The chief didn't understand. "No?" Legion had never withheld power from him before.

"We will give you the power you need, but do not eliminate this Sasha James. We want her alive. Bring her to us as a sacrifice, as our next pet."

Wouldn't it be easier to just kill her? The chief thought but dared not ask out loud. *It would certainly be more enjoyable.* "Your wish is my command," he said instead.

"Bring her to us, and we will give you the ability to complete your plan."

The chief certainly did want to complete his plan. Seeking revenge on all who had ever wronged him was an ambitious plan. The list was indeed ponderously long. He once thought it impossible to complete. However, since joining with Legion, it had become doable.

He had already made good headway. The child at his feet, for example, was the progeny of homecoming royalty from his high school days. That Getreide royalty had made his high school years miserable. Now, he was giving them a little payback by kidnapping one of their sons for Legion's whims. The other son would soon die as well. In fact, if it weren't for Sasha James, Daniel would already be pushing daisies.

Andrew Kahler was another example of one who had picked on him back in the old days. Andrew had no children, so he could not seek his revenge through that means. The original plan had been simply to kill the man in some diabolical and painful way, but Andrew was such a spineless coward that such an act had hardly seemed sporting.

Instead, he chose to use him as a tool seeing value in Andrew's position at Getreide Lutheran Parochial Elementary. He knew from the start that Andrew would be a good resource to find other children whose parents he wished to hurt. In this regard, his tool had not disappointed until recently.

"I will bring Sasha James to you," the chief answered Legion, daring to open his eyes. "You will have her as your new pet, but please bestow power on Clay to ensure success."

Legion did not answer, but the glowing red from the abyss brightened into a glorious crimson. The entire cavern bathed in that brilliance as did the chief.

A wisp of flame rose from the abyss - Legion's essence. Its many selves could not leave the abyss, yet its essence had more freedom to influence space beyond its prison confines.

That essence surrounded Clay like a dark cloud before entering into him. The chief thought back to Clay's birth. His name was fitting. Clay was a golem, a figure created from the dirt in the cavern, and given life through the secret arts of which Legion had knowledge.

In Clay, the chief discovered what he never could in humans. Clay never bullied him. Clay never abandoned him. Clay was loyal (though a bit slow). He was just what the chief required.

And, the best part was that Clay did not exist, not really. He had no fingerprints. He had no birth certificate. He had no flesh and blood parents. He was the ideal goon, because he was a blank slate able to do the dirty work. This freed up the chief to enjoy the more private moments with the prisoners, in his home and away from prying eyes and pointing fingers.

Of course, the old adage was true: nobody's perfect. This held true for Clay as well. The power that Legion filled him with was temporary, and the more strength he required, the faster the reserve drained away. Also, Clay could only work if the chief was in close proximity. This second flaw could be frustrating at times. The chief didn't like being at the crime scenes where witnesses could implicate him. It was a miracle that this had not happened yet. Then again, it seemed that Legion had a way to cover the eyes of Getreidians.

The chief liked the relationship he had with Legion. In exchange for providing Legion with pets when requested, Legion would give the chief what he needed to further his plan of revenge. It was a contract signed in blood and binding to all parties.

He watched as the essence of Legion returned to the abyss leaving Clay virtually vibrating with power. Seeing such a tool at his disposal brought a grin to his face.

"Go. Bring Sasha James to us. Bring us our new pet," the many voices of Legion rasped.

Together, Clay and the chief ascended from the cavern to the basement and then to the main floor. Once out of the house, they backed out of the driveway in the S-10.

Chapter 8

Sasha fled. The hypocrisy in this act frustrated her as she swore she would never run from Richard again. Yet, here she was, scurrying away like a beaten dog, her tail between her legs.

She hid in her shower behind the pulled curtain and sensed that he was near. She chastised herself for not finding a better hiding place, one that offered more avenues for escape. Now, it was too late to change her decision.

At least she had her bat which would be dead from strangulation, from the tightness of her grip, if it had been a living thing.

Tick, tap, tick. The moth returned. The sound it made haunted her. It seemed so loud, and she feared Richard would hear.

In terror, she heard the bathroom door open and saw a dark figure through the opaque view of the curtain. She had seen Alfred Hitchcock's *Psycho*. She knew her situation was dire.

She readied the bat. The shower curtain opened. She swung.

***

She awoke but didn't move a muscle. Fear kept her still.

Her attention angled toward her alarm clock. It was 12:34 a.m.

Such nightmares were not uncommon when under the effects of sleeping pills or so said the warning label on the bottle. Still medicated, Sasha's eyelids closed as her mind drifted. At that same incoherent moment, she registered a new sound.

The noise wasn't overly loud or particularly malicious. It was simply a noise - a quiet, scrapping sound -- like metal against metal, then the click of a lock disengaging. The first sound stopped but another replaced it: a quiet creaking.

After that, a soft scuffing noise indicated footsteps upon her floor. Someone was drawing near.

In her nightmare, somebody was removing her comforter. In her sleeping pill-induced, semi-dream state, she found herself glad she had gone to bed fully clothed.

She felt something touching her bare foot. It felt like flesh but not living flesh. This flesh was as cold as the grave.

At her core, she knew that this event should alarm her. She remained calm, though. After all, she knew it had to be a return to her medication-induced dreams and nothing more.

As the touch rose from her foot to her ankle and then her calf, she noticed a smell. It reminded her of high school pottery class, like modeling clay.

"Pick her up," a voice whispered.

This is no dream! she suddenly realized as adrenaline flooded her body. She wanted to scream, but terror took away Sasha's voice. Instead, she swung the bat and cracked a home run.

The connection of the bat reverberated through her body. Whatever she hit fell off to the side of her bed like a bag of wet cement.

She scurried off the opposite side and turned on the reading lamp beside her bed. In that faint glow, she saw a dusting of something reddish-brown upon the nearest wall. The same speckled her bat. It didn't look like brains. Keeping her bat in battle position she slowly moved around the end of her bed to get a better look at her victim.

She could see his feet sticking out from behind the far side of her bed, wide, large, and bare. The intruder was lying on his back.

One of the toes twitched minutely, a disturbing action. She crept closer. Leaned over the bed to get a better look. She was sure that the fallen one was dead.

His skull had been flattened where bat and cranium had met, yet something was amiss. The condition of the skull should have meant exposed gray matter and lots of blood. Yet she saw nothing of the sort only that strange reddish dirty substance.

Again, her nose caught the scent of modeling clay. She looked down at his face and stared into vacant eyes.

She did not like those eyes staring at her. She moved a bit to the left to remove herself from that line of vision, but like a portrait in a haunted house, that gaze seemed to follow her movements.

Sasha considered reaching down to force the lids closed but refrained. She couldn't bring herself to touch the corpse.

She needed to call the police, but the phone was on the end table beside her bed. Between that end table and herself was the deceased. The thought of reaching past that body in order to get her phone repulsed her.

Spinning from the victim, another noise drew her! It came from the bathroom and this time did not sound like a moth. She readied the bat.

The bathroom door was open just a crack revealing darkness beyond. The bathroom light was off. This was the same light that she left on earlier.

"Stay where you are!" She wished her voice sounded tougher than it did.

She jolted back toward the body beside her bed. The deceased began to stir. The body twitched. The dead man sat up!

Impossible, she thought to herself. She tried to scream, but terror choked it out. The bat dropped from her hand as her fingers went numb.

The man let out a moan as his eyes zeroed in on her. Those eyes were still lifeless and a bit askew because of the deformation she had cause him. Yet, he lived!

The intruders left her apartment door open. Sasha took the opportunity and fled.

***

The chief came out of the bathroom and helped his golem up. It always amazed him to watch Clay heal. His skull was already remolding back into the proper shape. In another few seconds, he would be as good as new.

They should have had her. It should have been easy. Of course the bat was a surprise. *Who sleeps with a bat anyway?* He only barely had time to duck into the bathroom before being spotted. The chief wondered how many more surprises hid up this woman's sleeve and vowed higher vigilance the next time he encountered her.

Without delay, the chief and Clay ran from the apartment so as to create distance between themselves and the crime scene. Even with the town under Legion's influence, it was likely that somebody heard Sasha's shouts, and he certainly didn't need any witnesses.

Plus, Sasha was escaping. Every second was precious in their pursuit.

***

Sasha slammed into the side of her Ford, frantically pulling on the door's handle. It was locked, and there was no way that she was going back for the keys hanging on a hook inside her apartment.

Standing under the glow of those sodium vapor security lamps normally made her feel safer but not now. Now, she felt exposed like an escaping inmate caught in the spotlight from the prison tower.

She heard footsteps and ducked behind her car, daring to peek around the corner just enough to see. Two figures emerged into the light. One was her attacker. His head was no longer misshapen, but she was sure it was him. Even from that distance she sensed those vacant eyes of his. The second figure was a stranger. The one from her bathroom? Perhaps.

She was fairly certain that they had not spotted her yet, but it would only be a matter of time. They were moving in her direction systematically checking around every car and clearing every shadow.

She glanced around, needing an escape route. She tried the car next to hers. It was also locked.

In the silence of the night she could hear the two hunters drawing nearer. One of the two had abnormally loud footsteps as if he weighed much more than his body suggested.

Her mind raced, trying to make sense of the nonsensical. One of those two should be dead without question. Her bat had hit a homer, right out of the park. His brains should be all over her bed right now. Yet, he not only survived, but appeared uninjured. The reality of that impossibility terrified her.

Sasha peeked out at them as they moved closer like two sharks following the scent of blood in the water.

She felt her heart pounding so hard against her sternum that it hurt. Her breathing quickened, her chugging lungs boomed loud in her ears.

It was suicide to stay as the circle around her tightened. She knew this, so she drew a deep breath, mustered her courage, and bolted.

Refusing to look back, knowing that doing so would only confirm that the chase was on, she ran. Around the corner of her building, she flew hoping she had enough of a lead to lose her pursuers.

She knew that in such situations, the victim should make as much noise as possible in order to get attention from neighbors, but she failed to draw in enough breath for a proper scream. All that came out was a sad wheeze.

Unable to resist the temptation, she glanced back. Two elongated shadows appeared black against the parking lot light from behind. Those shadows were drawing nearer. They were approaching.

Frantic, she looked for any avenue of escape. Her eyes rested upon an old Dodge Dynasty the only car parked on that street.

Running to it, and discovering it was unlocked, she slid into the drivers' seat. Apparently the owner of that vehicle wasn't concerned with thieves because the keys were in the ignition.

She started it up simultaneously looking in her rear-view mirror. She saw them in the street running toward her, quickly eliminating the distance between them and her.

Recollections flooded her mind, memories of being the victim and promises that she would never be the victim again. Instead of escape, she chose to attack. She put the car into reverse and slammed the gas pedal down. Tires screeched as the car lurched to life.

There was a brief moment when she could see the still-lifeless eyes of the heavy-footed one. Those eyes widened as the car connected with his body. The sound of Detroit steel reshaping itself roared into her ears and soul.

The man went down hard as the vehicle careened over him. She slammed on the breaks. All grew still.

The stillness shattered. Someone was shrieking, someone inside the car. It took a second before she realized that it was her own voice. "Dear God, what have I done!"

Something from her peripheral vision drew her. She turned and locked the car's door in just the nick of time. The second man was there trying the handle and staring maliciously.

For a moment, their eyes locked. His stare was also cold and lifeless but in a different way from the one she smashed with the bat and subsequently ran over with the Dynasty.

"Get away from me!" she screamed.

The man ignored her commanded, opting instead to punch his fist against the car's window. It was not enough to break the glass, but it got her moving.

She wrenched the shifter into drive and took off flying down the road like an escapee from the lunatic asylum. She took the next corner so quickly that two of her wheels lost contact with the road. Gravity brought them back down, and she pushed the accelerator to the floor.

She could no longer see the men. Still, they remained vivid in her mind. She did not slow down.

***

The chief stood over Clay's misshapen body. What a mess. His legs had been flattened to the asphalt where the car's rear tire had rolled over him. Other portions were smashed in and disfigured beyond recognition. On his forehead, the Dodge emblem had been embossed marking the spot where his head connected with the truck of the vehicle.

The chief was thankful that Sasha had hit Clay instead of him. Golems couldn't be destroyed by sheer blunt-force trauma. He, on the other hand, could and by the damage done to Clay's body, he was certain that it would have been fatal if he had been in Clay's shoes.

His golem consisted of mud. That mud now churned and bubbled as it strove to reconfigure. After a minute, the reconfiguration was complete and Clay sat up.

"Did we get her?"

"No, Clay, we did not get her."

The chief was more than a little perturbed. This kidnapping had not gone at all to plan.

It should have been so easy. They should have had her by now. Instead, she not only got away, but he had no idea where she was.

Legion would not be happy if he came back empty-handed. Legion asked for a new pet. Legion desired Sasha James. If Legion did not get what Legion desired, well, he shuddered to think of the consequences.

The chief pushed these thoughts away. It would do no good to dwell on such self-condemning prophecy. He simply needed to get Sasha. If he could complete that goal, then all else would be easy.

"My fingers are gone." Clay said, pulling the chief from his inner monolog.

"What?"

Clay held his hands up for inspection. What Clay said was true. Both hands had thumbs but no fingers.

"What happened to them?" the chief wanted to know.

Clay shrugged. "I tried to grab the bumper as she ran me over. I guess when she drove off, my fingers went with her."

Normally, severed fingers would require immediate medical attention but not so with Clay.

"My fingers are with her," Clay said matter-of-factly.

The chief nodded but didn't really care to have this discussion right now. He had more important things to worry about.

"My fingers are hooked to her bumper about a mile from here."

The chief tried hard to tune Clay out. He had to think.

"My fingers just took a left turn."

There had to be something he was missing. There had to be a way to locate that woman.

Clay chuckled. "My fingers just hit a bump in the road."

"What did you say?"

Clay's grin disappeared. "My fingers just hit a bump in the road?"

"How do you know that?"

"They are my fingers," Clay answered matter-of-factly.

"Can you see where your fingers are going?"

"Not with my eyes," Clay mumbled.

"With what then?"

Clay suddenly looked like a child that was in trouble but did not really know why. He scuffed his toe repeatedly on the asphalt. "With my feelings. Those fingers are mine. I feel where they go."

Finally, some luck. "And where are they now?"

Clay stuck his nose upward as if he were a hound dog on a hot trail. Then he pointed a stubbed hand straight out. "That way! She's going that way!"

Within seconds, the chief and Clay were in the S-10. It seemed laughable to him that Clay was now in charge, but on a certain level, that was exactly the case.

The chief drove. Clay directed.

The chase was back on. They would get their prisoner. Legion would have its pet.

Chapter 9

Sasha ignored both stop signs and red lights. Luckily, Getreide was a town that slept at night. All the intersections were deserted.

What to do now? That question pummeled her head, but the answer was foggy. Her first thought had been to go to the police, but what would she tell them? *Yes, officers, that it correct. Somebody broke into my apartment, so I bashed his head in with a bat. What's that? No, I didn't kill him. No, his brains didn't splatter. He just got up and brushed himself off, no harm done. How did I get this car? Glad you asked – I stole it. Oh, and I also ran over the man who was trying to kidnap me. Yes, sir, the same one that I had whacked earlier. No, I don't know if I killed him. Why not? That's an excellent question. To be honest, it was because I fled the scene. What's that officer? You want my jacket size? What does that have to do with anything? And who are these men in white coats?*

She looked in her rearview to see if she was being followed. She saw no one and let up on the gas.

Why would anyone want to harm me? she thought. *I have no enemies.*

As soon as that thought materialized, she knew it was a lie, because she did have an enemy. "Richard," she said through gritted teeth.

The early autumn night was cool, yet thoughts of her ex-husband brought heat to her face. It hadn't always been this way. Back when she had first met Richard, he had seemed nice enough. Sure, he liked to party, but that was no crime. In fact, she found it kind of exhilarating, dating a "bad boy."

It wasn't until after they were married a couple of years that his alcoholism really started to take over, and when that happened, things went down the crapper in a hurry.

Sasha tried to make things work, but it was so hard. The problem was when he was drunk, he was violent, and he was always drunk.

His abuse left Sasha afraid to act. It took six years of hell to muster her courage and leave, but once done it was like ripping off a Band-Aid - freeing and yet, exposing a nasty scar.

The divorce was bitter. Throughout most of the process, Richard was intoxicated. He threatened her whenever the divorce attorneys were distracted by paperwork and their own self-interest.

She never considered the fact that he was motivated to act on his threats. Now, she wondered if she should have taken them more seriously.

When she left Richard, she vowed never again to be a victim. With that vow renewed, she turned the car around and formulated her plan. It was time to confront Richard.

This decision was both brave and stupid. It was also necessary. She gripped the steering wheel with all her strength in order to stop her hands from trembling knowing that she was digging into the grave of her past and fearful of the phantoms that lurked there.

Chapter 10

Clay was like a hound on a fox hunt zoning in on the scent of his prey. The chief had never before seen him so focused.

He pointed with his stumped hand. "That way, Chief."

The chief turned as directed. "Are we getting closer?"

"I think so."

The chief sincerely hoped that Clay was right. They had to get this girl and soon. Legion would tolerate nothing less.

The topic of failure never came up in his discussions with the demons which lived under his house. There had never been a need for such discussion as he had never failed. Still, if he believed the old stories, demons did not take kindly to such breaches of contract.

"We are very close now," said Clay.

"How can you tell?" The chief was growing impatient.

"My fingers are pulling me stronger now. I can't explain it other than that."

He smirked. Clay never was too good with words.

"There! Over there!" Clay shouted.

"How about if you use your inside voice, Clay."

Clay nodded. "Sorry," he said barely above a whisper. "But, over there, Chief, over there." He jabbed to the right with old stubby.

"I don't see anything." The chief remarked.

"You can't see it with your eyes, but can't you see it with your feelings?"

The chief felt a headache coming on. Clay could do that to him from time to time. This was one of those times.

They rounded a corner. "See there!" Clay said throwing the inside voice rule out the window.

The chief looked. He saw. He smiled.

Parked on the street sat a Dodge Dynasty, the rear-end damage identifying it as Sasha's getaway vehicle. It appeared to be unoccupied.

He expanded his view and caught sight of her just as she was entering a nearby house. He drove by casually, so he wouldn't spook the prey.

"We're passing by!" Clay shouted.

"Shut up! What did I say about using your inside voice."

"I know Chief, but we are passing by."

The chief didn't acknowledge Clay's input but simply pulled about a block passed the Dynasty before selecting some street parking. The idea was that he wanted to be far enough away so as not to rouse suspicion, yet close enough that he could get back to the pickup quickly if needed.

He adjusted his rearview mirror so that he could see the house and considered the situation. He needed to ensure that she would not slip through his fingers a second time.

Speaking of fingers, he looked at Clay. His henchman was giddy like a child who had just arrived at the Zoo. "Are you eager to get your fingers back Clay?" he wanted to know.

"Oh, yes, Chief."

Together, they exited the S-10 and walked toward the Dynasty. The chief kept an eye on the mystery house. All of the windows he could see were onyx-black. If anyone was there besides Sasha James, they were either sleeping or simply fellow coinsurers of darkness.

A smile grew on Clay's face. "There they are Chief! There they are!"

It was true. The missing fingers were there dangling from the bumper like a family of fleshy leaches. Clay approached and as he did so, the fingers came to life, wiggling and squirming.

Clay extended his hands and the dismembered digits jumped to him suckling to their proper spots. Within seconds, he was his complete, old self again.

Well, not quite exactly complete. The chief noticed one of Clay's hands was short a pinky.

Momentarily, Clay stared at the void on his hand. Then, he began to examine the bumper, searching for the remaining lost appendage but came up empty-handed. "I guess one of them must have fallen off somewhere back."

The chief smiled. "Ah, it's just the pinky Clay. You'll never miss it."

"Can we go back and look for it?" Clay stared with a forlorn expression at the spot where his finger should have been. "I look weird without it."

"Not now, Clay. We have to prioritize our tasks, and right now, we need to get Sasha."

"I just don't look right without my pinky. It looks very weird."

The chief ignored his henchman's latest lament. Clay was weird either way. Besides, it was time to focus on the hunt.

He looked up at the house that he had seen Sasha James enter. It was time to go in after her.

***

Any doubt that Richard still resided here disappeared the moment that Sasha stepped onto the front porch. For one thing, the key was just where she knew it would be under the welcome mat. For another, when she tried to use the key, she found that the door was already unlocked as well as slightly ajar. Richard rarely locked doors as the fine motor skills required for such tasks were beyond the ability of his inebriated self.

The door creaked softly as she pushed it fully open. Immediately, the odor hit her, a combination of vomit, garbage, and rot.

Holding her nose, she entered the house leaving the door open behind her in hopes that the stench could escape. Plus, the thought of closing that door felt akin to lying in a coffin and closing the lid.

All of the lights were off in the front room, but by what she could see from the glow that shone through the front window from the streetlights beyond, she confirmed that the place was in shambles. One might suspect vandals, but Sasha knew better. She looked over the many empty bottles which littered the room. All of Richard's favorites were present and accounted for. He didn't adhere to a single brand just whatever was cheap and strong.

She took a step further into the space and gagged as the foul odor increased. One might have thought that Richard had died somewhere among the refuse, but Sasha knew better. If he had died, he would not smell. Years of self-pickling would have preserved him for all time.

She looked at the ruined living space, and a feeling of sadness overwhelmed her. This had once been her life. She had climbed out from that pit determined never to return. Richard, on the other hand, still lived there.

The question was had he fallen far enough to consider putting a hit out on his ex-wife.

If she was to press charges, she would need to get a confession. There was only one flaw in her plan; they were under court order to stay away from each other. The very fact that she was in his house slinking around put her in the aggressor's seat. She hoped once the truth came out that the courts would be sympathetic to her plight.

She entered the kitchen which was just as gross as the front room. From there, she only briefly peaked into the adjoining bathroom to ensure it was empty. It was a very brief peak. Her gag reflex kicked in and would have progressed to vomiting if she had stayed there any longer.

She stood there in the darkness, scanning the space to ensure vacancy. She refused to turn on any lights as doing so would increase the chances of her being discovered. She needed to remain undiscovered. She needed that element of surprise.

She ascended the stairs which led to the second floor. She climbed slowly, one stair at a time, using deliberate steps. The stairs were covered with garbage, and she could not afford to cause an avalanche.

It seemed to take an eternity. When she finally reached the summit, a sense of dread pummeled her. Part of her wanted to simply leave, but now she had progressed too far into the enemy's turf. There was no turning back.

The first room along the upstairs hallway was a second bath. She pushed the door open, her hand touching something sticky as she pressed against it. The door did not open freely because of the garbage behind it.

She pushed harder, gritting her teeth as the hinges squeaked. A different, but no less vile stench hit her nostrils. She tried to hold her breath, but it was too late. Her eyes watered.

She opened that door just enough to peak in. A nightlight was plugged in over the sink. It revealed what she needed to know. Nobody was there.

She knew the next two doors led to bedrooms. She approached the first door. It was closed.

She had to open that door. She wished desperately she still had her bat. In fact, she wished for a loaded AK-47, but in the end, she remained weaponless.

Richard liked guns. In her mind's eye, she pictured him on the other side of that door with a loaded weapon leveled waiting for her to enter, so he could blow her away.

She grabbed the doorknob. She turned it, letting it open.

It was very dark in that room. Even the moonshine didn't penetrate through the window, which was odd, because it was shining full and bright earlier that evening.

Despite her fears, Sasha did what was necessary. She flicked on the light but didn't see Richard. With the light on, she understood why no light came in through the window. It had been boarded over from the outside with a large piece of plywood.

All the glass was missing. She had no idea what had happened to the window, but she suspected it had something to do with the man who called the place home. He had probably busted it out either accidentally or on purpose when consumed by one of his drunken tantrums.

There was no bed in the room, just a stained mattress on the floor with a grimy comforter strewn beside it. Next to the bed was a cardboard box that served as a make-shift nightstand.

The item on that box drew her. The handgun which rested there concaved the top of that box with its weight.

The room suddenly began to spin as pain engulfed her head. Confusion followed. Pain radiated out from the rear of her skull to the rest of her body. Her legs wobbled.

She tried to stay on her feet but failed, landing face-down on the filthy mattress. Something had struck her, something hard.

"Hello, Sasha," Richard's voice came to her as if from the other end of a long tunnel. "Welcome home, baby."

***

Richard wasn't sure if what he saw was actually occurring. He spent quite a bit of time in his head these days and had trouble sorting the real from the fantastical.

He looked down at where Sasha had fallen. She looked real.

She let out a weak moan. She sounded real.

She had landed on her stomach on his mattress and was, at the moment, struggling to rise to her hands and knees. He watched as she fumbled. She certainly moved as if she were real.

He removed the cap from the heavy glass bottle which he had just used to whack her. He pressed the bottle's lip to his own and took a long, hard swig.

"Man," he said to her with slurred speech. "It's a good thing your head didn't break my bottle." He paused to focus on staying upright. "If it would have spilled, then I would have called the cops on charges of alcohol abuse."

He chuckled. "Alcohol abuse," he said again. "That's funny."

She rolled over onto her back and stared up at him. Her eyes cleared by the second seething with anger.

"Ah, now don't be upset," he mumbled. "I know you can't stay mad at me. Hell, you can't even stay away can you? That's why you're here right, baby? You just couldn't live without your hubby right?"

She answered him clearly enunciating every word. "I am here, Richard, because I had a little run in with your friends tonight."

"My friends?" he scoffed. "Honey, you know I don't have no friends."

"I am talking about the two goons that you paid to have me murdered."

This conversation began to hurt Richard's head. He rubbed his temple with his free hand and tried hard to push away the tendrils of confusion.

He noticed that she was slowly moving toward one side of the mattress. Did she want him to join her? That would make sense. She never could resist his magnetic pull for long.

He stood there, not sure what to do. This was a lot for his alcohol-soaked brain to take in. And, the question remained, was she even really there to begin with?

He decided it didn't really matter if this was real or not. He accepted her offer. But, by the time he made this decision, things had changed.

She was no longer on the mattress but standing beside it. The gun from his bedside table was in her hands and pointed at his face.

He forgot he left the gun beside his bed. He couldn't remember if it was loaded, but it likely was. With all of the aliens, government agents and what not out to get him, he had no choice but to keep vigilant.

Of course, if Sasha wasn't really there to begin with, then it wouldn't matter if the gun was loaded, empty, or filled with jellybeans because hallucinations can't pull triggers. On the other hand, if she was real, then he was in a mess of trouble. Or maybe, it wasn't her, but one of the alien shape shifters that paid him visits during the dark hours of night. If it was an alien, then he was as good as dead, because everyone knows that aliens are a crack-shot with guns.

Sasha began to move around to one side of the room. He could tell that her legs were still wobbly from the blow he had dealt, but she grew steadier by the second.

"Sasha," he said as calmly as he could. "Don't forget who I am. You don't want to shoot ME now do you?"

"I will do what I have to," she answered.

He detected hesitation in those words, an indication that if she was really there, then it was indeed his ex-wife. Neither aliens nor government agents hesitated. He took a step further into the room. He would have to charm her to defuse this situation.

"Hey, baby," he began. "I didn't mean to hit you earlier. I mean, when you just sneak into a guy's house unannounced in the middle of the night, what do you think is going to happen?"

She said nothing. The gun remained trained on him, but he noticed that her hands were shaking, a chink in her armor.

"I thought you were some stupid burglar or something."

"Shut up!" She barked. "Don't treat me like an idiot! You knew good and well what you were doing."

He feigned a hurt look as he took one more step toward her. If he could just get a little closer, then he could grab the firearm and redirect it. Then, once out of harm's way, he would teach her a little lesson about why little girls should not play with such dangerous toys.

He tried to keep his grin from showing as he didn't want her to anticipate his plan. "Calm down," he said. "Let's just calm down."

He looked into her face, trying to read her mind through her expressions. Was she calming? He couldn't tell.

An idea struck him. He still had the bottle in his hand and what was more disarming than the invitation to a friendly little drink between friends and lovers.

He held the bottle out to her. "You look tense, honey. I know, I have stress in my life, too, but this stuff really helps. Want a swig?"

"I want you to call off your thugs, or I'll go straight to the cops."

He stared at her unsure of what to say. He found her little act to be quite baffling.

"I'm serious. I will go right to the police. Is this getting through that thick skull of yours?"

"Let's say you do go the police, sweetheart. I would like to hear what you would tell them?" Richard responded trying hard to keep his rage in check. "Because, I don't have the foggiest idea as to what you're talking about."

She narrowed her eyes. He did not know what to make of that. He hoped that it was a sign that she was re-thinking her accusations.

He pressed the bottle toward her. "Just have a drink, Sasha, it's just what the doctor ordered."

He watched her eyes. When they were focused on the bottle, he took his queue and struck.

Grabbing the gun by the barrel, he redirected its trajectory. A boom deafened him. Plaster rained down from above. He swore but did not let go of the weapon. "Sasha! You are one stupid…"

His sentence went unfinished as his head involuntarily whipped around 180 degrees. He lost control of his body and collapsed to the ground in a disheveled heap.

The last thing he saw was a pair of shoes he didn't recognize. The last thing he heard was shrieking. Then he slipped into darkness and silence.

***

Sasha shrieked and staggered back as two familiar men entered the room. One of the two had just snapped Richard's neck as if it were nothing more than a toothpick. Then again, she would have expected nothing less from the one who had survived a bat to the brain and a car to the gut.

The second man was the one who had tried to break into the Dynasty just before she took off. Together, they blocked the doorway which left only one other route of escape.

With all of the momentum that she could muster, she slammed into the plywood that covered the glassless window. Nails ripped from molding as she bashed into it full-force. Pain overwhelmed her with the impact.

The plywood gave way. The next thing she knew, Sasha slid down the roof, riding the plywood like a toboggan.

The roof ended. She was falling.

She managed to keep on top of the plywood which was a good thing. She landed hard. The surface-area of the wood dissipated the force of that landing. Still, it hurt as she landed flat on the ground.

Something clattered away from her in the darkness. *The gun!*

She rolled off the plywood in the direction she thought the weapon bounced and found it quickly. Rolling onto her back, she aimed it at the window from where she had fallen. She did not fire. There was nobody to fire at. The window was vacant.

Hobbling to her feet, and hoping that the men had finally given up, she kept her attention trained on that window. They were probably navigating the garbage-covered stairs at that very moment. Ignoring her many pains, she took off. There was not a moment to lose.

The Dynasty was still parked where she had left it. She got in, revved the engine to life and squealed away.

In her peripheral vision, she saw the front door of Richard's home fly open as the two men emerged into the front yard. She slammed the petal as one of them took off after her on foot, and he was gaining on her!

She pushed the gas pedal harder, but it was already floored. He was only a few feet behind her now. She took a hard left, rounding the corner rough enough to send her right hubcaps flying free.

She let up on the gas as the car fishtailed. The tires caught. The car straightened. She slammed down the gas pedal once again.

The man was only inches from the end of the car as she completed the corner and gained speed once again. She glanced back. He stopped pursuing her.

Maybe he was tired? *Yeah, right.* She had no idea why he stopped. She was just thankful he had.

She watched him become tinier in her rearview as she fled. Finally, he was just a speck. Still, she did not slow down.

***

Unbelievable. Sasha James had slipped away once again. Sure, Clay had tried, but when the chase rounded the corner, the pursuit ended. The chief became too distant from Clay, and his golem could not continue.

The chief jogged up to where Clay stood. He stared down the road, but the only proof she had been there were the tire marks on the asphalt and the smell of burnt rubber.

"Hey, Chief," Clay said as if just realizing that he was there.

The chief ignored his henchman. He needed to think. There had to be a way to calculate Sasha's next move. He had to know where she was headed. He needed to triangulate the next point of abduction.

"Hey, Chief."

He ignored Clay. *If I were Sasha James, where would I run?*

"Hey, Chief!"

"What Clay? What is it?" he said with exasperation.

"Um, I think she got away again."

Why do Golems have to be so dim, the chief thought. "Thanks for the news flash."

Clay's face brightened which only frustrated the chief more. He made a mental note to remember that Golems do not get sarcasm.

Together, they ran to the S-10. The chief had no idea what his next move would be, but whatever it was, it would be good to move there as quickly as possible. He started the truck and put it into drive.

The chief was not a praying man, at least not to conventional deities. He prayed to the unknown that he would not fail Legion a third time.

Chapter 11

Sasha drove wildly. The car's dashboard clock said it was after 2 a.m.

It was not rational and she knew it, but she felt strongly that if she could just survive the night, she might stand a chance. She found the vagueness of her situation aggravating. Obviously, somebody was out to get her, but who? She was no criminal mastermind, but she guessed that if those goons had been on Richard's payroll, they wouldn't have offed him it. With Richard dead, she was out of suspects.

Despite her past, she felt a twinge of guilt as she thought about Richard's lifeless body lying on the ground back in that landfill of a house. If it wasn't for her leading the hitmen to that location, then he would most likely still be alive. She forced the guilt away. She had no time for it.

She had to plan her next move. Previously, she decided the police were not a good idea. Now, she reconsidered. The goons who killed Richard seemed invincible. She was on their hit-list. Overall, things had really gotten nasty.

What puzzled her the most was how those men had known where to find her once she escaped the apartment. It was unexplainable. For that reason, she still hesitated in going to the police, because she feared that they would not be able to adequately protect her from this caliber of enemy.

She felt like Sarah Connor from the old Terminator movies. Just like Sarah, she was chased by something that seemed beyond human. And like in the movie, that enemy seemed intent on killing her at any cost.

Her growing paranoia caused her to glance in her rear-view, fearing that the mysterious hunters had somehow located her.

Her heart fluttered.

She was being followed.

***

Officer Simon Birch, the newest addition to the Getreide Police force, emerged from the shadows. As the plebe, he had the night shift. Often, his job bordered on the mundane. Even on exciting nights, things were calm compared to larger metropolises. In fact, though he had been on the force for over two years now, he had never been required to draw his weapon other than to clean it or for target practice.

He was an excellent marksman under the right conditions. If he ever needed to shoot, he would not miss provided the target was an unmoving black-silhouette in the shape of a Police Academy-approved head and torso hanging on a wire exactly 30 feet away.

So, when a Dodge Dynasty careened by him at twenty miles over the posted speed-limit, Simon pounced on the opportunity. He pulled out from behind the billboard where he strategically parked and gave chase.

The first thing he noticed was that the plates were unreadable due to rear-end damage. The back end and crumpled plate were covered in some sort of red coating. He was told to keep his eye out for a stolen car reported earlier that night. This car matched that description.

Chances were this whole stolen car situation was just some mistake. The car had probably just been *borrowed* by a drunk neighbor who, although they should not be behind the wheel, did not intend to steal anything. Perhaps they were just too inebriated to realize they had gotten into a vehicle that was not their own.

Given the situation, he radioed dispatch, asking for backup. He hoped he would get his answer quickly.

Dispatch responded. The Chief of Police himself was on the way. He had no idea what his boss was doing out at this hour, but he was glad that he was. There was no one better to have for back-up and validation.

Simon gave dispatch his location, turned on his flashers, and waited for the perpetrator to react.

***

Sasha looked in the rearview mirror and panicked. Then the emergency vehicle lights came on, and her paranoia dissipated. It was not the others. Still, she was in a stolen vehicle with a loaded gun registered to a murder victim.

She slowed down and moved off to the shoulder. The patrol car pulled in directly behind her. She watched and waited, but nothing happened for minutes that felt like hours. *What was taking so long? Why wasn't the officer getting out?*

Her paranoia returned. Something wasn't right. *Had Richard already been discovered? Had she been implicated in the crime?* It didn't seem possible.

The patrol car turned on a spotlight. She squinted as light flooded the interior of her car. Under that brightness, she felt exposed, trapped. The Dynasty became an observation cell.

She tried to see in her rearview, but it was no use. It reflected only white light. She turned and looked back, shielding her eyes as best she could. She could tell that a second vehicle had pulled up behind the cruiser but could not distinguish make or model.

Her instincts screamed *run away! Flee! Escape!* She looked around, taking in the details of her surrounding, readying herself to bolt if the need arose.

Off to her right was woods. Beyond her sight, back in the trees, gurgled Getreide Creek. Sasha knew this from her childhood when she used to play down there and catch frogs.

On the other side of the road was a new housing development. In the glow of the searchlight, she could see the skeletal silhouettes of partially completed houses in different states of construction.

A figure emerged from the second vehicle. He got out of the driver's side and sauntered up to the police cruiser.

Sasha stared hard, but the spotlight prevented her from seeing any details. This lack of knowledge sickened her. She felt increasingly trapped, as if she were a mouse in a snake's burrow.

The figure leaned into the squad car, apparently conversing with the driver. Slowly, she reached over to the passenger seat. Finding the gun, she gripped the handle.

With the weapon obtained, she pulled it close. Then, she waited.

Chapter 12

In the darkness, below the chief's house, discontentment was brewing. The many selves of Legion had played with its current pet to the point of death and there was no ETA on the replacement.

Legion hated the abyss in which it dwelled. Even more so, it hated the one who damned them to this prison, this forsaken hole.

If it wasn't for Jesus Christ forcing them out of the man and into the herd of pigs, they would be free to this day. Instead, they spent their endless immortal years crammed into the abyss like a tin of sardines waiting to be consumed.

Things were getting better, though. Of all the servants it had recruited over the centuries, none were like the chief in terms of loyalty and commitment.

Humans like the chief were a rare breed. Legion had found many with a penchant for vengeance, but few with such a deep-seeded desire to commit those acts of revenge. Yes, the chief was a packed powder keg, and Legion was the spark torching his short fuse.

Within the chief, there was a void. Legion offered to fill that void and the chief had accepted the offer. Prices were negotiated and contracts were bound.

It smiled and thought of how stupid this man actually was. Legion was at an advantage because they understood the chief's psyche. The man thought that he had everything under control, that if he supplied Legion with the contracted number of pets, Legion was like a genie ready to grant his every wish.

The chief was delusional. Demons could not be controlled in that way. It was all an illusion and with time, even the chief would see through the ruse. Of course by then escape would be an impossibility.

Regardless, Legion did relish the little treats the man presented, if for no other reason, than knowing it pained their enemy. Jesus wants all men to come to him, and with every pet killed in ignorance of that grace, one less could bow before their messiah. As a bonus, the pets were a wonderful if short-lived pleasure and a diversion from the reality of the accursed abyss.

Legion grew frustrated because it had grown accustomed to such pleasures and wanted a new pet. Now.

For all the chief's strengths, he had a newly-emerging ineptness which Legion found annoying. Between providing a golem and blinding the town's citizens to the truth, Sasha's fate should have been easily sealed.

In its frustration, it grabbed the chain and yanked hard, but only a feeble whimper came from its current pet. This one was so near death that it would get little enjoyment in finishing the little imp off. Still, it was all that it had to toy with at that moment.

Using the chain, Legion pulled the sad little specimen toward them. It was playtime.

The pet began to squirm. Legion relished the squirming. This one, who had been raised without faith in God, had been doomed even before it became a pet.

The pet thrashed as Legion yanked him over the edge of the abyss in order to separate the physical from the spiritual. It was time to harvest the fruits of its labor.

The physical vaporized in the heat of the abyss and the pet's eyes were finally truly opened. The soul screamed for mercy but none was granted.

Chapter 13

"You did the right thing in calling for backup," the Getreide Chief of Police said to officer Birch.

Simon Birch smiled as the chief knelt down to his level to converse with him through the open driver's side window. Things were just that informal in the little berg of Getreide.

That was one of the reasons officer Birch liked his job. Simon admittedly was a simple young man and the Getreide Police Department suited him just fine. The layers of hierarchy that existed in larger towns simply did not exist here.

He glanced in his rearview as he spoke with his superior and wondered who was in the passenger seat of his boss' S-10. A glare off the windshield impeded his view.

"So, how do you want me to handle this situation?" Simon asked, deferring command to the higher rank.

The chief stared at the Dynasty before letting out a brief chuckle. "You won't believe it, but I know who's in that car."

"You do?"

"Yup. It's that new employee that they hired a few weeks ago to work at the Parochial school. I believe her name is Sarah James."

"Sarah James?" Simon repeated.

"No, that's not quite right." The chief paused in thought. "Sasha. Sasha James. That's her name."

Simon didn't know a Sarah or a Sasha, but that wasn't unusual. Getreide was small enough, but not so small that he knew all the residents.

"Yes, I am sure that's her," the chief iterated while rubbing his chin thoughtfully.

"How do you know that?"

The chief stared at Simon. That stare, for some reason elicited a chill. "When you've been on the force as long as I have Simon, then you just know things." He looked back at the car ahead. "You just feel them in your gut."

Simon nodded. "What's she doing in a stolen car?"

"I couldn't begin to speculate. Probably just hit the bottle too hard and made a poor decision."

Poor decision-making was nothing new in Getreide. He thought back to the time when a very drunk Mr. Handel came riding into town on his prized horse. Riding a horse in Getreide was not unusual, however riding one while wearing nothing but a tinfoil hat designed to deflect alien mind-controlling rays made the situation a little further into left field.

In the case of Mr. Handel, the police helped him off his mount and covered him in a blanket. After detoxing, he was released, required to pay a fine and issue a public apology.

That was the way the law was in Getreide - simple and straight-forward. It was no surprise to Officer Simon when the chief suggested that Ms. James be given the opportunity to be taken home with charges pending and only filed upon the request of the stolen car's owner. Of course, Ms. James would be required to compensate the owner based on blue book value regardless, but that wouldn't be much.

"Do you want me to escort Ms. James home then?"

The chief shook his head. "I'll do it. I want you to get back on patrol. You're the only officer we have on the nightshift and if anything else goes down, I'll need an officer who's ready to respond."

Simon nodded. "Who's your friend?" he asked as he glanced in the rearview.

The chief stared back at his truck. "Him? He's just an old buddy from the next town over. Actually it works out well. He can follow me in the S-10 while I drive the Dynasty back to where it belongs as well as drop Ms. James off at her place."

"He won't mind doing that?" Simon asked.

"Nah. He owes me anyway."

"He does?"

"Yes, he owes me his life."

They locked eyes and Simon saw no humor in his boss' stare. Finally, Simon broke the deadlock. "You sure you don't need me for anything?"

"Quite sure. Thanks for all of your help."

With that, Officer Birch turned off the spotlight, put the patrol car into gear and pulled away. As he drove by the Dynasty, he made a point to look into the driver's side window. Ms. James was an attractive enough woman. He guessed her to be in her early thirties. She didn't look drunk. She looked terrified.

He left the scene, but that look of terror stuck with him. Still, orders were orders, so he drove on.

Chapter 14

Reverend Xavier Hernandez could not sleep. He sat at his kitchen table and stared at the empty glass that had held warm milk. He heard drinking warm milk encouraged grogginess. Now, he assumed it was only a myth.

The reverend rarely suffered from insomnia. The last time was the night of September 10, 2001. That night, the need for prayer overcame his need for sleep. He prayed hard through the night, not knowing what for exactly. Everything became crystal clear the next morning.

He wondered what equally-significant calamity awaited him. Tonight, as before, his insomnia was more than an inability to sleep. A feeling of dread, a sense that something was unbalanced and about to come crashing down possessed him. This dread had heft, a crushing, suffocating weight.

He glanced around the room. As a man of God, he knew spiritual powers everywhere engaged in a cosmic war of good versus evil, God versus Satan, angels versus demons.

Usually that knowledge didn't bother him because he knew he was on the winning side. In fact, the war was already won, victory attained the day his messiah rose from the tomb.

Still, tonight, just as in September of 2001, he found the darkness of Christ's crucifixion overpowering the resurrection. Some hidden evil grew blacker, more malicious, and more powerful.

He pushed the empty glass aside. In the face of such darkness, he knew what must be done. He put his head down on the table, closed his eyes and clasped his hands to pray.

How should he pray? The answer eluded him. Without options, he began asking God to release him from this feeling of impending doom.

God hears all prayers. He knew this. Yet, he had the suspicion that God was not about to take away this burden, at least not yet. He prayed in earnest, trembling with effort.

A crashing sound jolted him from concentration.

The empty milk glass fell from the table and shattered on the linoleum floor. He didn't know if this was a result of his own alarm or something more.

He pushed past the interruption and resumed praying, changing tactics, no longer praying for relief. He prayed God's will would be done. If he was to endure this darkness, then so be it. He asked that the purpose of it would be to God's glory.

Xavier realized the spiritual attack that was upon him and prayed. He prayed. He prayed with all of his might, sweat and tears oozing from him, thick as blood. His hands ached from the effort taken to clasp them together, but he didn't stop.

He didn't dare stop.

Chapter 15

The patrol car took the spotlight glare away with it. Sasha recognized who had been speaking to the officer and felt the color drain from her face. She watched him saunter back to the S-10. He got in behind the wheel and closed the driver's door. The pickup's engine revved twice.

Sasha shook with terror. The fact that the officer left her alone with this killer only confirmed her fear that she couldn't trust the authorities. Preparing for the worst, she tightened her grip and kept the gun low and out of sight.

She glanced at the dashboard clock. Only minutes. It felt like hours. *Why don't they do something?* she wondered as she watched them through her rear-view.

How could this be happening to her? There must be something she could do, she reasoned. It felt like a nightmare. But she was awake and this was gut-wrenchingly real.

Those behind her were waiting for something. *Waiting for what?*

Her attention moved from the driver to the passenger side of the truck. That spot was vacant! Where was the second thug? The big, monstrous one?

Crash!

Glass sprayed her as her front passenger window imploded, followed closely by a large fist.

The fist belonged to the maniac she had both bludgeoned with a bat and run over with 3,000 pounds of Detroit steel. He was standing there outside her passenger door glaring at her with those soulless eyes. *I made him angry, not dead.*

He reaching in through the hole he created.

She shrieked as he groped for her, sparkling pellets of automotive glass somehow sticking to his knuckles like cheap rhinestones. Instinctively, her foot slammed down on the accelerator, rousing the car to life.

The engine roared.

The wheels squealed.

She went nowhere.

This man who had survived both bat and car demonstrated superhuman strength, keeping the Dodge from moving.

He grabbed at her. His feet came off the ground. The car moved. He leaned back to replant his feet on the ground.

The tires screamed. The air filled with the stench of burning rubber. His fingers brushed against her arm, trying to grab her shirt.

Burning rubber nauseated her.

If she could break the car free of his grip, even if it meant leaving him standing there holding the passenger door, then so be it.

She floored the gas pedal.

She heard a pop and ducked, but it wasn't gunfire. It was the sound of a tire exploding. In the rearview she saw the other get out of the vehicle, a slinking predator, growing ever nearer.

With both time and options running out, she unlocked her door, flung it open and fled. Her hand felt heavy. She looked at it realizing she still held the gun.

Without looking back or aiming, she pointed the gun behind her and pulled the trigger. The report deafened her, the force of the discharge almost shocking her into dropping the weapon. She had no idea if the bullet hit anything but wasn't optimistic.

She dared not stop, and look. Instead, she fled into the darkness, running toward the newly born, half-constructed neighborhood.

Behind her, a voice shouted, "After her, Clay!"

"Yes, chief."

She bolted around the corner of the first house. Then, she zigged around the second before zagging around a third.

Her lungs burned. Her muscles ached, but she refused to slow down. Doing so, she knew, was suicide.

The ground was soft beneath her. She hated the slapping, sucking sound her bare feet made as she slapped them against the moist earth. And hers were not the only feet slapping and sucking. She could hear those of her pursuers as well - loud, heavy, and foreboding.

Terror shot adrenaline through her body.

She ran like a hunted animal, desperate to survive.

Chapter 16

Reverend Xavier Hernandez prayed until compelled to stop and study the scriptures. Not knowing what God was leading him to read, he opened his Bible randomly. The book fell open to the story of Jesus and the man possessed by the legion of demons.

Jesus asked him, "What is your name?"

"Legion," he replied, because many demons had gone into him. And they begged him repeatedly not to order them into the abyss.

A large herd of pigs was feeding there on the hillside. The demons begged Jesus to let them go into them and he gave them permission. When the demons came out of the man, they went into the pigs, and the herd rushed down the steep bank and was drowned.

He read that passage a few times before closing the Bible and pondering its significance. As he thought on it, the darkness intensified around him, a spiritual darkness blacker than anything existing in the physical. He tried to push away that empty feeling, but it felt like he was losing.

He knew at that moment that no amount of warm milk would allow him to sleep, not with that darkness closing in. The weight of it overwhelmed him.

Like tentacles extending from deep-sea depths, the inky oppression reached for him, looking for a weak spot in his defenses through which to taint his soul. He could feel it slithering around, seeking entrance.

He had no fear of this satanic power for he was not standing alone against it. God stood with him albeit unseen strengthening him.

Xavier prayed. Only God could light the darkness. He sought salvation and as he did, a new feeling washed over him, a feeling of spiritual purpose. He sensed that he was to do something against this evil darkness. He wasn't sure what exactly he was to do, so he prayed that he would be ready when, where and how God needed him.

As if angry at him for seeking help from above, the darkness doubled its efforts, slamming upon him with the force of a tsunami. He countered by increasing the ferocity of his prayers. Straining from the pressure, perspiration poured from him.

The darkness appeared confident that sooner or later his strength would slip. Before that happened he would need to be ready.

Chapter 17

Despite efforts to calm herself, Sasha trembled. She found refuge in the open basement of a newly dug foundation. Above her, there was no roof only the great outside.

She was vulnerable here, yet she found nowhere safer. Staring at her mud-covered bare feet, she worked to suppress the panic growing within.

The night was cool but not frigid, still the mud on her feet leached the warmth from them. She would have given anything for a pair of sneakers. Rubbing her feet she tried to get better circulation. It pained her, yet she refused to whimper for fear the hunting party would hear.

The basement she hid in had a walk-out, less confining but the only way in or out. If those men came into the basement from the open side, there was no escape. With this fact recognized, she resolved to move out. Creeping in the shadows as much as she could, she edged herself nearer to the basement's entrance. Leaning just enough to meet the minimum requirement, she peered into the darkness.

There was no sign of her pursuers. The hope surged that perhaps they had given up the chase. *No.* She forced herself to be realistic. *They haven't given up yet, why would they*?

A shadow shifted nearby. She froze. Searched. A flashlight. She saw them. There, on a ridge about 30 feet away.

By the leisurely way that they moved, she was certain they had not spotted her.

Yet.

The time is now, Sasha thought as she raised the gun, wrapped her finger around the trigger and took aim. Mentally, she flexed that finger and fired, but physically nothing happened.

Sasha wanted to shoot, but something stopped her. Too many questions buzzed around inside her skull. *What if it wasn't them? It was dark and they were too far away for a positive identification. And if it was them, what if she fired and missed? What were her chances then?*

With her confidence in shambles, she lowered the weapon. The housing development beside this lot was comprised of finished and occupied homes. She could see lights on in a few of those distant windows. At this time of night, she doubted that the lights represented awake residents. It was more likely the lights had simply been left on, perhaps for safety when going on nocturnal bathroom trips, or maybe by those who had been lured into the temptation of midnight snacking.

Those on the ridge drew nearer. She had to move or be caught. She watched the swath of the approaching flashlight beam. She readied herself. When the swath of their light moved away from her direction, she fled.

Once again her feet slapped the soft earth, much too loud. But there was no going back now and no way to be any quieter. She ran. She ran as fast as she could refusing to look back.

***

The chief flashed the beam off to his left, following the slapping, slopping sound. His quarry was close.

He ran toward the noise keeping low, knowing his prey was armed. Clay followed. The chief stopped. Clay stopped. The chief listened. The noise was still present but fading fast.

It was gone.

Frustrated, the chief scoured the space about him, but his flashlight failed to uncover Sasha James. He turned and found himself standing at the entrance to a walk-out basement. He entered that darkened space.

The basement was empty, but she had been here. His light revealed a set of bare footprints recently sunk into the mud. The entirety of that evidence wasn't much, but it was enough.

Further inspection revealed more footprints. He followed them out of the basement with Clay close on his heels.

"Was she here, Chief?" Clay wanted to know.

He chose not to answer. His focus was elsewhere, and the stupid question did not deserve his attention.

In the open, the shape of her footprints changed. They widened from a walk to a run.

He shone the light ahead and saw that the footprints were leading into a newly developed neighborhood. "Come on, Clay," he said with an almost giddy sound in his voice. "The hunt isn't lost, not by a long shot."

***

Staggering with exhaustion, Sasha stumbled into the nearest residential avenue. The streetlights glowed down, bathing everything in narrow shadows. She both welcomed and hated the light. She would see them coming, but they could find her too.

She jogged down the road, passing house after house, hoping for some sign that those within were awake, but so far she came up empty. The few lights that were on exposed not a living soul.

Glancing back, she saw the persistent beam of that flashlight as it illuminated the night. It shone just over the ridge that separated the developed neighborhood from the construction area. With a wheeze she trudged on.

She turned left at the first intersection. This street was deserted too.

Under any other circumstance, she would have screamed as loud as she could while she ran. All the women safety classes taught such tactics. Anyone who heard her screams for help would likely call the police. But as she already witnessed, the police wouldn't help her.

The why's and how's of her situation continued to baffle her. This lack of knowledge exhausted her more than the physical regimen, but it too was taking its toll. She never considered herself to be athletic and tonight's escapades only verified that. She felt as if she were about to collapse from exhaustion. Only adrenalin kept her moving.

The stress took its toll. Unable to force it back down her throat, she stopped, bent over, and vomited.

Her heaving gut refused to relax. Even after the puking stopped, she continued to spasm for what seemed an eternity. Sasha stared momentarily at the bits of mustard-yellow bologna that now steamed upon the asphalt.

She wiped her chin with the sleeve of her shirt and looked back once more. The street was still quiet. Regardless, the flickering flashlight beam danced just beyond the intersection, evidence that the mystery men had not given up the chase.

She wanted to collapse. Her body begged for recuperation, but its cries went unanswered. She ran, this time cutting through a yard.

***

The chief had a hard time keeping up with Clay who was now leading like an overexcited dog pulling at his owner's leash.

"Clay!" the chief growled.

"Yes, Chief?"

"Let me lead."

"Yes, Chief."

They entered an intersection and paused. Sasha could have gone any direction. "Any ideas?" he said to his henchman.

Clay stood there. His only answer was a shrug. The chief wasn't surprised.

He shined the flashlight down all paths, but none of them revealed any clues that Ms. James had travelled that direction.

Clay spoke. "When I tried to reach into the car and get her, I caught the smell on her breath. It smelled like bologna."

"Not now, Clay."

"Definitely it was bologna," Clay continued.

The chief tried to ignore his henchman. Sometimes this was a hard task for him, like ignoring a child who consumed too much Pixie Stix powder.

"Also, something else. There was something besides bologna. What was it? Think, think, think."

The chief figured that she turned either left or right. If she had continued straight, he felt certain he would have spotted her in the distance. She did not have that much of a head start after all.

"Mustard!" Clay shouted.

"What?"

"I said mustard."

"Shut up." The chief had enough.

Clay shut up by putting his hand over his mouth and hopping on one foot. Then, he began frantically pointing with the free hand.

"Clay," the chief said, suddenly realizing that maybe, just maybe Clay had some information that might be helpful. "Do you know which way she went?"

Clay stared at him, keeping his mouth covered. He stopped hopping and nodded.

"Which way?" the chief inquired. It took all that he had in him to keep harshness out of his voice.

Clay looked unsure. He just stood there with his mouth covered and his hand extended. His legs vibrated as if the hopping was about to recommence.

The chief rolled his eyes. "I am sorry for shouting at you Clay. I really do want to hear what you have to say."

Clay removed his hand. "This way." And he was off.

The chief followed him down the road that led off to the left and went perhaps 30 feet before stopping in front of something warm enough to produce steam on that cool night. The smell of vomit entered his nostrils.

"This was hers! This was hers!" Clay announced while jabbing a pinky-less hand toward the pile.

"How do you know?"

"It smells like her breath. It smells like bologna and mustard."

The chief pointed his light down the street. Deserted. Then toward the nearby yard. The grass had been trampled and at spots torn free of the mud beneath.

In one of the exposed areas, he saw the impressions of five toes. Sasha's footprint.

"This way, Clay," he said. "Quickly."

Chapter 18

Legion's agitation was mounting by the moment. Being without pets simply did not agree with it.

"Where are they?" One of Legions' selves shouted to the rest.

"We don't know," came the answer from many of the others.

It was more than just a delay in the itinerary. Legion grew increasingly agitated for another reason as well. *Prayer* and *worship*. Both of these words repulsed and maddened Legion, boring into it like ravenous parasites.

Usually, Legion owned the night. Most humans slept and of those that were awake during the dark hours, a disproportionate percentage were up to no good. This night was different. The encroaching power of prayerful worship of its one true enemy filled the air. It stung like a million, venomous wasps. It would not be ignored.

Legion's many selves screamed out. Some screamed in terror. Some in rage. All screamed in pain. Regardless, they all screamed a glorious crescendo of bloody murder.

***

Reverend Xavier Hernandez opened his eyes. His body shook like an autumn leaf caught in a blizzard gale.

Something wrenched him from his prayers - a disturbance. He heard, or thought he heard, screams. The screams of a multitude in agony. But what was it? Where was it? Looking around, he saw nothing unusual. Silence surrounded him, but the memory of those tortured shrieks haunted him.

He felt queasy, as if the owners of those voices carried poison on their breath. Terrified, he stood up. His chair toppled. It struck the floor and he jumped. Straining his ears, he listened. All was silent. Only his heart pounded in his ears.

Trembling, he went to his front window, parting the blinds just enough to have a peek. Everything appeared as normal - just a typical, deserted street in pre-dawn Getreide.

He felt the emptiness of that street.

It was the same emptiness dwelling within him. He knew that his mood was the result of dark forces. He also knew that things were not as bleak as they appeared. He was not alone. Jesus said he would be with him always, even to the very end of the age.

At the window, he bowed his head. He closed his eyes and prayed for strength.

He felt watched as he stood there. The feeling was strong, interrupting his focus. Unable to pray, he opened his eyes.

A gasp filled his lungs as he jolted.

Someone was watching him. Through the still-parted blinds of the front window, a face stared in.

At first, he thought it was a mirage, a reflection in the glass. But no, the face remained.

Scurrying backward, he staggered and caught the blinds with his flailing hand. He caught his foot on the rug and fumbled to maintain balance while shaking the blinds from him.

All the while, that face pressed against the window continued watching.

***

Sasha James finally found somebody awake. Unfortunately, she may have just killed him.

He struggling to keep upright, wrestling the blinds away and tripping over something. His shocked stare never left her face.

She took a step back from the window and held up her hands, palms out, trying hard to look as non-threatening as possible. She wasn't sure how much of her the man could see through the window, but she hoped it was enough to verify to him she was no threat.

It didn't seem to help; he looked more frightened. That's when she remembered one of her raised hands still held the gun. Not knowing how else to defuse the situation, she dropped the weapon allowing it to land near her feet.

For the first time, he averted his eyes from her. She followed his glance to the table where a smartphone sat. *Dear God,* she prayed inwardly. *Please don't call the police.*

Staring once again at her, he managed to catch his balance, moved toward the phone and picked it up.

Dear God, don't let him call the police.

He didn't dial. Instead, with the phone in his hand, he walked to the front door. From her vantage point, she could no longer see him, but the click of a deadbolt disengaging verified his presence.

The door opened.

What to do now? she wondered. She wanted to rush into the safety of his house but knew such quick movement might invite panic which would result in the door shutting before she could get through. Instead, she just stood there trying to look as innocent as possible.

She could feel the gun as it rested against her feet on the cold earth and wondered how quickly she could grab it if those who chased her arrived. Would she be fast enough? Sasha had her doubts.

"Please, sir," she sobbed, "some guys are after me - real bad guys. I need a place to hide."

For what seemed an eternity, the man stared her down, unmoving, silent. The seconds ticked by in painfully slow progression, and the urge to retrieve her weapon intensified to almost unbearable levels.

"Please!" she pleaded.

Without saying a word, he came toward her, picked up the gun and ushered her into his home. It wasn't until she was inside and the door was safely locked behind her that her adrenaline-overdosed brain registered what happened. She was surprised. Who would take a mud-covered, shoeless, armed stranger into their home in the dead of night?

The answer suddenly came to her. Nobody would unless he was a lunatic. She took a step back toward the door, but it was already shut and relocked. He stood there, her gun in his hand, unspeaking, unmoving.

With her shoulder blades pressed against the door, she glanced about for an escape route but saw none. Even if she could get out, her escape would be bittersweet as those other men were somewhere out there no doubt closing in on her.

Then, she felt something heavy in her hand. He had given the gun back to her. "I hope you understand that giving this back verifies I'm on your side." His voice was gentle but serious.

She nodded her acknowledgement - amazed, relieved and a bit confused. She tried to say something. Words failed.

***

Xavier took a leap of faith. This woman clearly needed help. Normally he would have been reluctant to allow an armed stranger into his house. The fact was, he had nearly called the cops on her, but something softened his heart. There was something in her eyes that told him she was part of God's plan and possibly held answers concerning his sleeplessness.

So, he let her in. He gave her back the gun. Now, it was time to see if his choice to let her into his life was prudent.

Knock – knock – knock.

The woman's eyes widened with terror as the vibrations of the knocking reverberated through the door. Seemingly unable to speak, she pleaded with big, saucer-eyes. Xavier returned her gaze with a silent nod.

He sighed and whispered, "Okay. Here's the plan."

***

The chief peered into the front window as best he could without looking obvious. He saw an overturned chair from the dim kitchen light and the wrecked remains of a set of mini-blinds. He also glimpsed somebody standing near the front door, but the angle prevented positive identification.

Clay knocked again while the chief continued to stare through that window. The figure didn't move. Suspicious.

"This is the Getreide Police," the chief called out. "Please open up!"

He hoped those inside would comply. Bashing the door down would be the next step. It was a step he hoped to avoid as doing so would be a noisy affair apt to draw unwanted attention from neighbors.

Relief washed over him as the door opened just an inch, further opening hindered by the door's engaged security chain. "Good evening, um, officer?" a man's voice came through the crack. An eye peered out at Clay.

The chief spoke up. "Sorry to bother you, sir, but we have received some reports of a suspicious woman in the area. She's a suspect in a number of crimes and considered to be armed and dangerous. I was just checking to make sure you were safe."

That eye changed trajectory, looking at the chief. "I beg your pardon, but neither of you are wearing any uniforms. Can I see some identification please?"

"Of course," the chief responded without missing a beat. As he reached for his wallet, he kept his focus on that peering eye. This was not the eye of one who had been sleeping.

He opened his wallet and held out the badge close to that eye for inspection. He had no doubt that this would convince the one inside to open up. It was genuine after all.

That eye squinted as it scrutinized. After a moment, the door shut and the sound of the security chain being disengaged could be heard. Finally, the door opened fully, revealing the eye's owner.

The one who stood there was a 40-something male. The chief sensed this man was nervous but trying to hide it. "A woman you say?"

The chief nodded.

"I haven't seen anything out of the ordinary tonight."

The chief stared at this liar without emotion. He certainly didn't want to alarm him prematurely. "Nothing at all?"

The man chuckled. It was a nervous chuckle. "Trust me, officers, if I had met up with an armed suspect, I would have dialed 911 right away."

"Good to know." This interrogation was going to plan. He always loved it when he had somebody right where he wanted them. "Have you been here all night?"

"Yes, sir."

"You haven't even stepped out on the porch?"

The man scrunched up his face in thought before shaking his head. "No, sir, haven't even unlocked this door since the sun went down."

"I see." The chief rubbed his chin before continuing. "What about these muddy footprints that I see coming into your house?"

The man looked down. "Oh, well, I took out the trash earlier."

"So, you were out earlier after all."

"Uh, well yes. But, like I said that was before the sun went down."

"They look fresh to me," the chief responded almost as soon as the man uttered his statement. "And, yet the sun has been down for hours."

The man was sweating bullets, and the chief loved it. He lived for moments like this watching people squirm. The strange thing was, he couldn't figure out for the life of him why this guy would protect Sasha James.

"You went barefoot to take out your garbage?" the chief pressed.

The man looked down at the prints saying nothing.

"Because these are clearly barefoot prints. See, one of them shows toes." He paused for effect. "And might I add that they're kind of dainty footprints for a man your size, wouldn't you say?"

The man still said nothing. He just stood there dangling against the proverbial ropes.

"Sir," the chief continued. "I see now that you are wearing shoes. Can you please explain why you would go outside to take out the garbage barefoot just to go in and put on a pair of sneakers?"

The man looked confused, and so was the chief. This situation made no sense. Why would this man harbor Sasha? Maybe they knew each other. Or perhaps she was hiding nearby and had threatened to shoot this man if he gave her away. Of course what he knew about Sasha James hinted that she wouldn't hurt a fly unless it was absolutely necessary. She must be desperate. Perhaps hurting flies had become quite necessary.

"Sir, if you don't mind, I would like to take a look around your place."

"Oh, no thank you. I can assure you that I am quite safe here."

Okay, time to throw the good cop vibe out the window. "Listen up. Right now, I have a set of circumstances that leads me to believe that you are harboring a fugitive. Whether or not you are doing it willingly or under duress is yet to be determined. What I do have right now is sufficient evidence for probable cause. That means I can enter your home without a warrant with or without your permission."

The man said nothing. The look of defeat on his face said it all. Slowly, he backed away from the open doorway to admit them entrance.

The chief had Clay lead the way into the house just in case bullets began to fly. Clay could take a bullet much better.

From the beginning of this mission, he had gone unarmed. This was not an accident. Going unarmed meant he would not, in a fit of rage or accidentally damage Legion's prize.

The chief was having second thoughts about that approach. Sasha had proven to be far more resourceful than he anticipated. This left him feeling vulnerable. He hated that.

The man stepped aside keeping a nervous grip around the door's knob as he backed into the wall. "So, this woman, she is dangerous?"

The chief didn't answer. He was too busy listening for any noise that would give away the location of his prey.

"Well, if she is dangerous, then I am sure glad you are…"

"Shut up!" The chief interrupted. He needed silence.

The chief cocked his head. He heard something, a noise. It was coming from behind the closed door of the next room.

He looked at the man and smiled. "What's in there?"

"Nothing, that's just a spare room."

The chief eyed the man over. His nervousness was giving him away. "Then, you won't mind me checking it out?"

The man sighed. "I don't mind, but I would caution you."

"If you have something to tell me, now's the time."

"I have a few raccoons in there."

The chief never heard anything so ludicrous. "Raccoons?"

The man nodded. "I found them under my porch. In fact, it's a whole family of raccoons."

The chief wasn't buying this cockamamie story for a minute, but he played along just the same. "What are you doing with raccoons in your house?"

"I have a soft spot for God's creatures," he said sheepishly. "With the land being developed into neighborhoods, they lost their habitat. When I found them, they were malnourished. I took them in to nurse them back to health. I was planning on returning them to the wild when the cubs were big enough."

"So, you say you have a whole family in there?"

"Well, just a mom and her cubs. I wouldn't go in there, though. The mom thinks she owns the place."

Frankly, the chief had expected a more believable story than that. Regardless, the one that was actually hiding in there was as unpredictable as ten territorial raccoons if not a thousand times more valuable.

"Clay, go check out the – um – raccoons." The chief made sure and paused at the right moment. He wanted this man shaking in his boots.

Clay moved forward and put his hand on the door. He turned the knob; he pulled the door open.

"What do you see, Clay?" The chief wanted to know.

"Nothing. It's pretty dark in here."

"The raccoons prefer it that way. They're nocturnal." The man chimed in.

The chief knew better than to believe the raccoon story. This man was a liar.

He made a mental note to add this one to the list for elimination at a more opportune time. He inched into the room behind Clay.

Clay flicked on the light switch and instantly, something growled. The chief turned back just as the door slammed shut in his face. At the same moment, the mother raccoon attacked Clay springing up and scratching at his eyes.

Clay grabbed it, peeling it away and holding it out by the scruff of its neck. The coon was hissing like a cobra. Smaller coons were scurrying about. One bit at his ankle, but the chief kicked him off while trying to work the door's knob. The knob turned, but the door was stuck.

The chief screamed as the raccoon lashed out at him from the end of Clay's arm. He felt a sting, and his face grew instantly warmer.

"Kill it!"

Clay obeyed, snapping its neck with a quick flick of the wrist. The animal dropped to the ground where it twitched but no longer presented a threat.

"Get us out of here!" the chief ordered.

Clay turned and plowed through the door smashing to splinters both it and the chair that had been propped up under the knob. Blood was dripping down into the chief's eyes from where the coon had sliced his brow, but even through the blood, he could see his error.

"Well, I'll be," he said as he looked at the muddy footprints near the wall just behind the front door. "Sasha James was behind that door the whole time."

She wasn't there now, though. The front door had been left open. Both Sasha and her accomplice had escaped.

He stepped out of the house just in time to see a red Toyota Rav4 barrel down the street. They skidded around the corner and were gone.

"What now, Chief?" Clay wanted to know.

The chief said nothing in response. He was not sure what to say. One thing was sure, Sasha James was one massive pain in his plan.

Chapter 19

Officer Simon Birch's gut sunk. It started the moment he left the woman with the chief and had been sinking ever since.

The look in that woman's eyes as he drove off haunted him. They looked so terror-struck, so forlorn. But it was more than her eyes that enticed his uneasiness. He didn't like how things had gone. It just didn't quite mesh even by the Getreide Police force's laidback standards.

So, he made a decision. He turned his car around and headed back to where he left Sasha James. He just needed to convince himself that everything was kosher. As he drove, his uneasiness grew, and he knew it would take considerable convincing.

He arrived on the scene, and that feeling spiked within him. Something was amiss. First, the Dynasty was still there but now it had a busted passenger window and a blown tire. The road beneath the car was streaked black. Somebody had been running the tires bald.

Maybe Sasha James resisted them, he said to himself. That was plausible, but if that happened, why had he heard nothing about it over the police frequency?

Behind the Dynasty sat the chief's S-10. It appeared deserted. He thought hard to come up with a rational, legal explanation, but no matter how hard he tried, the same nagging fact resurfaced. Something was rotten in Getreide and all fingers pointed to his boss as the prime suspect.

He wondered who the chief's friend was, the one who sat in the S-10 with him. Whoever it was, Simon hypothesized he was more than just a friend from the next town over as the chief claimed.

He also wondered how far up this thing went. The veins of corruption could run deep in small-town America. Simon sighed as he thought of the fact that everyone suddenly became a suspect in his new, under-the-table investigation.

He sat there in his patrol car rubbing the back of his head as he often did when deep in thought. Normally, he would call dispatch and relay the situation, but this case was no normal situation. Could he trust dispatch? The answer was unclear.

Even if dispatch was free and clear, any communication with them would be the same as communicating with the chief, which was something to be avoided. The element of surprise was his only advantage and must be kept close.

Something caught his eye.

Off in the distance, a glow emerged. Somebody flashed a light and that light seemed to be drawing closer. In fact, it was just over the ridge that separated the new neighborhood development and the road.

He rolled down his window, knowing sound carried in the silence of night. He heard, "Are you okay, chief? That coon sure messed you up."

Quickly, he turned off his headlights and drove perhaps thirty feet before rounding a bend in the road and pulling off into the tall grass beyond the shoulder. He hoped he would go unnoticed in the darkness.

Exiting the car, he crept along the banks of Getreide Creek back to the spot where the Dynasty and the S-10 still sat. The trees and tall grass that grew on either side of the creek's banks gave him cover. He was thankful. Because of the foliage, he was able to get within a few feet of the cars without much chance of being noticed.

He didn't have to wait long. Those with the flashlight approached.

Two figures emerged, coming to within a foot or two of him as he lay upon his stomach concealed by darkness and foliage. Neither of the figures spoke. The one with the light flashed the beam toward the creek, the shaft of light cutting through the darkness only a foot above Simon.

"Clay," one of them finally spoke. It was the voice of the chief.

"Yes, Chief," came the response.

He couldn't identify the responder by his voice and guessed it to be the mystery guest seen earlier in the chief's truck. Now he had a name.

"Get the first aid kit out of the tool chest," the chief commanded.

"Yes, Chief."

While Clay got into the back of the pickup and opened the chest, he watched as the chief grabbed the radio receiver from the cab. "Dispatch, are you there? Over."

"This is Zelda on duty. Go ahead – over," the response came over the police frequency.

"I need to know who lives at 322 North Rolland Road."

"Checking, sir."

While Zelda checked, the chief waited and Clay delivered the first aid kit. "Thank you, Clay. Now, get some gauze and iodine out of there. I need to disinfect the gash from that raccoon."

Raccoon! What in the world have they been up to? Simon wondered.

Zelda's voice came across the radio. "I have the information when you're ready - over."

"Go ahead."

"The owner of that residence is one Xavier Hernandez."

The chief flinched as he applied the iodine to his wound, hissing a curse word or two.

"Come again, sir?" Zelda's said.

"Oh, nothing. I just have a bit of a headache tonight. Any additional information on Mr. Hernandez?"

"Actually, it's Reverend Hernandez, and his records are clean."

"He's clergy?"

Simon's blood went cold as he listened because he knew the reverend. In fact, he was a member of his church.

"Affirmative," Zelda responded.

There were only two churches in Getreide. "Lutheran?"

"No, sir. He's at the other church."

The chief paused in thought before finally continuing. "Thank you, Zelda. You have been a real help."

"No problem, sir. Do you want me to call in Officer Birch for any sort of assistance?"

"That won't be necessary, Zelda. I'll let you know if anything changes to that parameter. Until then, don't contact Officer Birch or inform him regarding Reverend Hernandez. I want to keep him on his nightly patrol if at all possible."

"Understood, sir."

With that, the chief ended communications with dispatch. "Clay?"

"Yes, Chief."

"Where do preachers go when they've been chased from their homes?"

"Um, I don't know, Chief."

"Well, I have a hunch that we should check out his church. What do you say?"

"You're the boss, Chief," Clay answered.

The chief threw to the ground the cloth he had used to clean his wound. Little did he know that Officer Simon Birch was close enough to catch that cloth in the face. The smell of iodine burned Simon's nostrils, but he refused to react.

Clay and the chief got into the truck, made a U-turn, and took off. As soon as the taillights faded from view, Simon swatted away the chief's cloth and emerged.

Within moments, he was back in his car peeling out from the weeds and heading for the church. On the way, he radioed Zelda. "Dispatch, this is officer Birch, do you copy?"

"I copy you, Officer Birch."

Simon paused. "How's things at headquarters?"

"Just an average shift, sir."

"Have you heard from the chief this evening?"

Zelda didn't respond right away.

"Do you copy?"

"Negative, the chief has not communicated this evening."

Zelda failed his lie detector test so could not be trusted. He checked his watch. He should be at the church in a matter of minutes. He only hoped he would arrive in time.

Chapter 20

Reverend Xavier Hernandez sat in his Toyota at the far end of the church parking lot staring at the old church building. Dark, it appeared vacant.

The Rav4 passed quite a performance test. Throughout the trip, he obsessively looked in his rearview, expecting to be followed. But as far as he could tell, no one pursued them.

He only slowed down when the woman who sat in his passenger seat begged him to do so. She pointed out that the police would have a reason to pull them over. With his own recent experience with the police in mind, who could blame her?

During the short journey from his house to the church, he learned much about the woman he knew now as Sasha James. Recently divorced, she had a new job at the Lutheran school as a paraprofessional. She also apparently had a hit out on her life, and she had no idea why.

He knew it sounded crazy, yet under supernatural compulsion, he asked, "have you ever heard of Legion?"

She shook her head. "No, I have no reason to believe that the American Legion is involved."

The reverend nodded, being too frazzled to laugh at such a misunderstanding.

Now that the car stopped, she put on shoes which she grabbed from his front room as they exited. They were a pair of old hiking boots and too big for her feet. She laced them tight to keep them on.

He looked at her now, boots and all, knowing that her life was in great danger. He believed that God put him into this situation as her protector. So, he would protect her.

Not being used to thinking like a fugitive, he had not been sure where to flee. So, he fled to the church which was where he always fled when troubled.

There were two churches in Getreide, a Lutheran one associated with the school and his, which was non-denominational. Getreide, being a town founded by Germans, was overwhelmingly Lutheran. His church, by comparison, served only a small speck of the population.

The building itself was much older than the congregation that attended. In fact, it was the original Lutheran church before the new and current building was erected about 50 years back.

In size, it was nothing spectacular. It did however exude an air of grandeur. It was built in the traditional German, gothic style, complete with spire, stained glass windows and gargoyles glaring down from the roof-peaks.

He parked at the far end of the lot so that he could observe from a distance and decide if it looked safe to approach. It appeared safe.

Together, they exited the Toyota and hurried across the parking lot, feeling exposed. The distance from his car to the front doors of the church was maybe 30 feet, but at that moment, it felt like 300.

He wanted to run as fast as he could to the safety of that church but restrained himself.

The front doors of the church were massive hardwood doubles that towered above their heads in an arched shape. At the pinnacle, it was maybe fifteen feet from the ground. *Leave it to the Germans to make things larger than life.*

He pulled on the doors, and they opened. He rarely locked the church. He wanted the people to feel free to enter any time they wished. Plus, this was Getreide, Iowa, - just a small town where he felt safe. That opinion was changing for him with every passing minute.

They entered. The doors closed, and darkness surrounded them.

They were now in the deep shadows at the rear of the sanctuary. At the front, a light flickered. It was the eternal candle which stayed lit, a symbol that Christ's light always shines in the darkness.

The eternal candle didn't have a real, burning flame. Modern fire-code prevented unattended open flames. Instead, the light consisted of an electric bulb inside a red glass shade. Nondenominational churches didn't usually have eternal candles in their sanctuaries. That was more of a Lutheran thing. Then again, most nondenominational churches had not been converted from old Lutheran buildings. This one had been hardwired into the wall years ago, and it had been determined it would be easier just to let it remain.

That night, he was thankful for the red glow. It cast enough light to see what he needed to see. The sanctuary looked empty.

At the front of the sanctuary, stood the altar. In the crimson light, it looked more towering than normal. Even in the daylight, it was a hulking mass of carved mahogany, a piece original to the church and another example of sturdy German craftsmanship from a past time.

Above the altar stood a larger than life statue of Jesus. The Christ looked down upon the altar. A kind look gentled his face in the harsh-colored light. His hands, complete with nail holes, were extended in welcome.

This was a white Jesus, but what else would one expect from Germans? In truth, the Messiah transcended race. Xavier believed this, so the blonde Jesus was as good as any for his church.

He felt a tug on his arm. It was Sasha. She was trembling like a leaf.

He looked at her, but she wasn't looking back. She was looking out the one clear speck of glass in an otherwise stained-glass window. Her eyes grew wide as she let out a whimper.

***

The chief was on edge for good reason. The prey was armed and dangerous. He had no idea how many bullets were in her firearm or if she had extra beyond what was loaded.

He'd parked beside the Rav4 at the end of the church's parking lot. When he sighted the Toyota, it confirmed his hunch was correct.

The chief exited the vehicle. Clay followed. Using his golem as a shield, he approached the Toyota.

"Do you think they are in that car?" Clay asked.

The chief didn't know. He suspected not. Who would stay in a car when there was a perfectly good church nearby? However, Sasha James had proven to be full of little surprises. So why wouldn't she be in the car waiting for him, drawing a bead, preparing to pull the trigger?

"What do you think?" Clay pressed.

"I don't know. Go check it out," the chief responded.

He took cover behind the S-10 while Clay walked around the pickup without evidence of fear. He strolled directly up to the parked Toyota and cupped his hands around his eyes as he pressed his face against the windshield. The lack of fear didn't surprise the chief. Clay never showed fear as it was not imbedded in the DNA of a golem.

The windshield didn't disintegrate. Sasha's bullets did not pulverize it to glittery bits.

Clay shattered the silence. "They're not here."

Using his sleeve, the chief wiped a thick layer of sweat from his brow as he emerged from the far side of the pickup, making sure to stay low to minimize himself as a target. He peeked around his golem, staring at the darkened church building. He loathed the idea of entering a house of worship, that bastion of Christianity which he opposed so fervently.

He scrambled for other options. Perhaps he could draw them out to him. If he torched the church, he could smoke them out.

No. Doing to the church what he did to Andrew's place would only draw attention from the community. Plus, what if they don't come out?

What if they choose to be martyrs? How would he explain to Legion that he had incinerated its pet? He shuddered to think of those potential consequences.

The chief ordered Clay to the front of the line making sure his "shield" was in place. He hated this need to cower for protection, but he hated the idea of being mowed down by Sasha's bullets more.

In Getreide, many doors remained unlocked as the citizens simply felt safe. He hoped that would be the case with the church. They approached the door. Clay reached out, grabbed the handle, and pulled. The door opened.

Quickly, they entered the building, finding themselves at the rear of the sanctuary. As the chief stood there, the disgust he felt within doubled. He had no doubt that Legion would catch the scent of a foreign god upon his countenance when he returned. He only hoped Legion would tolerate it.

Everything was bathed in a dim, red glow, the consequence of a single-bulb with a red glass shade extending from the wall at the front of the sanctuary. They walked toward the light.

The chief still had his flashlight, but he dared not turn it on. The sanctuary possessed too many hiding places. Light would make them an easy target.

Despite the danger inherent in hunting armed prey, he was glad that he remained defenseless. He just could not risk shooting Legion's pet even if it were in self-defense. A dead Sasha James was a worthless Sasha James.

He snuck along the side aisle making sure he kept Clay between himself and the pews. Although glad of his decision to go unarmed, he was kicking himself for not having any other protection besides his golem.

There were many less lethal options available to him from pepper spray to tasers to chloroform, not to mention body armor for self-protection. When he started out on this little mission, body armor seemed like overkill. Of course, that was before Sasha James proved her resiliency.

Every row of pews offered a hiding place for the enemy and with every additional row they cleared; his heartrate hit a new crescendo. Inside, the chief's mind screamed. *I'm a trained law enforcement officer. I have a certain level of expertise pertaining to handling stressful situations.* Yet now, the only thing that kept him moving forward was the thought of what might occur if he lost his cool and fled back to Legion empty-handed.

After what felt to be an eternity, he arrived at the front of the church. He turned and looked upon the pews which he now knew were empty. From behind Clay's body, he redirected his gaze to the altar, the pulpit, and the pastor's study.

Any moment, he expected the barrage of bullets to fly. When that happened, he wanted to be ready for the capture.

He considered simply having Clay smash all the hiding places to bits, but that would expose him as a target, not to mention jeopardize the safety of Sasha who simply could not be damaged. Together, they crept up to the pulpit. It was a massive, old monolith.

As the chief approached this ancient monument, he felt his nerves tighten. There was plenty of room for the hunted to hide behind that pulpit.

They crept up the steps that existed just in front of the pulpit. The chief dug his fingernails into his golem as the tension mounted.

Clay leaned around the pulpit so that he could see what lurked there, the chief pasted to him like a piece of macaroni on a kindergarten art project. He dug his fingers deeper into Clay's flesh. The tension was crushing.

"It's empty, Chief," Clay reported.

"One down, two to go," the chief said as he looked back and forth from the altar to the Pastor's study and back again.

He wasn't sure which to check next. Finally, he directed Clay toward the altar. He thought he could keep an eye on the closed door of the Pastor's study while they checked behind the altar. He didn't want to do it the other way around. What if he entered the study and they were behind the altar? Then he would open an escape for them once again.

His jitters intensified as he neared the altar. He felt small under the stare of a ridiculous-looking, blond Jesus. The gaze of those carved, blue-painted eyes compounded the stress and knotted his gut.

He assumed the sculptor of that statue had been trying to convey a feeling of benevolence and grace in the statue's face. In the chief's opinion the sculptor failed.

In this statue, he saw only the look of a condemning judge. What else could the chief see but that? He chose his allegiances, and they did not align with the teachings of Christ.

Further tension mounted as his vulnerability increased. He could only hide behind Clay from one angle at a time but two angles now presented themselves. He kept his golem between himself and the altar.

He jolted as Clay spoke. "They're not here either."

The chief blinked. In his stress, he hadn't realized they had gotten close enough to check behind the altar.

"Are you sure?" he asked.

"Yes, Chief."

So, it's the study then. He eyed the closed door considering the best way to enter with the least amount of risk.

One step, second step, third step - they drew closer to the study.

"Did you hear that?" Clay asked in a voice much louder than necessary.

The chief turned back. He *had* heard something. It might have been nothing, just a mouse scurrying behind the altar. *Then again...*

There was only one way to discover the truth. Together, they backtracked.

***

Sasha's hand remained over her mouth hoping her sneeze went unnoticed. Beside her, Xavier cringed in fear.

They stood in a secret space behind the altar. The secret space was not original to the church but had been retrofitted in back during the First World War.

The church back then was predominately German, and Germans were not well liked in the good old United States during that time in history. It was for that reason that the congregation secretly installed this room and the connecting escape tunnel. Such were the fears that dominated German-American culture at the time, that a non-Aryan mob would come and simply exterminate them.

About a year or so ago, Xavier had stumbled across the hidden space accidentally tripping the latch holding the secret panel in place while he cleaned. Now, he was glad he found it. At the time of discovery, he hadn't known what its purpose had been. But Xavier had been curious. His only clue had been the year 1917 followed by a sentence in German, which had been engraved in the wall of the secret room.

There were a few elderly men and women still in Getreide that didn't know about the secret room first-hand but had heard rumors of it from their parents. Through these second-hand accounts, he had found the truth about the secret space.

He never imagined he would use it himself. He looked past Sasha down the narrow escape passage.

Through a stained-glass collage separating his space from the sanctuary, he watched the two who stood only feet from him no doubt searching for the source of Sasha's sneeze.

By the meager light of the eternity candle, the enemy approached. The red glow from that light cast a demonic hue upon the two scoundrels. They drew close, within a foot of the glass wall, staring intensely, their eyes roving analytically.

Xavier felt the urge to run. One of the men unknowingly stared into his eyes through glass artwork separating the two rooms. *They can't see me. They can't see me. They can't me,* he mentally chanted.

Unable to look away, the reverend stared down the other in terror.

There was something odd about the one called Clay. Clay's face looked unnatural. His facial movements were stiff and manufactured. It was as if he wasn't real at all but a cheap knockoff impostor from an inferior creator.

More than anything, the man's eyes gave him away. They say that eyes are the window to the soul, and these eyes indicated a vacant body.

The chief joined Clay in the stare-down. Four eyes glared.

The reverend noticed the chief also had an empty look about him, but it was different from Clay's. It was not a lack of soul that made this one appear so vacant. This was the look of a soul damned - one in league with demons, perhaps even an entire legion of demons.

Clay reached up and put his hands gently against the stained glass. His soulless eyes continued to search.

The reverend trembled slightly as a strange smile grew on Clay's lips. They were only inches from each other with only the most fragile separator between them.

Beside him, he heard Sasha's heavy breathing. He glanced over at her. She still had her hand over her mouth. She seemed to be less stifling a sneeze now and more containing her screams.

Xavier's trembling increased as he watched those powerful-looking hands press against the glass.

Clay's smile broadened as he turned and whispered something to the chief. On a certain level Xavier would have given anything to hear what had been whispered. On another lever however, he already knew.

"Run!" the reverend hissed as he grabbed Sasha and dragged her down the escape tunnel.

As they began to move, the glass exploded into a thousand shards.

Clay's fist protruded through. Those sausage fingers splayed outward, grasping for anything they could find.

They caught nothing but air. Xavier and Sasha vacated at the right time.

The other hand smashed through creating a bigger gap in the glass. Then came Clay's head and torso. They rounded the corner of the passageway, but not before getting a look at the one who stared at them, flecked with bits of glittery shards which stuck from his flesh like pins in a cushion.

They rounded the corner just as those soulless eyes grew wide with recognition. Behind them they heard more smashing and knew the chase was on. They ran as fast as they could navigating the narrow passageway. Behind them, more smashing.

Chapter 21

Officer Birch pulled up next to the pair of vehicles at the end of the Church's parking lot. He recognized the chief's S-10 as well as his pastor's red RAV4. Seeing both of those vehicles together intensified his uneasiness.

He emerged from the patrol car keeping a vigilant eye. All was still, yet he couldn't shake the feeling that chaos was on the verge of erupting.

Resting one hand upon the holstered, standard-issued sidearm on his belt, he reached with the other into the squad car and retrieved the Beretta 1301 Tactical 12 Gauge shotgun that all of the town's police cars came equipped with. The switch that released the gun from its holder resisted at first, a testament to the fact that Officer Simon had never before needed that kind of firepower. He pushed the switch harder, and it clicked. He picked up the gun. It was a far cry from his Grandad's 410. Then again, he was hunting something more than pheasants.

Being a police officer in Getreide meant you had to take a fair amount of ribbing from time to time. People called him things like Barney Fife or Enos Strate. They called him things like that when he was giving out some sort of citation or serving a warrant.

Despite being compared to these and other bumbling TV deputies, Simon had always taken his career seriously. So, it irked him that his hands trembled while loading the shotgun's chamber.

He began the trek from his car to the church and his hands trembled more violently with every step. The lot suddenly seemed outrageously large, or maybe he had instantly shrunk. Regardless, it felt vast as he crossed it.

His walk became a jog. His straight-line route became a serpentine pattern that only ended when contacting the exterior wall of the church. He pressed himself against that wall. He stood still, barely breathing. He thought he heard noises from inside the building, the sound of breaking glass.

Slowly, he peeked into one of the windows, but the stained glass prohibited any visual contact. Knowing he needed to gain access to the building, he scurried under the window and over to the main door. He tried the handle and found it to be unlocked.

Forcing his hand to stop trembling, he pulled the door open. It swung easily and silently. Simon entered the church.

He entered further into the building, keeping the shotgun at the ready, trying with all he had to keep from shaking. He was glad he had this weapon. The great thing about shotguns was you didn't have to be an expert marksman to hit things. The spread of the shot ensured damage if only it were aimed in the general direction of the target. This was a good thing, because with his nerves frayed as they were, he felt that the broadside of a barn would stand a fair chance of escaping the fury of his onslaught.

The darkness within the sanctuary wasn't relieved by the eternal candle. The red glow only added to his anxiety, casting everything into diabolical shadows in varying shades of crimson.

He wanted to turn around. He wanted to run away, but the badge he wore prevented this.

Scurrying down the side aisle, he stayed low, keeping the shotgun trained on any spot where he felt an enemy might be waiting. He would give anything to call for backup but refrained. He had no way of knowing who was caught in this web of corruption.

He needed to see better. Reluctantly, he held the shotgun in one hand as he flicked on the flashlight he kept on his belt next to his holstered sidearm. He didn't like giving away his position and only turned on the light out of necessity. The beam bounced because of his twitchy nerves. This frustrated him, because deep down it made him wonder if he really was nothing more than a Barney Fife or an Enos Strate.

Officer Simon neared the front of the sanctuary and laid his eyes upon the Malay. Somebody smashed to bits the stained glass behind the altar.

With his shotgun at the ready, he crept past a statue of Jesus, hearing the sound of grinding glass under his feet. With caution, Simon leaned in and looked through the void where beautiful glass had once been. Deserted. Upon the floor, evidence of activity. The disturbed dust revealed fresh footprints.

He knew what he had to do. He entered the space and proceeded down the passageway. He really had no choice.

Claustrophobia bombarded him as he entered the confined space. He forced those crushed in feelings away and willed himself to move forward.

The passage was dark and narrow, so narrow his shoulders brushed dust off of the walls as he progressed. In that cramped space, he had trouble keeping his shotgun at the ready.

He considered pulling his sidearm from its holster. His handgun would certainly be a better choice given the restrictions of this narrow space. But, he only had so many hands and would be unable to hold this handgun, his flashlight, and the shotgun all at once. He managed, keeping the shotgun close to his body with the barrel pointed toward the ceiling hoping it could be aimed and fired quickly if needed.

Step after step, he progressed deeper into the unknown, feeling like a tunnel rat from Vietnam. He pushed forward. Despite his fears, he pushed forward.

Chapter 22

Xavier's advantage was that having explored the tunnel upon discovery, he was familiar with what existed in that pitch darkness. He didn't remember this many spider webs a few months ago.

He wasn't afraid of them, but their webs altered the tunnel just enough to make it feel foreign. Having no time to clear the path before him, he moved through the silky filaments, shivering as they brushed against his face.

He tried hard to remember what was ahead. About 20 feet in, he recollected the passageway took a sharp right turn keeping in line with the thick exterior wall of the church. It was here they began crawling to get under frames that held the massive stained glass windows.

"Are you back there?" he whispered as he crawled.

"Yes," Sasha answered.

That relieved his fears somewhat. He wished he could somehow put himself between Sasha and those who hunted her, but he felt more comfortable taking the lead in this secret passageway.

He reached up and felt the stone that held the windows. Ahead, the tunnel would slope downward fairly steeply. Because of the limitations of the small crawlspace, they would have to take it on headfirst.

Silently, he flew down the slide. It wasn't far, maybe ten feet or so down that smooth shaft of granite. He landed and waited. She didn't follow.

"Sasha?" he hissed.

"Where are you?" she responded.

She sounded frantic. "Just keep going. You're coming up to a slide. It's okay. Just go with it."

A second later, she came skidding down to meet him. He could hear the panic in her voice as she spoke. "How are we going to get back up?"

"We're not going back up. The ones who built this meant it to be a one-way escape."

"Where are we?" she asked.

"Right now? We are under the church parking lot."

"What is this place?"

"There's no time to explain. All I can say is this escape route is a gift from God. Now, move. We must keep ahead of the others."

***

Sasha's paranoia flared, but who could blame her considering recent events. As she crawled along, she became acutely aware of the fact she was following a stranger down a dark tunnel to an unknown destination.

She didn't like putting such trust in somebody with so little history. *What if he is on their side? What if he is only leading me into a trap?*

Her knees hurt as they continued crawling along, but the diameter of the round-shaped tunnel didn't leave room for her to walk. Her efforts were hampered by the solid grip on her gun.

Holding the weapon pacified her paranoia.

She tightened her grip as she pictured the two who followed. In her mind's eye, they were just behind her, right at her heels, reaching out, their fingers missing her by only inches as she struggled along.

Claustrophobia invaded. Vertigo ensued. Suddenly the walls of the tunnel constricted upon her.

Her fear overpowered her. She swore she could feel grasping hands reaching around her throat, but it was her imagination. She tried to push them away so as to catch a breath, but the air itself seemed against her.

She found herself on the verge of hyperventilation.

"It's okay, Sasha. It's going to be okay," the reverend spoke.

She said nothing in response. Her breaths came in wheezes, her heart pounded like a drum.

"Do you know how I know it is going to be okay?"

How could he know? she thought.

"Because God never forsakes his people. You do believe in Jesus don't you?"

"Yes," she managed to whisper.

"Good. Let's pray."

"Yes," she wheezed.

"Father, we know that even when things are at their darkest, we don't need to fear. We know you are always with us. Even now, as we scurry along in the dark like worms in the garden, we know that you are with us."

As the reverend prayed, she felt freed from those throttling hands. The air thinned. She breathed easier. The dizziness passed.

"We don't know how, and we don't know when, but please deliver your servants from this present tribulation. In Jesus' name we pray, amen."

"Amen," she chimed in, being aware that her voice sounded much clearer than before.

She continued to pray with all her heart as they silently continued crawling.

Chapter 23

Legion's many selves were throwing a tantrum. Enraged, Legion shouted curses from the abyss under the chief's house.

Legion was angry for many reasons. First, there was the issue of their servant's incompetence. The chief should have had Sasha James in custody by now. In fact, at this moment the many selves of Legion should be having their fun with her.

They were furious of the fact that even with Clay's assistance, the chief lacked the skills to capture this one mortal woman. Her name rung out within their collective consciousness, "Sasha James! Sasha James! *Sasha James!*" it spat through gritted teeth.

The demons' rage continued to build upon itself like a brick and mortar combination designing its own tower of Babel to rage at God himself. It was a rage so forceful it flowed from the abyss into the world.

That essence found the vile woman with the man of God as they crawled along that tunnel like a pair of beaten dogs.

Legion sensed that Clay and the chief were closing in and had a chance to overtake them if only the fleeing prey could be slowed down. For that reason, Legion's essence reached into the tunnel and grabbed at the woman, wrapping invisible claws around her mortal throat.

It enjoyed the feeling of her throat tightening. They delighted in every wheeze that she let escape.

Legion's satisfaction was short-lived. The man of God tempted her to pray. At first, Legion's essence choked her harder, hoping to dissuade her from joining. Despite that effort, she did join and Legion could do nothing but release her.

It took so much energy to find Sasha in the hidden tunnel, they had no choice but to retreat to the abyss and regain strength. Now beaten and writhing, Legion curled up among its many selves like an intertwined orgy of mating vipers.

Legion needed recuperation and would have to rely on the chief to bring the pets to the abyss; a fact that frustrated them to no end. For now though, it could do nothing but lick its many wounds and wait for a more opportune time.

Holding court, they judged the chief may not be worth his service for much longer. It may be time to eliminate their servant.

Chapter 24

The chief hadn't been so humiliated since his childhood. Not only had Sasha James eluded capture yet again, but he found himself crawling along some unknown passageway and looking at nothing but the flashlight beam emblazoned butt of his golem.

Sadly, there was no other option. Clay had to go first. The tunnel reeked of booby trap and ambush potential.

Clay made a great shield, but he made a lousy leader. Repeatedly, he would stop and ask if he was going the right direction insinuating there was any other direction to go in this one way passageway.

"Yes, Clay, you are still going the right way," the chief responded while searching for his ever-elusive patience. "In fact, I am so sure that you are going the right way that I think you should crawl faster."

"But it's dark down here. I can't see."

"Who cares," The chief dug as deep as he could but found no additional patience.

Suddenly, Clay disappeared. "Clay!"

"Down here, Chief." Clay's voice sounded distant.

The flashlight beam revealed a hole in the tunnel. He pointed the beam down and could see Clay's butt staring back up at him.

It looked like about 10 feet of a drop. Reluctantly, he followed.

He was fairly sure the slide had brought them below ground level and the round tunnel which they now crawled through was below grade. But where were they headed exactly? He had no clue.

Never in a thousand lifetimes would the chief have thought that capturing one little woman would be such an undertaking. He had a golem at his command. He had Legion on his side. Capturing Sasha should be easy.

As he crawled, his fears turned toward thoughts of Legion. He wondered if it grew anxious. He wanted to keep those demons happy. Happy demons were agreeable demons, and as long as they were agreeable, they would continue to serve his purpose. Not killing him was a plus, too.

He suspected Legion had already helped him far more than he was aware. The demons gave him a golem to do his dirty work. However, he always had to be in close proximity for his golem to remain animated. Being in such proximity to the crimes would surely implicate him as a suspect. Even with his position in the town, he would not be able to avoid incrimination.

He had the feeling Legion had unseen influence upon Getreide. The citizens had the proverbial wool pulled over their eyes.

The chief saw evidence of this may times. It was evident yesterday during the attempt to murder Daniel. The crowd just stood there watching.

The chief frowned at that thought. Not everyone just stood there. Sasha James had taken action. What was so different about that woman that she should be immune to Legion's influences?

He suspected her actions weakened Legion's hold on the other bystanders as well. Once that happened, the mission had to be aborted.

People like Sasha were rare, being resistant to demonic influence. Her resistance made her dangerous. Therefore, she had to be eliminated.

This woman was an enigma. How was it she still roamed free?

He had to try harder. "Come on, Clay. Let's pick up the pace."

"Yes, Chief."

With renewed vigor, they crawled along. If he concentrated hard enough, he could almost sense the fear wafting from those he chased. Or was that his own fear he sensed?

He could not fail Legion. He *would* not fail Legion.

***

Officer Simon Birch didn't like his position. He had squeezed himself into the narrow passageway. Because of that limited space, he was vulnerable, unable to keep his Beretta 1301 Tactical 12 Gauge shotgun at the ready. Now, as he found himself forced to crawl under what he suspected was the church's stained glass windows, he found the gun more cumbersome. Instead of carrying it in front of him, he had to hold it under his body as he scooted along.

He cringed as the space reverberated with the sounds of the shotgun scraping along the bottom of the tunnel. Deep down he knew it was a quiet noise, but considering the situation, it sounded like a 100 decibel alarm in his ears.

To the best of his knowledge, he was headed in the right direction. Then again, he knew that even a Barney Fife should have no trouble with such a task. The passageway was either forward or backward. No other options presented themselves, at least not yet.

He considered radioing into dispatch. Standard procedure required him to take that action, but distrust gave him pause. He remembered the earlier communication with Zelda. Dispatch could not be trusted. He left the radio on his belt unused.

He thought that he heard something akin to voices. Simon froze, listening. Maybe the unique acoustics of the tunnel were playing tricks with his hearing. He listened harder, straining his ears but those sounds--if they had ever been--had vanished into silence.

He remained motionless, waiting for the sounds to begin again, but they didn't. After a time, he started forward, trying to keep his Berretta off the ground and trying with all his might to stay vigilant.

Besides the fact that the passage only went one direction he was encouraged by the fact that only broken spider webs existed here. That told him he was on the right path.

The illumination from his flashlight was sorely inadequate, revealing only a radius of a few feet. *What if the batteries failed?* The thought came to him like a mallet to his head. The darkness would be absolute. Involuntarily, he shuttered.

Ahead of him, as he scooted along, something emerged into the light. It was a hole.

He drew close to it and peered down into the depths. It was not a 90 degree hole but perhaps 45 degrees. The floor and sides were made of some slippery material--perhaps polished granite?

He could see the bottom. It wasn't far.

With apprehension, he realized he would have to follow like Alice on her way to Wonderland.

Like Alice, he couldn't see past the bottom of the slide. What if it was an ambush? What if sliding down there was the last thing he would ever do on this side of eternity? Then there was the dilemma of how he'd manage getting back up. The sides were steep and smooth. There would be no way to claw himself out.

Overriding his inhabitations, he took the plunge head first, trying to brace his feet against the walls to slow his descent while keeping his gun from scraping. In both these objectives he failed.

Too fast and too loud, he landed at the bottom. Unable to bring his weapon up, he did the only thing he could; he covered his flashlight, held his breath, and prayed no one was waiting for him.

Once assured he was alone, he dared point his light toward the space in front of him. He found himself in a new stretch of tunnel, round in shape and perhaps four feet in diameter. After a moment to catch his wits, he continued onward.

He shuddered to think about how his actions this night would be evaluated. He had not followed standard protocol, not by a long shot.

Under normal circumstances, he would not be in this tunnel at all. He would have called in for backup. But this was Getreide, and his backup, he had determined was likely corrupt. He was on his own and would use the radio only as a last-ditch effort.

He tried to figure out his location but could not. Where did this tunnel lead? He had no clue. All he knew was that he had to continue. So, he continued, and his terror increased with every inch.

***

The reverend led. Sasha followed. The destination remained a mystery. At least she was still alive; that was miraculous.

Her head felt lopsided from holding too many questions and too few answers. *Why were these people after her? Why was it seemingly impossible to kill them? Who were they working for?*

Like laundry in a perpetually-running dryer, the questions tumbled about. She hoped answers would stick to the tumbling questions with the static building, but no revelations came.

The most relevant question at the moment related to the reverend. Why was this man risking his neck to help her? She learned his name. She learned his occupation but knew little else about him. Could she trust him? She didn't know.

Why get involved? Why did he stick his neck out on the chopping block when it was easier to walk away? She tossed those questions into the proverbial drier. They joined in the tumbling but answers remained hidden.

The only reason she could think of was the same for her when she intervened for Daniel the afternoon before. It was the right thing to do.

She hoped she was right in that thinking. She hoped that Reverend Xavier Hernandez was a man of honor doing the right thing. Still, doubt ate at her. *Good Samaritan or wolf in sheep's clothing?*

Once again, she felt the unseen hands of panic reaching toward her, scraping jagged nails against the nape of her neck. As before, she prayed sensing those unseen hands losing their grip and slipping back into the oily darkness.

***

Legion, Xavier thought as he crawled along the tunnel. *How did Legion fit into this bazar puzzle?*

He tried to fathom the connection but could not. He felt there was a connection however well masked it was.

He wondered about Sasha James. Having only just met, he was surprised in the trust she apparently put in him. He only hoped her trust was not misguided. Silently, he prayed he could point to God for trust since he was only an instrument of the Almighty's.

He knew escaping those who hunted them would not be easy, not if they had connections to Legion. According to Sasha, these men seemed to possess a resiliency beyond that of mortal men. It was a resiliency that only could be explained through a connection with supernatural means.

Without warning, the tunnel ended. He fell.

Deep coldness overwhelmed him. He knew where he was. He was in Getreide creek. This was an optimal exit point for those who had built the tunnel all those years back. The high banks provided camouflage. The shallow water was never more than three feet deep. The creek was a perfect way to get out of town quickly without being noticed.

Sasha plopped into the shallow water beside him and let out a gasp. "My gosh! That's cold."

Xavier agreed. "In another month, the creek will be frozen over and harder to navigate on foot."

"We have to get out of here before they find us," Sasha said. "Come on, let's go."

Xavier stood up from the water, and a thought struck him. There was no way to outrun these men who had Legion on their side. They needed to take God's way. They needed to stand against this enemy. The main challenge now would be convincing Sasha they needed a new strategy. "I think it's time we take the offensive."

She seemed to ignore him, pulling on his arm, and pleading with him to run. The desperation he saw in her tugged at his heart.

Grabbing her hands in his, he told her his new plan. When he finished, he waited, knowing it would take a moment for the new objective to sink in. She said nothing, but her trembling fingers spoke volumes.

"It's the only way, Sasha," he added.

He wished he could see her face, read her expression, but the darkness prevented it. Letting go of her hands, he prayed she wouldn't run.

Finally, she let out a sigh. "Okay. We'll do it your way."

Chapter 25

"Are we there yet?" Clay asked again. Some people might have found his childish mind endearing, but the chief was not one of those people.

"Are we there yet? Are we there yet? Are we there yet? Hey, Chief."

"What!"

"Are we there yet?"

"No, Clay," the Chief finally responded through clenched teeth. "We are not there yet."

"Are we getting closer than before?"

Well, obviously. "Yes, Clay."

His nerves were frayed and not just because of Clay, but because of the larger picture. He fretted about the possibility of failure. If he did fail to requisition Sasha James, then what? Would Legion quit helping him? Would Legion do worse than quit helping him? He shuddered.

His face bumped into Clay's butt. His golem had stopped. "What's going on?"

"I think we're finally there," Clay answered.

"How do you know?"

"I can smell the night."

"You can?" This was news to the chief.

Clay didn't respond but knowing who he was talking to, the chief assumed his golem was nodding vigorously, oblivious to the fact that his nodding could not be seen from the chief's angle. Clay's special abilities never ceased to both amaze and annoy. *He could smell the night and track down his dismembered fingers, but he could not track the scent of Sasha James? Go figure.*

He heard Clay inhale. "Yup. That's the smell of the night alright. It is directly ahead of us."

"What does it smell like?" the chief asked.

"It smells like me."

"And what does that mean?"

"You know, it smells like the outside. It smells like dirt, and mold and earthworms."

The Chief wondered. "Does it by chance smell like a frightened woman?"

Clay inhaled loudly three times in a row. "Nope."

Of course not.

***

Sasha and Xavier hid 15 feet above the ground within the foliage of a large pine that grew from the creek's bank. Here the moonlight failed to penetrate, leaving the duo in near-absolute darkness. Together, they peered out like owls watching the tunnel's exit point, waiting.

Now as they huddled in the tree, a crucial flaw became evident. If they were discovered, there was no escape unless they miraculously sprouted wings.

That problem nagged her, but there was nothing she could do. Changing hiding places now was too risky. The gun in her hand gave her little consolation. Cars, bats, and angry raccoons did nothing to stop these men. She had no reason to believe bullets would be more successful.

Sasha looked at Xavier perched one branch away. In the darkness, he was nothing but a dark silhouette within a collection of shadows. "Look," he whispered.

She looked. She felt a lump of fear build in her throat as two dark figures emerged from the tunnel.

***

The chief was glad to be out in the open. He stood upright massaging his back and ignoring his pained knees. Beside him stood his golem seemingly unaffected by the trek.

He didn't want to give away their position but had no choice. He flicked on the flashlight knowing that his prey could not be far ahead and hoping to catch them in full retreat.

The light confirmed what his water-logged boots hinted. The tunnel deposited them into Getreide creek. The light didn't reveal the whereabouts of Sasha James or her new companion. They couldn't be far, probably just around the bend. *Which direction had they fled and which direction should he pursue?*

"Do you see any sign of them?" he asked his golem.

"No, Chief. Do you?"

The chief bit his lip with agitation. He contemplated his next move denying that the trail had grown cold.

He checked for tracks in the mud along the banks of the river, but his light revealed nothing. Perhaps the footprints existed but without the benefit of daylight, they would be exceedingly hard to discover much less follow with any speed or accuracy. Maybe Sasha and the reverend plodded along in the creek itself. If that were the case, then there would be no prints to follow at all.

Out of the corner of his eye something caught his attention, a slight shifting in the darkness. He turned. Off to his right stood a large pine. He shone the light at it, staring hard, but the dense foliage of those branches obstructed his view.

He saw it again, a minute movement that might have gone unnoticed under other circumstances. He took a tentative step closer, staring hard.

A crucial fact popped into his head. Sasha James was armed.

"Clay," he said with little more than a whisper. Calmness was the key to this situation. No sudden movements that would panic the one with the gun.

Clay came up to his side. "Yes, Chief," came the booming response.

The chief cringed, expecting bullets to fly. None did. He leaned in close to Clay not wanting to be overheard. "I'm going to take cover behind that tree."

Clay followed the trajectory of the chief's finger with his eyes staring at a large oak about fifteen feet from where they stood. "Once I am behind that tree, I want you to check out this pine and catch whatever is hiding in there. Do you understand?"

"I understand."

With that, the chief began to walk over to the big oak, deliberately keeping his pace calm, steady, and without any sudden movements. The oak was about four foot in diameter which was more than adequate to provide cover from any bullets that might fly his direction. It was close enough to the pine so that he would be close. Clay would not slow due to distance from his master.

He plastered himself against the far side of that tree, peering around the trunk enough to see his man of the earth in action. As instructed, Clay started his task and a second later, tranquility devolved into chaos.

Something growled, then hissed. Clay let out a scream, an act uncharacteristic of a golem. He staggered away from the pine. Something was on his head, and it was not happy.

The chief couldn't tell what it was, but knew it was not Sasha or the preacher. Whatever it was, it was giving Clay a run for his money.

The growl came again, low, and ominous. The chief shone the flashlight at the spectacle, but the glare only added to the chaos, casting devilish shadows and distorting shapes.

The battle was short and over the instant Clay was able to grip his adversary. Clay squeezed and the sound of crushing bones silenced the growls and hisses. With a huff, the golem threw the lifeless lump to the earth.

The Chief approached, keeping the light on Clay who had deep gashes etched on his face with one penetrating deep into his throat (right where the jugular would have been in a normal human). Clay's wounds looked gruesome, but his earthen face was already in the process of remolding. Within seconds the golem would be as good as new.

The Chief directed the beam to the dead thing at Clay's feet. There, periodically twitching, was the broken body of a male bobcat.

The chief swore. He'd been sure the tree housed Legion's pet. No doubt Sasha and her new companion used this distraction to escape.

"What now, Chief?" Clay wanted to know.

The chief looked toward the east. The sun lightened night's horizon.

"I'm getting really sleepy," Clay mumbled.

Ah, nuts, the chief thought. Legion bestowed Clay's energy. With the night's activities, he burned through his reserve.

They had to get back to the house quickly for replenishment. He had never tried to carry Clay, but a six foot pile of mud would not be easily lifted.

He looked at the pine where the bobcat had been and let out a long sigh. "Let's go back to the house, Clay. Perhaps Legion will be merciful."

Chapter 26

Xavier and Sasha watched in disbelief. Bobcats were uncommon in Northern Iowa. They were also solitary, skittish creatures. What were the chances one lived one tree away from where they hid?

During the long crawl through the tunnel, Xavier had already told Sasha a little bit about himself. He wasn't just a preacher; he practiced what he preached. The reverend believed a spiritual war was going on all around them and had been raging since the beginning of creation: angels versus demons, God versus Satan, good versus evil. He believed everything that occurred in someone's life was a result of spiritual warfare and that included what was happening to them right now.

That's when he told Sasha about Legion, the demons that Jesus cast into the herd of pigs. He told her how God revealed to him the connection with Legion and their recent plight. It was a connection he did not quite understand, but he believed understanding would come later.

Sasha didn't know what to believe. Did she believe in Jesus? Sure, but this seemed almost like the script from a badly-written science fiction movie.

Still, Xavier's theory made about as much sense as any she had come up with herself. Assuming that the reverend's theory held water, why would demonic forces be after her? She tried hard to find the answers but came up empty.

"Did you see how that bobcat attacked him?" she whispered to Xavier as they continued to sit in the tree.

"I did," he answered.

"That cat was angry."

She saw him nod in the dim light of early dawn. His face was stone-cold serious. "It didn't seem to do any real damage to him though."

Xavier added "And, he killed the cat. Do you know what kind of strength it takes to kill an angry bobcat?"

"The strength of a demon?" she asked.

"Maybe even an entire legion of them," he answered.

Those words chilled her.

He said nothing more but began his descent from the tree.

"Wait," she said as she stared at the tunnel. There was something strange going on there. The early morning light was not sufficient to illuminate anything well. Yet, the tunnel was aglow.

They re-ascended the tree and waited for the next surprise.

***

The shock of being immersed in icy water overtook Officer Simon Birch as he fell out of the tunnel. Frustrated in the sound of his own splashing, he sat still and acclimated to the cold. Stealth was to his advantage. It was an advantage he did not want to give up.

After a moment, he stood up shivering. Finding the morning light sufficient, he turned his flashlight off.

He climbed out of the creek and bumped into something warm and sticky. In the dimness of the dawn, he couldn't tell what exactly it was. He touched it again. It was fury and comparatively warm but the dim light hampered any identification.

He stood up beside the warm whatever-it-was and caught a glimpse of the chief and his strange friend cresting a ridge. He watched them disappear over the hill. He knew the chief's house was at the top. That mystery solved, he turned his attention to the thing at his feet and flicked on his light for just a second.

A dead bobcat. By the way its head flopped, its neck had been snapped. *What kind of person could do such a thing? And why?* With new apprehension, he continued his pursuit, keeping a good distance between himself and them. He didn't want to be detected by these men who had the strength to overpower wild bobcats.

As he followed, he glanced up the hill and caught a glimpse of the chief's secluded property. The house stood alone on the top of the hill overlooking the creek and as he stared at it, he couldn't help but wonder what secrets were there waiting to be uncovered.

The chief lived alone and had often mentioned he preferred it that way. Now, given what he had learned of his boss, he wondered if his secluded lifestyle had a more sinister element-- a darker side hidden beneath the surface.

He crept along, keeping to the foliage as much as possible following those two dark shapes against the brighter tints of a dawning day. He followed them as they crept ever closer to the sinister house. It was not hard to keep pace. One of the two seemed sluggish, as if injured or intoxicated.

Officer Birch stalked forward, silent as the creeping light of a new day and as stealthy as a prowling bobcat--one that would not die.

Chapter 27

They watched the chief and Clay head out. Then the surprise lurker came and went. Only then did they dare descend from the pine. Down wasn't overly-strenuous, yet Sasha's heart pounded.

Not yet light enough to identify the third wheel, they still knew for certain that things kept getting stranger and stranger.

The reverend stood beside her. They stared at the hill.

In the stillness of that morning, Sasha's brain shouted, *Run away!* She took one tentative step when she felt the Reverend's hand wrap around her arm as if he knew her thoughts, as if he knew she was considering reneging on her commitment to the new plan.

The morning light glinted off his eyes as he stared into hers. "We can't outrun these men. I think we can both agree on that."

"There's got to be another option," she hissed back.

He did not increase the pressure of his hold on her but did not he release her. "Where will you run? Where can you possibly go where these men can't follow?"

She opened her mouth to speak, but no words came out, because she had no answer.

"Doesn't sound like you have much of a plan."

"I'll run to the end of the world if I have to."

"Our enemy is not of flesh and blood. They will not stop until they have you even if they have to chase you to the end of the world."

"You just want to see if you can find out what this Legion business is about," she grumbled.

"The way I see it, it's the only way to save ourselves."

Sasha looked at the gun in her hand, knowing it was a useless weapon against her current enemies. "We can't win. These guys are invincible."

The reverend shook his head. "No, they are not invincible. Something hurt them. Did you see the way Clay was walking? He seemed barely able to stay on his feet."

"I don't see what good it will do to follow them."

The reverend looked away. "Honestly, I don't know either. I do know for a fact we are not alone in this mess."

She stared at him.

"We have a power infinitely greater than Legion. We have God on our side. Jesus made a promise to us he would never leave us nor forsake us. He says so in the Bible. I believe that fact, and I believe he will protect us now as we face this tribulation."

She sighed as tears of frustration trickled down her cheeks. He wiped away her tears with the sleeve of his shirt as a father would to a crying child. "With God's help, we can overcome this. We can find their weakness."

She sighed again. "But what if they don't have a weakness?"

"They do have one," his voice sounded confident.

"What's that?"

"They are not men of God."

He said those words with such conviction. She wished she shared that level of belief, but at the moment her faith pool was barely a puddle.

He continued, "Do you think you and I crossed paths by coincidence? Do you think it was random chance that there were raccoons in my spare bedroom or that a bobcat had been so precisely placed?"

Sasha said nothing.

"Do you feel the escape tunnel created by another generation in a past time wasn't meant for you and me last night?"

Sasha remained silent.

"These men are against God. As such, they can't stand for long. Their foundation is on sinking sand."

“Then, let's get help.”

“Who would we tell? Who would believe us?”

She looked beyond the creek, staring ahead as far as she could. The morning light was now sufficient to see the hill of trees before them. Nestled among those trees a house stood dark against the morning light. She had never been on that property. She had no idea whose it was, but for some reason she shivered at the prospect of playing follow-the-leader to that spot.

Chapter 28

The chief half-carried his golem along. A laborious job, his only motivation was to get Clay inside before the energy reserve completely depleted. He needed his henchmen away from the prying eyes of the public. He needed Legion to replenish the power within the lump of clay. He only hoped his wish would be granted.

To Clay's credit, he helped as best he could, using the chief as more of a cane than a wheelchair. This didn't decrease the chief's mental burden. He didn't have Legion's new pet and knew it would not take his failure well.

Working with Legion was precarious. He supposed this was always the case when dealing with their kind. If the old stories were true, demons were usually more than happy to help mortals in a symbiotic relationship.

There was an old German legend about a man named Faust who sold his soul to the Devil in exchange for unlimited knowledge and pleasures. He grinned as he thought about this. Faust, if he had been real, was a fool. The dope made a crucial mistake in selling his soul. Selling a soul to the devil is a guaranteed death sentence. That's common knowledge.

The chief was smarter than Faust. He hadn't signed a pact to sell his soul, agreeing instead to provide other souls in lieu of his own. As long as this supply to Legion was met upon request, then the demons would continue deceiving the town and give Clay the power to commit acts of revenge.

Arriving without a soul breached his agreement. He must smooth-talk Legion. This was his first failure with the demons. Because of this, he felt confident Legion would allow him a second chance.

Perhaps he could negotiate a suitable alternative. Surely there were others in Getreide worthy of Legion's whims: others he could catch easier than slippery Sasha James. But no, Sasha's intervention in Daniel's sacrifice was unforgivable, and by being so elusive she had angered him further. There could be no suitable alternative. He would get this one for Legion and would enjoy watching her suffer as she paid for her crimes.

He had been so engrossed in his thoughts he hadn't realized how far they had progressed until his foot caught on the lowest porch steps. He fumbled with the keys while trying to keep Clay upright.

"Are we there yet?" the golem mumbled.

"Yes, Clay. We are home."

"Good, I need to sleep."

The chief didn't answer but disengaged the lock. He opened the door. They entered the house and the chief locked the door behind him.

They immersed themselves in the silence of the place, then proceeded further into the entry. The chief took note that Clay was better able to stand on his own. Their proximity to Legion was already having a positive effect.

Of course, it would take way too long to fully recharge here. He needed to get Clay closer to the abyss and closer to the immense power of the demon-gods.

As they neared the basement steps, Clay reached out and grabbed his hoodie off the nearby hook. The chief shook his head as Clay fumbled the garment onto himself. This hoodie had always been Clay's security blanket. He never slept without it. Sometimes, he wore it out as he had yesterday in the Daniel scenario.

The chief allowed him to wear the hoodie out. It worried him a little that the garment might be traceable. In the end, he felt the risk was minimal with Legion's blinders deceiving the town's citizens.

Why hadn't Sasha been caught up in Legion's spell? he wondered. *Everyone else seemed caught up in it with the possible exception of her new friend. Why was she so special?*

The only explanation was the woman was immune. That would also explain why she was so slippery, sliding through his fingers time and time again.

He frowned as he thought on this. If Legion had no grip on her, then she was dangerous. In fact, his whole plan could implode because of her.

His only hope was that she didn't realize the extent of her power. As long as she remained ignorant, then he held the advantage. He simply needed to apprehend her before she realized her strength.

He helped Clay down the stairs, laying him down at the entrance to the tunnel which led to Legion's lair. He dared not venture any closer to the abyss, not yet anyway.

He would get Legion's pet, but first, he had much to do. He needed to retrieve his pickup and would do this while Clay rested.

He watched momentarily as Clay curled up and began to suck his thumb. Satisfied that his golem was recharging, he exited the house through the garage entrance.

Within seconds he straddled his vintage 1983 Honda Hobbit 49cc moped which he had obtained years ago at a swap meet. He raised his garage door and zoomed down the driveway at top speed.

He wore no helmet, but that did not worry him. Top speed on this vehicle was only about 25 miles per hour.

He wished he could go faster because time was of the essence.

Crap. In his haste, he hadn't closed the garage. He didn't turn back. Staying on schedule was crucial.

Within seconds, he was on the road. The morning sun was bright and beginning to peek above the horizon.

The sun blinded him, and he put one hand above his eyes to shade them from the brilliance. He cranked the throttle and the little Hobbit lurched forward.

***

Officer Simon Birch watched from the shadows as the chief flew by on what he could only describe as a bicycle on steroids. The buzz of that little engine faded away as the chief departed, leaving Simon to wonder where he was off to.

Even with the chief gone, Simon used caution. He had not seen the one named Clay leave. Simon assumed he was still in the house.

Summoning his courage, he peeked around the tree where he was hiding. He estimated his distance from where he stood to the front porch was about 20 feet. Focusing on the windows facing him, he tried to determine if anyone was watching. But the glare from the rising sun made it impossible to know.

With the sun up, he made a decision. He set his flashlight down so he could better handle the shotgun. Sweat oozed from his palms and dripped from this weapon.

He took a deep breath, forced his nerves into submission and bolted from hiding like a paranoid squirrel-- seconds later diving onto the porch. He slammed hard, stomach-side down, keeping the barrel leveled at the door.

His goal had been silent infiltration but as he clattered upon that porch, he knew he had failed. Skidding to a stop and ready to defend himself, he waited. No response came from within the house. If anyone detected his presence, they chose to remain incognito.

He scurried beneath a large picture window to the front door. Staying as low as possible, he reached up and tried the knob. Locked.

One thought presented itself. He raised the gun and put the barrel squarely over the lock. Surely, a 12 gauge shot would be sufficient to pulverize anything keeping that door shut. He prepared to pull the trigger.

He had no warrant. He had no authorization from dispatch. He had no probable cause. Slowly, he released his finger from that trigger.

He realized he needed to enter without leaving blatant evidence of his intrusion. Keeping low, he ran off the porch and around to the side of the house to where he had seen the chief fly off.

He stood there staring at the open garage. Maybe he was a Barney Fife or an Enos Strate after all but at least he had the sense to check the garage door. Staying vigilant, he crept into the garage and tried the door leading into the house. The knob turned. The door opened.

He entered the house and closed the door. The latch engaged behind him and he realized there was no going back.

***

They followed Clay, the chief and the stranger to the house at the top of the hill. Now that the sun was fully up, the light was sufficient to identify this man as Simon Birch.

There was no question it was him. Xavier knew Simon was a police officer, and he also recognized him from Sunday morning service as Simon was a member of his own flock.

The presence of Simon was both a relief and a source of worry for Xavier. Simon represented the law, and the law in Getreide could not be trusted. On the other hand, his experience with Simon told him he *should* be trusted.

He leaned toward Simon being innocent. His stealthy entry into the house was not normal for one in cahoots with those inside. He couldn't write Simon off the suspect list, though, until he had more evidence.

Xavier and Sasha crept as near to the house as they dared, taking cover behind a woodpile. From that spot, they had a clear view of the open garage where Simon entered.

"What now?" Sasha hissed.

"I suppose we should go in."

"What? Not on your life." Sasha clearly did not like that suggestion.

"Do you have a better idea?"

She opened her mouth, but no rebuttal came out.

"Look, we can't go to the cops. Plus, the people who are after you seem to be in league with Legion. I hate to be a Debbie Downer, but I think our best chance lies with taking the offensive."

She closed her mouth and looked at him. Unable to look at the terror in her eyes any longer, he brought her into a hug. She buried herself into his shoulder and began to cry. They were silent suppressed sobs that shook both of their bodies.

"I don't want to die," she finally managed to say.

He pulled her back so that he could look her in the face. "Personally, I don't think we have anything to worry about there. If it had been God's will for us to die, I think he would have already allowed it. No, I think we are to go in there and get a grip on this situation."

They hid behind the woodpile for what seemed an eternity while Xavier gave her time to accept what he was proposing. He prayed that she would accept it. He prayed hard.

Finally, she looked at him. The fear in her eyes seemed to lessen. She rose from the woodpile. Her breathing was heavy. Her chest heaved.

Then, she bolted from their hiding place to the garage.

He barely had time to register what just happened. In a sprint, he followed.

The darkness within the garage was unsettling. Even after his eyes adjusted, the gloominess seemed greater than it should have been.

"What was that all about?" he whispered.

"I just figured if we were going to take the offensive, we better get going."

Sasha stood by the door leading into the home. She tried the knob. He found himself suddenly wishing it were locked, terror spiking despite his faith.

The knob turned. It wasn't locked. The door opened.

She entered.

He followed. It was, after all, his idea.

Chapter 29

The Hobbit puttered up to the chief's truck, which was right where he had left it by the Toyota the night before. Unfortunately, there was an additional vehicle here now. There was his pickup, the reverend's Toyota, and a squad car.

The car's number confirmed it was Officer Birch's cruiser. He looked into the passenger window. Empty. Even the standard issue Beretta 1301 Tactical 12 Gauge shotgun was missing.

With a sigh, he stood and glanced at the church, wondering how much Simon knew. If Simon knew even a little, it was too much.

He needed to gather Intel.

He used the radio in his pickup. "Dispatch, this is the chief, do you read?"

"This is dispatch, over."

The chief recognized the voice. It was Gary, the day-shift operator. That was a good thing. That meant Zelda had likely gone home.

"Any word from Officer Birch this morning?"

"Negative, Chief. Do you want me to radio him?"

"No need. He called me at the end of his shift. He has the flu or something." He paused as an additional idea stuck him "Actually, I just relieved him of his duties and gave him a ride home to get some rest."

"Copy that, Chief, but if you just took him home, then why did you ask if I had received any word from him?"

The chief paused. That was a good question. "You know Officer Birch. He's such a workaholic. I gave him orders to stay home and suck down some chicken soup. I told him not to even think of coming back to work until he was better, but you know how he can be." There, that should be vague enough to discourage additional inquiries.

The pause on the other end of the line was nerve-wracking. Hopefully, that meant that Legion was doing its magic, clouding any suspicion Gary may have. "Do you copy, dispatch?"

"Roger that," the response finally came.

"His patrol car is parked at the little church over on Fourth Street. Can you send Gill out to tow it back to the station?"

There was another pause. "Affirmative."

"Also, if Officer Birch does call in later, get his location and contact me right away. I want to make sure he stays home today."

"Copy that."

Confident things were being taken care of, he loaded the Hobbit into the back of his pickup, climbed into the Chevy's cab and drove away toward his next task.

In a town like Getreide, everything was only minutes away. Still, the drive from the church to the Dodge Dynasty felt longer than usual.

He finally arrived.

In the light of day, he could see the damage. The back end was a total mess due to the collision with Clay. He was surprised the car had been drivable at all. Crashing into Clay like she did was like hitting a hard-packed adobe wall, and she had hit it while in a full-reverse acceleration.

With the blown tire and busted passenger window, the result was quite a scene. Chances were good that if anyone had noticed the car, it would not have been noted as particularly suspicious thanks to Legion's influence.

Regardless, he didn't want to get sloppy or take his anonymity for granted. Using a handkerchief to avoid leaving fingerprints, he reached in and jimmied the Dynasty into neutral. He got into his pickup and pulled up behind the Dodge until their bumpers met. Slowly, he pushed on the gas pedal and pushed the wreck off the road and into the ditch until it was completely engulfed in the tall grass.

Now that the car was out of the way, he got out and fastened a note to the driver's window. It was on official Getreide Police Department Letterhead. The note indicated this car had been involved in a search and seizure operation and would be impounded. The note further warned against tampering with the car as it was a crime scene-- a punishable infraction.

He wrapped the car with a generous amount of crime scene tape and got back into the pickup. Satisfied, he drove off.

Later, he would have Gill come and tow the car to the Getreide Police Impound lot. He would have to alert the rightful owner of the car and let that person know it sustained significant damage.

He would also have to let out the fact that the car thief escaped but the police would diligently follow up every lead until the perpetrator was apprehended. He smiled as he thought of that last statement. Sasha, the car thief had indeed escaped, but as sure as the sun was yellow, he would soon capture her and hold her accountable for her crimes.

He thought of what Legion had planned for her. The things he had seen Legion do to past pets were unspeakable.

Thinking about such things made him a bit queasy. It wasn't what Legion did to those pets that nauseated him but more the thought of what they might do to him if he failed to deliver Sasha James.

He could not fail.

He needed a plan.

One should always have a plan when negotiating for more time to complete a task. That rule applied doubly when the other party was demonic.

Step one of his plan: own up to his mistakes. He would take responsibility for the fact that Sasha was not yet the pet of demons.

Step two: he would explain his plan for capturing her. As long as he had a plan in place to get Legion what it desired, then he was sure it would be merciful. After all, no one else was standing in line to do its bidding and it couldn't just hop out of the abyss and get the job done itself.

He drove toward home. The morning sun was bright, and so was his optimism. He would not fail Legion, and Legion would not fail him.

He felt confident.

Chapter 30

Simon crept along, his sweaty palms wrapped around his shotgun like a vice, as if loosening that grip invited the weapon to attempt an escape. He glanced back at the garage door and contemplated his own escape. No, he knew too much. Turning back now would be cowardly and against the badge he wore.

He slunk along a long narrow hallway keeping a low center of gravity in order to minimize himself as a target. Call it a vibe. Call it a hunch, but the place had a quality that made him uneasy.

One thought permeated his mind as he crept along. *This is no academy simulation. This is deadly real.*

The first room revealed itself as he neared the end of the hallway. A couch came into view along with a reading lamp beside it on an end-table. There was also a free-standing coatrack with something on it that reminded Simon of a bride's veil made of gossamer threads dyed red. Beside the coatrack was an ornamental umbrella stand.

A large window behind the couch looked out onto the front porch. Looking out at that beautiful morning, one would never suspect anything dark lived for miles.

To the left of the window was an exterior door. He filed that info into his mind, knowing the value in being able to use alternative escape paths if the need arose.

As he entered the room, the air felt thicker. His lungs burned as they struggled to suck in the oxygen his racing heart craved.

Keenly aware that a gunman could be hiding in the blind-spot existing behind the end of that couch, his gut screamed, *beware!* He became still as stone, terror planting him to the floor. In the silence of that stillness, a ticking noise filled his ears.

His finger tightened around the trigger of the Beretta as his focus pinpointed to that hidden space on the far side of the couch. He neither moved forward nor back into the hallway.

The air felt solid and he willed himself to suck it into his lungs and churn it back out. *Just breathe,* he told himself. *Relax and just breathe.*

Procedurally, he had been taught to announce his presence and give the perp a chance to come out peacefully. That was back when he operated under the terms of the law, but now no such procedure applied.

He plastered himself against the wall and prepared. Inhaling the gravy-thick air, he burst around the end of that couch drawing a bead on what was there.

Vacant. The ticking continued. That noise conjured thoughts of time-bombs and images of his body blown to smithereens.

He looked up, following that sound. It came from a novelty clock upon the wall behind the couch. It looked like a cartoon cat. With every tick-tock, the eyes and the tail shifted. Tick, to the left, and tock to the right.

He pointed the barrel of the Berretta at the plastic feline feeling compelled to stop its incessant tick-tocking, but he refrained. It would only leave evidence of his presence in a place he had no business being. He exhaled as he lowered his weapon.

Movement!

He turned, bringing the shotgun back into position. His heart lurched with terror before ratcheting to a new rate of excursion. A second cat. This one was not a clock.

The black feline observed him with intense green eyes. It didn't run. It didn't attack. It simply observed.

After a moment, it slinked off in mild disinterest. He was glad it had been a cat. A dog would more likely see his presence as a territorial challenge, and that could have gotten ugly.

The cat disappeared from view, strolling down the hallway which led to the garage. Simon crossed the room quickly, his footfalls masked by the rhythmic sounds of that clock. On the opposite end of the living room, there was a door. Closed. He nudged it with the barrel of his weapon and found it to be a free-swinging model.

He pushed the door open. A kitchen. He entered, checking the far side of the small countertop island to ensure no one was hiding there. No one was.

He listened. He could still hear the clock from the previous room, although it was quieter now. No other noises were evident.

At the far end was another door, identical to the last. He pushed through it and found himself in a dining room.

This room, like the others he had gone through, was unoccupied. An Ouija board sat on the table.

He never played the game. The premise contradicted his faith. This version didn't look like the average, store-bought model; it looked homemade from white pine with black-ink letters stamped upon it.

The letters were faded in spots. A few of the letters had almost entirely disappeared. On top of the board sat the planchette.

It pointed toward the word, "hello." He regarded it but did not return its greeting.

Being a member of Reverend Xavier Hernandez's church meant he had heard many sermons about the dangers of such toys. They were not toys at all but tools of the devil. Looking at the board now, confirmed that fact.

Surrounding the board, five black votive candles sat evenly placed as if they were points connecting the invisible lines of a pentagram. The candles appeared burnt almost to their base looking like melty blobs that were now one with the tabletop.

He moved around this table of witchcraft as if the board were going to strike out at him. At the end of the room were two doorways. He opened the first and saw a staircase leading to the basement. He opened the second which showed stairs leading up.

The basement route was dark and gloomy. The upstairs was lit by the natural light of the morning. There must have been a lot of windows up there.

Down into the depths or up toward the light. He glanced back at the macabre scene on the table before turning back and choosing a door. He closed the basement door. Then he went up the stairs purposely leaving the door open behind him. If he needed a quick escape, he didn't want to waste precious seconds fumbling with a knob, because sometimes a few seconds are all that separate life from death.

***

Sasha watched as Xavier closed the door that led back out to the garage. That closing held a sense of finality. Everything felt like a dream as they edged along the gloomy hallway. No, dream wasn't the right word. This was the makings of nightmares.

She gripped Richard's gun in both hands keeping the barrel pointed downward but ready to raise it at a moment's notice. It felt strange to her that she wielded such a weapon. Her firearms experience before yesterday was nonexistent. Now she wielded the gun like one of Charley's angels.

Perspiration coated her skin leaving her cold and clammy. She thought, *If I need to, can I pull the trigger?* She didn't know.

She felt Xavier's hand rest upon her shoulder from behind. She was glad he had her back. Even though they only recently met, their shared experiences created ties as tight as family.

She trusted him. He had a unique outlook on this situation. She believed he truly felt God was on their side, and she took encouragement from that. She didn't know if she completely believed that herself, but she took solace in the fact the reverend did.

The end of the hallway opened into a living room. She peeked in around the corner only enough to ensure nothing was about to attack. The room appeared empty.

The space was minimalistic. There was a couch, a lamp, and an end-table. Beside the couch was an ornamental umbrella stand beside a free-standing coatrack. On the rack was a hat with something dangling from it. Was it hair? Was it a wig? She couldn't tell for sure, but she felt a familiarity enter her as she stared at the oddball object.

It suddenly occurred to her that the end of the couch presented a blind spot in the room. With her gun quivering in her grip, she rounded that corner. The space was empty. She exhaled, realizing she would have to remember the enemy could be anywhere.

There was a gimmicky cat-clock on the wall and a lamp on an end-table. Also on the end-table sat a stuffed cat.

This particular taxidermy specimen was black with green eyes. Whoever stuffed the feline had done a professional job. The cat had been set in a relaxed pose, curled up with its tail against its face as if getting ready to take a little cat nap. It looked so peaceful and out of place within Sasha's world of chaos.

Everything was silent with the exception of her inner workings which were humming into overdrive.

Her focus moved to Xavier. The door to the next room was shut. Xavier pushed against it, confirming it swung freely. She watched as he opened it enough to peek through.

She caught the sound of movement and spun around raising the gun, nearly tripping over her own feet. She knew that this wasn't very Charley's Angel-like, but it was too late to do a retake.

She caught her balance with the gun quivering in her trembling hands. It was the cat. The tail was no longer curled up to its face but extended behind swaying slowly like a cobra-charmer's snake. The cat was alive!

It seemed unconcerned with how close it had come to losing one of its nine lives. It simply purred, stretched, and slinked down from its perch.

As Sasha tried to get a grip, the animal began rubbing its body against her legs. Its warm-blooded heat contrasted harshly with her chilled gooseflesh.

Sasha lowered her weapon, exhausted by the episode.

She hated herself for her fears which seemed all too ready to bubble up with the slightest provocation, and she vowed to keep a tighter rein on them in the future.

The feline moved past them, pushing the door open just enough to slide its silken body through. They followed it into a kitchen.

The cat, in one single pounce, landed on the island countertop in the middle of the room. From there, it watched them. Its tail continued to do the charmed cobra act.

Sasha stared, mesmerized momentarily by the swaying tail, and unsettled by the greenness of that stare. Xavier's nudge brought her from the moment. This room, like the one previous, had places to hide which they would have to search.

With hand signals, he indicated he would go around one end of the island countertop and she should go the other way. Again, her fears spiked.

They crept around the island. They peeked around the corner. Her terror lessened. Nothing was there.

The cat pounced to the ground and once more began to rub itself against her legs purring with satisfaction as it did so. She gently kicked it away.

They opened the next door and entered the room.

There was no place to hide in the dining room. On the table was an Ouija board that looked homemade, old, and well-used.

Perhaps it was the placement of the surrounding candles or the fact that the game had superstitious connections, but shivers invaded her as she regarded the game. The arrow piece pointed toward the word "Hello".

The reverend picked up the piece and set it aside. Then, he picked up the board.

Sasha was confused. Why would the reverend disturb this game? Why create additional evidence of their presence in the house?

He held the board on each end. Then he brought up his knee, splintering the board into two pieces.

In the short time of their acquaintance, she had never seen the reverend act out with such an expression of hatred. With disgust, he threw the pieces to the floor where they clattered to a standstill. Then, he threw the piece on top of the broken board.

Perhaps because of the noise, the cat entered the room and joined Sasha in her shock. She looked at the pile of pieces and then looked up at the reverend.

The reverend glared at the pieces. "Witchcraft," he hissed.

Sasha let that word sink in. To her, witches had always been those pointy-hatted broom riders that kids dressed up as for Halloween.

She knew real witches existed, but she never thought about one living in her town. It would explain much about recent events. Still, it was a lot to consider.

Ahead of them stood two doors, side-by-side. One door was closed. The other was open. The open door revealed stairs leading up. She opened the closed door and saw stairs leading down.

"Meow," called the cat at her feet.

She looked down, her brown eyes locking with the feline's. For some reason, she did not like that creature.

The cat moved past her and hopped down the stairs that led to the basement. Sasha took the opportunity and closed the door behind it.

"This way," she hissed to the reverend.

She ascended the stairs. She heard the sound of a door being shut and turned back to see the reverend closing the door. This made her uneasy. Closed doors would only slow her escape if an escape became necessary. Still, for silence's sake, she said nothing.

As if he could read her thoughts, he offered his reasoning. "If somebody comes through here, we'll hear the door opening and maybe that will buy us enough time to hide."

She nodded. That made sense.

Strangling the gun with her grip, she continued up those stairs with trembling hands.

Chapter 31

The chief arrived home and entered the house through the garage. Opening the door was a challenge as he held thick stacks of envelopes in both hands. He retrieved them from the mailbox that stood at the end of the driveway. This wasn't a task he did every day. It was pointless to do so as most of what he got was either bills or scams.

He set the mail down on the kitchen island and turned toward the fridge.

His recent activities had been quite the calorie-burner. When the chase was on, his adrenalin levels hid his hunger, but now his pangs multiplied.

The chief pulled out a large bowl of leftovers from two days ago. Setting it on the island, he removed the plastic wrap and began to gorge himself on sauerkraut and sliced brats.

He ate without utensils, too hungry and pressed for time to worry about table etiquette. Within a minute, the bowl was empty. Checking off that agenda item, he moved on to the next.

Putting the empty bowl in the sink, he picked up the mail and walked into the dining room, flipping through the various envelopes as he entered. He never once looked up from the mail as he rounded the table, opened the basement door, and descended to the lower level.

One step down, he shut the door and stopped. Something was amiss in his dining room. Or was it? He had been so engrossed in the mail he could not recall what it was that felt so wrong.

He was about to turn back to investigate further but stopped himself. He had left Legion waiting too long as it was. He descended toward the abyss and the legion of demons that congregated there.

This would not be a pleasant meeting. He was confident, however, that Legion would allow him more time to collect Sasha James.

Legion was powerful. But, that power was not absolute. The chief knew that Legion could influence the citizens of Getreide, but its demons could not rise up from the abyss in their true form and go forth among men.

It needed somebody to work for them. The Chief smiled as he descended the stairs.

In the basement, he found Clay and tried to wake him up. This proved difficult.

"I'm still tired, Chief," he muttered as he rolled over. "Can I just sleep another ten minutes?"

Clay's whiny schoolkid routine irked the chief, but he kept his cool. It would do no good to go ballistic on a slow-witted golem.

He shook Clay awake not roughly but firmly. "No, Clay. I am sorry, but we have got to get up. It's time to go visit Legion."

At this, Clay sat up. He pulled back his hood and looked around blinking the sleep away.

The chief smiled. He knew that the promise to visit Legion would get his golem moving. It always did.

He set the mail down nearby. Paying the bills and viewing the scams was not a priority. Together, they descended into the tunnel leading to the entrance of the abyss.

Chapter 32

Simon's climb up the stairs felt harrowing. He didn't know what awaited him.

He arrived at the top, finding that his fears were unfounded. Nothing was there, at least nothing that he could see. A hallway ran the length of the second floor. The stairs he had just climbed connected to the hall directly in its middle.

He glanced first down one side, then down the other. The hall was dotted with six closed doors, three in each direction.

With the Beretta at the ready, he turned left and opened the nearest door. A study. The morning sun shone in through a curtain-free window. The walls were lined with packed bookshelves.

At first glance, this room looked almost inviting, but then he looked at some of the many book spines and his own gave a shiver. Those tattered tomes had titles like *Beyond Death*, *The Satanic Bible*, *Magick*, *The Satanic Rituals*, *The Power of your Mind*, *The Satanic Witch*, *The Devil's Notebook*, *Satan Speaks*, and *The Book of Lies*.

Besides those shelves, the room was nearly empty with only a desk and chair. The desktop was piled with more books along with pages upon pages of scribbled notes. He knew that handwriting; it was the chief's.

A bad feeling came over him as he examined these things. Almost as if being pushed by an invisible hand, he backed out of the room, closed the door, and moved on.

The next room was less disturbing, an ordinary bathroom, a sink, a toilet, and a shower without a curtain. As with the study, he backed out of that space, shutting the door, and moving on.

Upon reaching that last door on that side of the stairs, he felt that invisible hand once again pushing against him. Fear spiked as he reach out and turn that knob.

He held the crystal knob on that door with such force that he was sure it would shatter at any moment. Simon turned the knob and opened the door just a crack. The space beyond was dark.

He reached into the room-- his arm entering the darkness and terror grabbing him as he did so. He hadn't believed in goblins ever since he was a kid, yet visions of their grasping hands reaching toward his own now penetrated his thoughts.

He found the light switch and flicked it on. The darkness fled. He opened the door further and took two steps into the room.

This bedroom was not normal. For some reason, the window had been painted over with a thick application of black paint which accounted for the complete darkness prior to turning on the light.

The walls were painted a light green, almost a mint color, reminiscent of old hospitals and insane asylums. The floor was almost as black as the windows, a dark-stained wood. Those floorboards shined with a highly polished gleam.

The room's furnishings were sparse, a twin bed mattress on a simple wood frame. The mattress had a white cotton cover but no comforter or other blanket. A pillow sat on the mattress covered with a plain white case.

Besides a dresser and a narrow door, he assumed represented the existence of a closet, the room was empty. It gave Simon the feel that a monk who had sworn off worldly possessions and the comfort of blankets had taken up residence here.

The uneasiness that had begun on the stairs and which germinated more with every room he discovered, now reached epic proportions. The painted window and the blanket-free bed could have been the culprit, or it could have been something more.

He was about to follow his urge to leave the room but stopped short. He heard sounds in the hallway. Quickly, he closed the door to the room, hoping whoever was out in the hall would not enter. Then, he turned off the light.

In the absence of light, the room gave up a secret, a horrible, nasty secret. What he saw in the darkness made him dizzy with terror. He wanted to scream but refrained if for no other reason than to remain undetected to those beyond the door.

He couldn't exit the room, but he couldn't stand to exist here where the darkness showed him such terrors. In horror, he stumbled, flailing his arms, searching for the closet door in order to escape the room and hide from it.

He closed his eyes wishing he could un-see what he saw, knowing he could not. What he saw would stay in his nightmares forever. He opened his eyes beholding yet again the sickness covering the walls and ceiling of the room.

One thing was clear. The question regarding the Chief of Police's sanity had been answered. The place was a window to his soul, and it was a window best boarded over and locked for eternity.

The glow-in-the-dark paint was everywhere, a mint green glow that no doubt matched the wall color so as to be invisible in the light. The largest of the writing was on the ceiling. Only three numeric characters - 666.

The walls were covered as well. One wall described heinous crimes, the likes of which Simon had never before even conceived. Next to the writings were stick-figure illustrations depicting sadistic acts.

A second wall seemed dedicated to chants, mantras, spells, and symbols associated with satanic ritual. There were pentagrams, inverted crosses, as well as a crudely painted horned head.

The third wall was the worst, a list. The names went almost from the ceiling to the floor and some of them had been crossed out by a thin glowing line of paint, yet still visible through the phosphorescence.

He recognized the list. These were citizens of Getreide, many of them children. The ones with the lines through them were ones who had gone missing. Simon felt like vomiting.

The last wall simply read *I pledge allegiance to Legion*. Simon had no idea who or what Legion was, and he really didn't want to know. At that moment, he simply wanted out of the room, but the sounds from the hallway were growing louder. Those outside were nearer.

In the darkness, he found the knob to the closet door. He opened it. He stepped inside and closed the door behind him. A second later, a bar of light appeared in the space between the bottom of the closet door and the floor. Somebody entered the room.

***

Xavier pushed open the door just enough to reach in and turn on the light. He couldn't explain why but that dark space frightened him. He didn't open the door any more than he had to, just enough in order to reach in, flick the switch, and eradicate the blackness.

With the light on, his fright lessened. He stood aside as Sasha pushed open the door further and entered the room.

She kept her gun at the ready. Xavier didn't put much confidence in that gun. Sasha had admitted to him she had little experience with firearms. Plus, he knew their spiritual enemy could not be defeated with such conventional weaponry.

Resist the Devil and he will flee from you, he remembered. He knew this scripture was sound. Yet, fear persisted and festered within him.

He forced himself to enter the bedroom. His uneasiness increased.

He looked at Sasha. She looked as fear-stricken as he. The gun in her hand quivered in evidence of her fears. Her face was pale. Her eyes were wide.

"We should go," she said.

"Agreed," he answered.

They began to back away toward the door never once turning their backs to the room. It felt that maintenance of eye contact was crucial in preventing the unseen evil from pouncing.

They re-entered the hallway. The door was half closed. His hand was on the switch about to turn off the lights when he heard something from within the room.

He stood there like stone not knowing what to do. Slowly, Sasha readied the gun.

"Did you hear that?" she asked.

"Yes," said Xavier.

Not wanting to but knowing they had come to confront that which haunted them, he re-entered the room with Sasha by his side.

The room appeared unchanged. The sound he heard resembled a bag of marbles spilling onto a linoleum floor.

Reluctantly, he turned toward the closet door and pointed toward the knob. Sasha's eyes screamed no, but she nodded.

She took a step toward the closet. Xavier shimmied up to the closet's door from the side.

His mind was giving him simple commands: *Just open the door and get out of the way. That's all you have to do.*

Sasha nodded to him, indicating that she was ready. He nodded back that he understood.

For some reason, his hand upon that knob did nothing. He just could not force his hand to turn that knob.

Sasha nodded again, her eyes wide. He prayed for help. He wrestled with the terror inside-- terror he needed to overcome.

He gripped the door harder as perspiration dripped from his hand to the knob to the floor. The latch disengaged. The door opened.

***

Within the darkness of the closet, Simon stood trembling. Something fell on him from the shelf above. He knew the racket had given him away and now the closet had become his coffin. In the darkness he had no idea what he had knocked over, but it was raining on him like ping pong balls.

His finger wrapped around the trigger on the Beretta as he planted his body against the back wall of the closet. Leveling his weapon, he braced himself for the inevitable showdown.

The knob turned. The door opened. It was go time.

Chapter 33

As the chief neared Legion's abyss with Clay, he noticed that the glow from that crevasse seemed brighter than normal. This made him uneasy, especially given the fact that he was entering a negotiation situation.

Against the red glow, stood a black shadow. At first, the chief thought it was some great big wriggling worm. He looked closer. It was not a worm; it was a tail.

He recognized the shadow of the body connected to that tail. It was Shedeem.

Shedeem was his cat by default, the only animal ever to defeat him. Long ago, he had found it scrounging around on his property, a mangy stray.

A childhood of being bullied had given the chief a penchant for torturing those with lesser power. Any creature he could catch, he would torture. Usually, he received great satisfaction from destroying life. After the victims' death, the afterglow often remained with him for days.

Shedeem was different. The chief first tried to drown him only to receive the fury of his claws. He tried to strangle him, but he always managed to wriggle free. He thought about simply shooting him dead, but what would be the sport in that? Eventually, the cat simply wore him out, earning his right to live.

The strange thing was, Shedeem seemed to hold no grudge, choosing to stick around as opposed to fleeing. Without the passion to kill the creature what could the chief do but allow Shedeem into his life. Honestly, he admired a creature who possessed such tenacity. He could not say that this admiration was akin to love, but it was the closest thing he had ever felt to that emotion.

Shedeem never before ventured down below. The fact that the cat was there now only added to the chief's sense of uneasiness.

The cat's head turned, looking at the chief from where it sat next to the abyss. In the midst of the red glow, Shedeem looked more the green-eyed phantom than the mortal cat he was.

Acting nonchalant, Shedeem broke the stare-down and slinked over to his owner, staring first at him then at Clay. With a single pounce, it leapt onto Clay's shoulders, curling its body around the back of his neck as if it were the most natural thing in the world. There it made itself comfortable releasing purrs of contentment.

Clay didn't seem to mind. The chief simply shook his head. He had never understood this attraction Shedeem had for Clay. Golems, after all, were not warm or fuzzy, but only cold earth animated by the power of demons.

Shedeem purred in Clay's ear.

"Ya don't say," Clay responded.

This was the first time the chief had ever witnessed these two communicate. "You can talk to Shedeem?"

Clay nodded carefully so as not to dislodge the feline from its perch. "Shedeem says he has good news."

"What is it?" the chief asked, suddenly very alert to the fact that this cat had been near Legion's abyss.

Clay leaned into the purring cat. "Shedeem says to go ask Legion. Legion knows all. Legion will tell you the good news."

Good news? The chief didn't like this little unforeseen development, not one bit. He had his sales pitch all ready to go. He was prepared to give Legion a play by play regarding his plan to obtain Sasha. Now everything had been turned on its ear.

He walked toward the edge of the abyss. The heat from that crevasse was intense. Yet it didn't burn his skin. It never did when he approached. He felt the presence of Legion flowing toward him, fondling his soul, caressing his mind, and dabbling in his thoughts.

The many voices of Legion became audible. Whenever Legion spoke to him, he could never tell if the voices came to him audibly or if it was somehow telepathically sent to him via direct route input to his brain.

Regardless, the many voices coalesced into one mighty voice. "Come closer," it hissed.

He drew nearer with small apprehensive steps, as if he were Dorothy approaching the great and powerful wizard. The great and powerful Oz was exactly what Legion reminded him of, although he never witnessed a giant disembodied head. Also, he knew that here, there was no man behind the curtain, no slight-of-hand or trickery. He was not in some made-up emerald city and Legion was real.

He stopped just short of the drop-off and gazed over the edge. The abyss was bright with demonic energy. If he stared hard enough, he could almost make out the silhouettes of membrane-thin wings as they flew back and forth against the ruby light. Likewise, his ears could virtually hear their flittering.

"Do you have our pet?" Legion inquired.

The chief was at a loss. He needed to respond. Legion would demand it. But what should he say? What could he say?

"Where is the one called Sasha James?"

The chief stood on precarious soil. He needed to tread softly in order to avoid an avalanche. *What to say? What to say?*

A wave of heat billowed from the abyss laced with sulfuric fumes. It wasn't scorching as the chief had feared, but it hinted at Legion's great power and seething anger. "You will have Sasha James soon," he uttered.

Legion responded conversationally enough. "How soon?"

"As soon as Clay is fully rested, we will resume the hunt."

Legion said nothing and the chief found himself to be both relieved and irritated at the same time. The silence was broken only by Shedeem, who meowed softly as it leapt from Clay's shoulders to the ground, slinking against the chief's leg.

"Tell me," Legion hissed. "Where do you plan to pick up the trail? I certainly hope, for your sake, it has not grown cold?"

"The trail has not grown cold. I will get her for you." The chief hated the pleading sound in his statement. He had vowed he would not grovel. He was Legion's equal, for Pete's sake, not just a servant.

Shedeem purred and rubbed his neck against the chief's legs. The chief nudged him away.

Legion began to laugh. It started out low and sinister and grew until the chief covered his ears in an attempt to block it out. Covering his ears did nothing. The voice of Legion was something more complex than simple sound waves traveling through space. The laughter culminated into a crescendo-roar before ceasing, like a clap of thunder that is full-blown one moment and gone the next.

Within the void, a whisper came to the chief. "Indeed, the trail has not grown cold. We know this because Shedeem has reported such. In fact, your prey is close. Would you care to guess where Sasha James is now?"

The chief didn't respond. He had no idea where Sasha was.

"Would you believe that Sasha and her companions have followed you to your very home? Would you believe that they are inside your house right now? Would you entertain the idea that they may be in the top floor at this very second? Perhaps in your bedroom right now?"

"What?" His bedroom was sacred space. That was where he slept. That was where he schemed. That was where he kept collections and wrote on the walls and meditated on his gods.

"Sasha James is somewhere above us inside your abode."

The chief did not respond. He was not sure what to say. *Could this have been some mean-prank? Could Legion be toying with him?*

"All you need to do is go and get them. Do you think you can handle this small task?"

"Them?" The chief managed to say.

"Yes. Sasha James has friends, two to be precise. One is a man of the cloth and the other is a man of the badge."

The reverend and Simon, The chief thought as his anger rose. "Clay, we have work to do," he said as he backed away from the abyss. "Come."

For the first time ever, Clay didn't obey his master. He simply stood there, staring at the red glow of Legion's home as if that light mesmerized his simple mind.

"Do you feel ready, Clay?" Legion asked the golem. "Do you feel that my power has sufficiently resuscitated you?"

"Yes," Clay answered.

"Go with him, Clay. Be a good Golem. Obey your master."

Legion's voice seemed to wake Clay from his stupor. He blinked once and then joined the chief.

Together, they left the cavern. The chief with a sinking feeling in his gut. The meeting did not go as planned.

He worried that this second chance to get Sasha would not go well either. Then what? How would he be able to continue in Legion's favor and what would it mean for him if he were not?

He shook these self-condemning thoughts from himself and pressed on. Without choice, he pressed on.

Chapter 34

Xavier sidestepped, pulling the door open and initiating a precarious showdown. In the opening, a shotgun's barrel emerged, aimed directly at Sasha as Sasha's gun pointed back.

From his angle, Xavier felt fairly certain his presence was unknown to the mystery gunman. He considered his ability to redirect that barrel before the trigger was pulled. Would he be fast enough?

He hesitated with that question pummeling his mind. If he acted, he would only get one chance. Success would brand him a hero, but failure would brand Sasha Swiss cheese.

He couldn't risk failure. Plus, his chances of success were limited by the fact that the one in the closet had a shotgun, not a rifle. He would have to redirect the angle of that firearm considerably in order to avoid Sasha being hit by the spread pattern of that shot.

"Why are you after me?" he heard Sasha ask, her voice sounding detached and distant.

The closet-dweller answered. "Take it easy. I am not after you. I am here only for the truth."

That voice was familiar to Xavier. It wasn't the voice of the chief, but one he had heard before.

"I don't believe you." Her voice was shaky.

The closet-dweller said nothing.

Sasha narrowed her eyes and took a wide stance, one that would not send her falling if she pulled the trigger. She looked determined. Still, Xavier thought he saw cracks in her steel facade.

"I'm here to protect and serve. That's all."

Sasha did not respond. Xavier could hear her breathing. It was the loud, rhythmic breathing of someone psyching themselves up to doing something beyond their normal capacity. In this case, Xavier suspected she was preparing to kill.

"Listen to me…" the familiar voice spoke, but Sasha shut him down.

"No! You listen to me! I have no reason to trust the Getreide Police, and I have no reason to trust you!"

Xavier saw the shotgun lowering. It continued to lower until it settled upon the floor. "There, I am unarmed. I don't want to hurt you."

"You still have your sidearm."

The silence seemed infinite to Xavier. After what seemed an eternity, he saw a handgun appear on the floor beside the shotgun. He knew who was in there but for some reason, he had lost the ability to communicate.

"Come out of there," Sasha said with power. The fact her opponent was now vulnerable must have given her rejuvenated levels of bravery.

Simon Birch walked out of the closet. His hands were raised and his eyes locked with Sasha's. Still, she did not lower her weapon.

Xavier knew that she was running on fumes. Lack of sleep and the constant anxiety she endured had obviously taken its toll. Plus, the Getreide Police's ethics had been in question. She did not know Simon like he did, however. If she did, she would not suspect him of being in league with the others.

"It's good to see you, Reverend Hernandez," Simon said, momentarily glancing his direction before resuming the stare-down between himself and Sasha.

"Sasha," Xavier said. "This is Simon. He's one of my parishioners."

"He's one of them," she responded. "One of the others."

"If I may," Simon said. "Before last night, I had no idea what was going on with the chief. The fact is, I am trying to get to the bottom of this whole mess just as you are."

Sasha said nothing.

"Well, I smell a rat and I'm here to get some answers." He paused and then added, "as long as you will allow me to do so."

A twitch of her trigger finger would spell the end. Xavier would not be able to live with himself if that occurred with him doing nothing to stop it.

In good faith, he reached out to her and took hold of her gun by its barrel. She looked at him momentarily, pain in her eyes. Finally, she let go of the weapon.

Xavier exhaled, not realizing until that moment he had been holding his breath. The gun felt so heavy. He dropped it. It landed on the floor with a thud.

Overwhelmed, he lost his balance, crumpling to the floor, exhausted by the strain of the moment. Simon helped him back up.

"What are those?" Sasha asked as she stared into the closet.

Simon shrugged. "Don't know. They fell on me from the shelf above."

The closet floor was riddled with a scattering of pale orbs in various sizes. None of them were perfectly round. None of them were perfectly white.

One was about the size of a baseball. Xavier picked it up. As he turned it around, horror struck him. He was eye to eye with a vacant stare.

The skull he held was too small to be human. It had an elongated nasal cavity and shallow cranial slope. Possibly, it once belonged to a cat.

"There's something very wrong here," Sasha's voice came to him disconnected as if she spoke from the opposite side of a long tunnel.

"I've worked under this man for years," Simon chimed in. "He always acted so normal, so in control of himself. It's hard to fathom."

Xavier felt faint as he looked over the pile. Their very existence represented the deep psychosis in the one who resided here. Then again, he expected nothing less from one in league with demons.

He mentally estimated the number of skulls. There were perhaps 15 in all. Some were small like those of mice. Others were larger with lupine traits. One drew his attention more than the rest.

This one had landed in the back of the closet, its eye sockets facing a corner as if it had misbehaved and been put in a timeout to think about the wrongs it committed. Unlike the other skulls, this one did not have a low-sloping cranial ridge or an elongated nasal cavity. It was larger than a softball, but smaller than a volleyball.

It landed upside down with the mandible absent so that the top teeth could be viewed. Xavier felt dizzy as he looked upon those teeth, those eerily human teeth!

Sasha's gasp verified she saw the same skull. He looked at her. Her eyes were wide. Her finger was pointed at that closet-corner dweller. She was trying to speak, but no words came. Instead, she buried herself into his chest in an apparent attempt to remove the horror from her vision.

"And that's only the half of it. You need to see this, but I warn you it's a lot to take," Simon said as he turned off the bedroom light.

The walls shone their satanic secrets in all their glow-in-the-dark glory. Xavier tried to keep Sasha facing his chest, but she pulled free, moaning as she beheld the sickness upon the walls and ceiling.

Chapter 35

The chief stepped into one of the basement's side rooms and grabbed The Judge. The Judge was the crown jewel in his firearms arsenal. He looked it over, happy some genius invented it, a revolver pistol that shot 410 shells. It worked great in close quarters or when in situations where there was no time to aim. Just point, pull the trigger, and obliterate.

Up until that moment, he had promised to remain unarmed so as not to unintentionally kill Legion's precious pet. However, things had changed. It was Clay and himself against Simon, Sasha, and the reverend. Two against three, even with the golem on his side he didn't like those odds, not with the stakes so high.

He was also angry. *How dare they invade his sanctum? How dare they enter his abode?*

He loaded the cylinder one chamber at a time… slowly with deliberate moves. Each shell slid into place becoming part of the well-oiled machine. He put on a Kevlar vest and riot gear helmet. He lowered the face-shield of the helmet and commenced the filling of his pockets with more 410s. Finally, he grabbed a Getreide Police riot gear shield which leaned against the nearby wall.

In a town like Getreide, there was really no reason for such ordinance, but in a post 9/11 society, hysteria for such things can be infectious. The town granted the funds to expand the police force's firepower but courtesy of Legion's spell on the town, the entire arsenal remained in his basement waiting for a reason to be used.

Satisfied the odds were once more in his favor, he and Clay ascended the basement stairs. Despite the seriousness of the situation, the chief grinned. There were three intruders in his house, but only one had to be delivered to Legion. The others were expendable. The fun was about to begin.

Step by step, he led his golem up those stairs, no longer needing Clay to be his shield. Of course there was always the chance he could die. Improbable? Of course, but still possible.

His mortality was a nuisance, like a pebble in his shoe, but he was able to overlook it for the time being. That small chance of failure was just part of the fun. He had a golem. He had the armor. He had The Judge locked and loaded. Plus, he had Legion on his side. He was a safe bet.

Entering the dining room, he saw why he had previously felt something was out of place. His grin vanished as he bent toward the pieces of the broken Ouija board. *How dare they disrespect this most sacred thing, this direct line to Legion*?

They would pay for their disrespect. He would guarantee it.

He returned the broken pieces to their home within the sanctum of the black candles, fitting them back together like pieces of a puzzle. Then he returned the planchette to its spot on the board gently placing it over the word "Hello".

He stared at the reincarnated board momentarily before moving on. Hatred now welled up inside him like a fountain, and he promised himself to repay eye for an eye.

Going to the front door, he connected the first of three hasp and staple latches. He had installed these years ago when he first anticipated bringing unwilling guests into his house. He had one at the top of the door, one in the middle, and one near the bottom. He inserted a padlock into the latch. He locked it. He repeated the process for the other two, putting the key safely in his pocket.

From there, he went to the door that led to the garage and did the same thing. Three padlocks inserted into three hasp and staple latches. Once secured he felt the key in his pocket ensuring its presence. One key fit all the locks and only one other copy of the key existed. In the hallway as the chief locked up, Clay began to sniff the air like a dog on a trail.

"What is it, Clay?"

"It smells like barbeque over here."

The chief sniffed the air. He smelled nothing. Then again his sense of smell, unlike that of his golem, was only human.

Clay sniffed again. "Yup. It smells like barbeque."

The chief inhaled deeply; still he detected nothing. Not that it mattered. He would rather occupy his mind with thoughts of what he would do to those who had invaded his home and desecrated his sacred Ouija board. He went back to the dining room and then to the stairs that led to the second floor. He began the ascent. Clay followed.

He was going for stealth but failing. Clay could not step lightly.

The hallway at the top of the stairs appeared deserted, deserted but not undisturbed. Just as the intruders had desecrated his sacred Ouija board, he sensed desecration here as well.

Keeping the Judge at the ready in one hand and his riot-shield in place with the other, he moved toward that undefined wrongness. At the end of the hallway, he saw what was wrong. His bedroom door stood open.

This room was a window into his mind, private and intimate. He never left that door open, yet here it was gaping like a dead man's jaw.

This was where he slept and dreamed and when he could not sleep, it was where he schemed. It was a sacred space just as his Ouija board was a sacred object. He raged again at the idea that the intruders had violated this inner sanctum.

"Sasha James, are you in my personal space?" he mumbled as he pushed the door more fully open.

The door creaked until silenced by its knob hitting the wall. Darkness met him along with the prolific glowings that he so enjoyed.

He entered the room, shut the door behind him and turned on the light. The room was empty. His closet door was ajar just an inch.

Flinging the door wide open, he readied himself for those hiding in that closet, but the enemy was not there. They had been there, though, and they had ravaged his collection. His precious craniums were scattered all over the floor. "Unforgivable," he mumbled. "Unforgivable."

Setting down The Judge, he reached for his skulls, picking them up with the utmost tenderness and cradling them in his arms as a mother would her baby. Yes, these were his children in a way. He remembered the day he got each of them. He remembered taking away life and preparing the skulls for collection-status. He remembered it all as if it were only yesterday.

"Clay, keep a lookout while I clean this up." With effort, he kept his voice from cracking.

So many memories flooded his mind as he gathered his children to him. He remembered killing the mice when he was still a boy. Those mice had been his first victims. That was when he realized killing dulled his own pain.

Over the years, he gravitated toward bigger animals, cats, dogs, opossums, and raccoons. He remembered every killing and the high he got from such actions.

Last of all, he gathered the human skull that rested back in the corner. This had been his first human and therefore worthy of his special collection. This had been his first act of revenge against those who bullied him as a child, and the first Legion-sanctioned murder.

"Do you remember him?" he asked Clay as he picked up the Homosapien's skull.

Clay nodded. "I do remember."

The chief stared into those vacant ocular cavities before placing the skull on top of all the others in the bucket. He put the bucket back on the shelf in the closet. He closed the closet door, resuming the hunt.

Turning off the room's light he momentarily bathed in the glow of his inner sanctum. The sacred glowing scriptures gave him strength. He soaked it in quickly, knowing he could not stay.

With sadness, nostalgia, and anger, he put his hand on the knob and began to open the door. "Come on, Clay. We have to find these perpetrators and teach them a lesson."

Chapter 36

The trio heard the heavy steps coming up the stairs and barely found time to escape from the bedroom to the hall, and then into the adjacent bathroom. They now cowered there with the lights off and nothing but the closed door separating them from the enemy. They stood in the windowless room with near-total darkness.

Simon found himself wondering if any one of them had closed the bedroom door. In the stress of the moment, he could not think clearly enough to recall.

Thankfully, the bathroom had no glow-in-the-dark messages glaring out at them. It was only ordinary darkness that surrounded them now. Still, the knowledge of that other room haunted him.

He stood between the door and the two he had been called to serve and protect keeping the Beretta leveled and ready to discharge at a moment's notice. With his finger wrapped around the trigger, he waited.

A strange feeling crept in, one of disbelief. Never in a million years would he have guessed that the citizens of Getreide would need protection from their own Chief of Police. Yet here he was.

Simon strained his ears but heard only silence. He looked down at the narrow bar of space that existed between the bottom of the bathroom door and the floor. Shadows flickered. Somebody was passing by on the far side of that door.

Within a second, the shadow passed, leaving that light uninterrupted. Whoever had been there was now absent.

A chillingly calm voice shattered the silence. "Sasha James, are you in my personal space?"

The voice belonged to the chief. It sounded foreign. This was not the man he thought he knew.

Before today, that voice that had always represented truth and justice. Now, it conveyed only the psychosis of the criminally insane.

"What do we do now?" Sasha hissed from behind.

"We wait," Simon whispered his answer.

He heard the sound of a door opening, and he suspected the chief was investigating the bedroom. It would only be a matter of time before the mess in the closet became known.

He wondered if now was a good time to bolt. What were the chances he could get himself and the other two down the stairs without detection? *No.* It would be too risky. So, they stayed in the bathroom and prayed the investigators would not expand their search to adjacent rooms.

The chief either had company or he was talking with himself. The details of the conversation were muddled by the walls which separated them. He could only tell conversation was commencing.

A thought struck Simon, one that created a sinking feeling within him. He had inadvertently led himself, Sasha, and Xavier into a dead-end. There was only one way out, the hallway.

Knowing the chief to be a meticulous investigator as well as psychotic, it stood to reason the search for those responsible for entering his room and disturbing his collection would be exhaustive. Their chances of escaping notice would be slight.

He reconsidered his original plan to stay put in this corner. "Listen," he whispered to Sasha and the reverend. "We need to get out of here. When I open the door and burst into the hallway, I want you two to run as fast as you can down the stairs and out of this house. Do you understand me?"

"What about you?" he heard Reverend Hernandez hiss.

"I'll provide cover."

"I don't like this plan," Sasha said.

"There's no other option." That statement shook Simon, but he continued nonetheless. "Whatever happens, don't stop. Just run like mad. Do we understand each other?"

Only silence answered his question. *"Do we understand each other?"* he repeated with all the intensity he could muster within whisper levels.

"Yes," they both answered in unison.

Simon choked down a big wad of courage and readied his Berretta. He put his hand on the knob and turned it. He flung open the door and burst from the darkness into the light.

***

The chief jumped as the bathroom door flung open, mere feet from him down the hallway. He had just stepped out of his bedroom when the sudden chaos erupted.

It took his brain only a fraction of a second to register the emergence of his prey. Everything felt as if it were moving in slow-motion. He saw Simon's eyes lock in on his own. He saw the Beretta's barrel pointed at him. He saw the two others run out behind Simon. There was a flash as the Beretta discharged. He felt the force of that shot and instantly time returned to its normal velocity.

The riot shield took the brunt of the blow transforming it into garbage. Shot pellets smacked into his Kevlar. A few of them lodged into his exposed hand instantly bringing pain.

He staggered back a few steps, wanting to retaliate but unable. He needed his balance before anything else.

"Run!" Someone shouted.

His sight zeroed in on Sasha James who was almost to the stairs. The chief threw aside what remained of the shield and returned fire.

Two rounds erupted from The Judge. The first was a direct hit to Simon's chest, causing him to teeter backward. The second landed directly over the first.

A sickening sound came from the victim as he took those shots. Flying back and landing on the floor, he toppled over himself, coming to a rest at the opposite side of the stairway. He would have rolled further, but the radiator at the end of the hallway halted his momentum.

The chief smiled as a pool of blood began expanding around him. He didn't need to confirm Simon's death. Those direct hits painted a fatal picture.

His victory was tainted, however, because Sasha and the reverend were escaping. He could hear their feet scurrying down the stairs.

He looked momentarily at Simon's Berretta. Common Sense told him to retrieve it but doing so would increase the distance between him and his prey. Decision made, he left the shotgun where it was and gave chase.

***

Sasha was in shock. She saw Officer Birch open fire upon the enemy but got no opportunity to see if those bullets had any effect because the reverend dragged her down the stairs and out of sight.

Her ears rang as more shots boomed. She turned back in time to see a body summersaulting past the stairway and down the hall. She tried to run back up, but the reverend disallowed it.

In her panic, time seemed skewed. In the blink of an eye, she was on the main floor of the home. Footsteps echoed from the stairs. Someone followed. She hoped it was Simon. She feared it wasn't. Regardless, she obeyed the officer's last command to run.

They bolted from the dining room into the kitchen. Through the kitchen into the living room past that stupid cat clock, and then to the hallway.

She no longer heard the footsteps on the stairs which meant that the follower had either turned back or was on the main level and closing the distance between them.

Xavier reached the door to the garage first slamming into it with all his momentum. Grabbing the knob, he cranked it and pulled.

From Sasha's perspective, he was moving in slow motion. "Come on. Come on! *Come on!*" she shrieked as he pulled on the door.

"It's stuck!" he screamed back.

That's when she saw the hasp and staple latch complete with the padlock smack dab in the middle of the door.

"Stand back!" she screamed as she drew her weapon and pulled the trigger again and again until the last bullet fired.

The blasts left her ears ringing to the point of vertigo. It took a second for her to regain herself.

In all the television shows, it had seemed so easy to blow the lock off a door with a well-placed bullet. Most of her shots however missed the padlock. Large portions of wood veneer from the door and frame were missing where her bullets had gone, but it only revealed the fact that the exit was steel-reinforced.

Luckily for her, she had hit the padlock with one of her rounds. She grabbed it and flung it free from the door ignoring the fact that it was scalding hot.

Xavier plowed into the door, but it still wouldn't open. That's when she saw the other two locks, one near the bottom and one near the top of the door. *Crap!*

She looked back toward the living room expecting to see the enemy. She saw no one. The hall was empty.

"The front door!" she heard Xavier shout as he ran past her.

She followed him, but deep down she knew what was there, just a door with more locks. Still, she held tightly to that gossamer thread of hope.

They arrived at the door, trying it as that gossamer thread evaporated. The locks stood solid.

Xavier picked up the ornamental umbrella stand. It looked to be made of brass. More importantly, it looked heavy. He heaved it at the picture window. The glass vibrated with the impact but didn't break.

"It's a polycarbonate window. Quite expensive but worth every penny, in my opinion."

Sasha and the reverend turned in unison toward the chief's unsettlingly calm voice.

"All the windows in this house are made of polycarbonate," he said with a smile. "That's bulletproof glass to the layman."

Sasha gasped and glanced around the room, seeking a miracle.

Chapter 37

Legion grew more agitated by the second. It sensed things were commencing upstairs but had no details.

It wanted details but was too exhausted to reach their influence beyond the abyss. They had used all their energy choking Sasha in the tunnel and fending off the power of prayer that their act instigated. They tried to stop the intruders from going into the chief's bedroom, but barely had the strength to do more than create a foreboding in those mortal's minds. Then, after charging Clay, they were completely spent.

Shedeem purred nearby, basking in the warmth of the abyss. Legion lamented not sending the feline to watch and report back. Now, however, it was too late. Things had already happened.

Legion knew the chief was doing his best to please them. As long as he was able to please, he was as safe as a mortal can be when dabbling in dark powers.

Legion laughed among its many selves as it considered the chief's long-term future. Regardless of how well the chief obtained pets for them, it would eventually turn on him.

That day would be a total surprise to the chief. Legion knew the chief well enough to know what would happen then. He would start by bartering and when that failed, he would beg. In the end, the chief would lose as the chains of slavery shackled him for all eternity.

Legion held counsel with its many selves. It would need a plan for the arrival of the latest pets. It planned on taking all three regardless of the original agreement.

They found the man of God to be most infuriating. If his faith in the Christ was as strong as his profession suggested, there would be no getting at him.

Legion laughed at this. Legion would simply test this man of the cloth. On occasion it discovered such men's faith was not as strong as the image they portrayed.

"And what about the woman?" Legion asked themselves. "What about Sasha James?"

Legion was unanimous in their vote to pick apart the woman piece by piece in an orgy of pain and terror.

It would be more difficult if her companion, the man of God, was true to his faith. Not only could they not harm him, but his faith could act as a contagion and grow within the woman as well. If that happened, then all would be lost.

Legion chastised its many selves for questioning the supremacy of their own power. Men and woman were mortal and could crumble if the right amount of pressure was applied.

It thought of the policeman. He would be a pushover. That man already had doubts he could do much of anything. His insecurity would make him an easy target.

Shedeem purred, enjoying the heat from the abyss. Legion forced its feelings of impatience into more productive expressions. Impatience morphed into expectation. It waited with a feeling of euphoria descending over its many selves.

It waited.

Chapter 38

The chief stood before the frightened pair of would-be escapees. He regarded them, anticipating their next moves.

Clay remained around the corner beyond the prey's sight. He wanted Clay close enough for summoning but out of sight until the right moment for maximum effect. Of course, he might not need Clay at all. He held The Judge. He wore Kevlar. He wore his riot-helmet. The odds were overwhelmingly in his favor.

He eyed Sasha's weapon and wondered. He had counted quite a few shots earlier and had seen the damage to the door that led to the garage. Was the gun now empty?

She raised the weapon and pointed it directly at his head, her hand shaking, her eyes showing a total lack of confidence. "Let us go," she said with a voice that shook as much as her hands.

The chief tried hard to mentally count off how many shots had been fired. The Kevlar protected much of him, but her weapon was aimed at his face. He doubted the riot-helmet face-shield would stop flying lead. Regardless, a game of chicken had been initiated, so he would play along.

"Let us go!" she enunciated every syllable as if the words were painful.

"Well, it certainly looks like all the bets are on the table," he said as he removed his helmet, tossing it to the floor and calling her bluff.

His heart rate quickened. His face flushed. He loved these little cat and mouse games. The tension reminded him he was alive.

He took a step toward her. She took a step back.

"So," he began. "Do you have the guts to blow mine to smithereens?"

"Stay back!" she said. Her voice was shrill.

He glanced at the reverend, and his smile widened. "What do you think, Churchy? Do you think she can break the commandment? Do you think she will do what God says she shalt not?"

The reverend said nothing.

He looked back at Sasha who now had both hands on the gun. "And even if you can bring yourself to kill, can you live the rest of your life knowing you were that cold-blooded?"

"It would be self-defense," the reverend's voice trailed to him.

The chief looked once again at him. "Are you sure? I am not the one pointing the gun. Even if the law says it was self-defense, would you believe it in your hearts?"

Again, he locked eyes with Sasha. This woman was such an enigma. Her unpredictable nature made him wonder what was to happen next. His heart quickened more. His face felt hot. This was really living.

"Now, the question you should be asking is how many bullets are in your gun? Is there one left in there? You squeezed off quite a few earlier."

She swallowed in a way that informed him she had not thought that through. Every line of worry on her face deepened.

"This isn't like in the movies, Sasha. In real life you have to reload eventually." He watched her countenance as this information sunk in. "Now, if you have the stomach to pull your trigger, then by all means do it. But, if you do, you better be sure there's a live round in there because if there isn't, and you pull that trigger, it will be something you regret. That's a promise."

He saw it for a split second. It was more of an aura than something physical. In this deadly game of poker she held the losing hand, and she knew it.

He hesitated. If he took another step toward the reverend and the woman, he would be farther away from Clay than he liked. If he lost proximity, his golem would be useless within a matter of seconds. This distance rule was not an exact science and the parameters varied from moment to moment. He couldn't risk too much distance, not now.

"Why are you doing this?" she asked.

The chief simply smiled. He would tell her but not yet. He simply enjoyed watching her squirm.

Though he was well protected and the enemy was out of ammo, the odds were two to one. He called Clay.

Clay entered, and Sasha James began to scream.

***

The second entered. She recognized that hoodie and instantly clues fell into place. This was the one who tried to murder Daniel! It was so obvious now, so plain. She was shocked she hadn't made the connection before.

Her memories flew to the coat rack in the living room. She remembered the strange hat and hair combo resting on it.

She stared at the chief, mentally taking the ensemble from the coat rack and putting it on his head. Like magic, the chief became the one she had thrown aside in order to save Daniel. This was Mr. Linebacker. This new knowledge overwhelmed her. When Mr. Linebacker gave chase yesterday, he wasn't trying to capture Clay but escape with him.

Her screaming started the moment Mr. Hoodie (aka Clay) entered. Unable to stop the screaming, it continued as shock took over.

Chapter 39

Legion heard the screaming which drifted to their many ears from the world above. It was a pleasing sound.

Legion should not have had to wait this long. The delay had been agitating. Listening to those screams helped.

They desired to leave the abyss and see the chaos first-hand but knew such a journey was beyond it. The abyss was its prison. God was its judge, and Jesus was the executioner who had cast all of them from the man into the herd of pigs. That day, its cell had been locked, the key thrown away.

"Here, Shedeem. Come here," Legion's voices echoed out of the abyss. "Come here, my little Shedeem."

In response to his calling, Shedeem slinked up to the edge of the crevasse. His green eyes peered into the abyss, wide as saucers as Legion whispered commands.

The cat twitched and fell back over his own feet. It rolled twice before gaining his footing and shooting away from the abyss like a speeding arrow.

Legion called after it. "Yes. Run. Run to the world above, my little Shedeem. Be our eyes. Be our ears."

***

Shedeem moved quickly away from Legion and toward the world of the living. His green eyes remained watchful, his ears perked.

Exiting the underworld, he entered the basement. Stopping, he sniffed the air. Something here was abnormal. He sniffed again to make sure he was correct in what he thought he smelled. The chief liked to barbeque. Sometimes the man cooked beef. Sometimes it had been pork. And sometimes, it was the flesh of victims. Shedeem had been with the chief on many barbeque occasions, and he was certain what he smelled now was just that.

Why was this smell present here and now? Shedeem had no answer but felt compelled to investigate.

He knew his assignment from Legion took precedence over something as trivial as investigating a new smell. This, however, was a suspicious smell. It didn't belong in the basement. Maybe Legion would want the smell included in the report?

He sniffed the air, bounded a few feet, and sniffed again. The smell was stronger now, an indication he was nearing the source.

The basement had a room off in one corner. It was not a large space but judging by the amount of time the chief spent in there, it must be an important space. He sniffed again. The smell was definitely coming from that room.

He entered warily. The lights were off. No windows existed. The only light came from the doorway, but that light was sickly and weak. Under such conditions even his green feline eyes couldn't see much.

He took a whiff and tasted the air. It was like barbeque but not quite. Regardless, the smell didn't belong here, and it puzzled him.

Shedeem bent down and sniffed the floor. Then, he licked it tasting the odor upon his tongue.

The barbeque had recently been on that spot. Smells and tastes do not lie.

Shedeem looked back toward the entrance to the room. He thought of Legion. Perhaps he had deviated from the mission long enough.

He was about to turn and leave when an unexpected sound stopped him in mid-stride. It wasn't a loud noise, barely perceptible by his enhanced feline hearing, still it existed. *Curious.*

With pricked ears and poised body, he stood still as stone, listening with all intensity.

He didn't like this game of hide and seek. Luckily, it only lasted a moment.

Before he could react, something out of the darkness grabbed him. At the same moment, the barbeque scent became intoxicatingly strong.

Shedeem felt his body rise into the air, being yanked up by the neck. He tried to meow in protest but before he could do so, his head fell free and rolled to the floor.

From where Shedeem's head came to rest, his green eyes beheld the strange sight of his executioner. It was no more than a silhouette in the doorway against the light from the space beyond. In the creature's hand was a dripping knife, the very blade that had beheaded him. In the other was a twitching something or other. It took a second to recognize that twitching thing as a cat's body.

The murderer dropped Shedeem's body so that it landed near his head. The smell of barbeque and death was strong upon it, residual from the one that had so recently held the headless corpse.

The scene grew blurry as the last molecules of oxygen evaporated from Shedeem's brain. In a grab of greed, death claimed all nine lives, devouring them in one gluttonous gulp. As his green eyes glossed over, he felt the sensation of being picked up by his left ear.

Then, nothing.

Chapter 40

The chief allowed Sasha to scream herself out. That was the beauty of his house. You could scream and scream, and no one would hear. It had taken a while for her voice to crack but now in the comparative silence, he was content.

He kept The Judge trained on the reverend, keeping him at bay. Then, he ordered Clay to requisition the exhausted woman who now only wheezed a residual scream sporadically.

The golem grabbed Sasha from behind, wrapping one of his tree-branch arms around her waist. The other going higher, his spade-shovel hand covering her mouth, silencing even those wheezes.

"Careful, Clay, we don't want to suffocate the pet now do we?"

"No, chief," came Clay's characteristic response.

Satisfied the woman was getting air, he focused in on the reverend. He hated this man, this defender of the supposed Messiah. His faith was misguided.

The chief worshiped true power. Unlike the reverend, who represented the God of love and forgiveness, his deities were of vengeance and hate.

Before the days of his association with Legion, he had been a lonely man, Shedeem being his only companion. Those lonely years used to weigh him down, nearly crushing him with their weight.

Those days of misery and pain were now dead and gone. In these post-Legion times, he had taken on a new life; and in exchange, he pledged allegiance to his benevolent redeemers.

The rage within the chief continued to swell as he glared at this man. He struck the preacher hard.

He towered over the reverend who crumpled to the floor under the force of his blow. Victory was his, and it was sweet.

The victim looked up without rising. He wanted the man to rise, so he forced him to his feet grabbing a fistful of hair to provide the motivation.

Yanking him up, he looked him in the eye. His rage continued to grow because he saw that sick look of forgiveness in his eyes. He needed to destroy that look but, for now, he simply looked away in disgust.

He would deliver the pet to Legion, but first he would have some fun especially with this one that Legion had not claimed.

With a fistful of the prisoner's hair, he pulled the reverend along. "Come on, Clay. Follow me to the dining room. We have games to play."

***

Sasha's heart broke as Xavier fell. It was because of his kindness to her that he now suffered. That's when it struck her how much suffering was happening because of her. Xavier was being beaten. Upstairs, Officer Simon lay dead. Then, there was Richard. She had disliked her ex, but he hadn't deserved murder.

She struggled to break free from Clay, but there was no give in his vice-like grip. Such strength didn't surprise her. In fact, she expected nothing less from one who survived bats to the head, angry raccoons, angrier bobcats, and a Dodge Dynasty.

Clay led her along, bringing up the rear of the sadistic parade. They finally stopped in the dining room.

"Here, Clay," the chief said as he handed off Xavier.

Clay removed his hand from her mouth, gripping the reverend around one wrist with that massive hand while holding Sasha's in the other. The chief took a step back and regarded the trio before him as if he were admiring a fine piece of art.

Setting down his gun, he took off the Kevlar all the while maintaining that look of concentration. "No need for this any longer," he said as he tossed the armor aside. "I'm glad, too. Do you have any idea how hot and uncomfortable these things can get?"

Sasha said nothing in response. Neither did Xavier. "Sure, Chief," Clay said.

She still held her gun and had no idea why. It was empty and useless.

The chief continued staring. "Clay, what's your favorite game?" he asked as he retrieved his weapon.

Clay's eyes brightened. "That's easy. It's Twister."

"Do you want to play Twister?"

"You mean like we did the last time we had guests?"

"Yes. Exactly like the last time."

"Oh, yes. I do want to play very much."

The chief smiled. "Well, don't go anywhere. I will be right back with the game." With that said, the chief exited the room.

"I do love Twister," Clay said with the enthusiasm of an elementary student at recess. "Although, I don't know if you two will get as much fun out of it. The last folks we had over didn't seem to like it as much as I did."

Sasha felt ill as her thoughts drifted to the collection of skulls they found earlier. The room felt hot. It began to spin, and she knew she was losing that last bit of rationality. Regardless, she seemed incapable of reeling it back in.

Her knees buckled and she would have fallen to the ground if Clay's grip hadn't prevented it. She heard a clattering as her gun fell free. As it fell she sensed her sanity fall with it.

She began to scream once again, knowing that her grip on reality was gossamer thin. She tried to keep those screams bottled up but a new reservoir had been released. She screamed again and again.

Chapter 41

Simon heard a horrible howling that invoked horrific images. Banshees evil and devilish surrounded him. Their hair was disheveled, and their mouths were like hellish vortexes.

They surrounded him, constantly circling as if they were a storm, and he were the eye. With every revolution, they drew closer.

Their eyes flashed red, kindled by unholy fire. Protruding from their bloody gums were jagged teeth that they gnashed in a sickening display. He could feel their airborne spittle colliding with the flesh of his face as they screamed bloody murder, drawing ever nearer.

Simon cowered as they drew close, his eyes searching for a weak spot in the tempest, an opening through which he could escape. He searched frantically but no opportunity for escape was apparent.

They were close enough now to touch him and touch him they did. They probed deeper than the physical, groping inside him, as if his flesh were nothing but air, his bones nothing but water. They seemed to be looking for something . . . searching.

It only took a moment for him to realize what it was they were searching for. They were searching for the man within the Barney Fife. They were searching for the hero within the Enos Strate.

Their howls grew and expressions of frustration appeared on their hag-like faces. He knew why they were frustrated. They were searching for something that simply didn't exist.

The truth was, there was no real man within him. There was no true hero in the body of Officer Simon Birch. He was 50% Enos and 50% Barney which left 0% for anything more.

He began to cry as the fact hit him that he did not have what it took to be a hero. He cried bitterly.

***

Opening his eyes, the Banshees vanished. It had all been a dream, one bad dream.

Upon awakening, he found one nightmare had been replaced by another. He let out a moan, because he knew this later dreamscape would not allow him to simply wake up. Escaping this reality would require more than simply opening his eyes.

With the vanishing of the Banshees, pain arrived. It was a whole body kind of pain. He sat up with his back against the hallway wall and looked down. His badge was nothing but garbage now having been pulverized by shotgun pellets. His shirt had been riddled with holes which exposed the black Kevlar underneath that had saved his life.

The funny thing was, he had never worn it before last night's shift. It was not required, and Getreide had always been such a laid back town he never bothered to wear the awkward and heavy garment.

He wasn't sure exactly why he had decided to wear it that last evening. At the time, it just seemed like a good call. He had no idea then how much of a good call it would be.

His chest felt as if it had taken the brunt of a batter's homerun swing. He tried to breathe in but only managed shallow breaths. Anything deeper only intensified his pain. Best case scenario, he had some major bruising going on under that vest maybe even a cracked rib or two.

He looked at the floor where he had been laying. A puddle of red haloed where his head had been resting.

He reached up and touched the back of his head. Wincing, he pulled his hand away. He must have hit it hard against the nearby radiator.

Gingerly, he explored the wound with his fingers. It seemed to have scabbed over for the most part and felt to be superficial. He knew how head wounds could bleed. His injury probably looked worse than it was.

In a perfect world, he would have liked to go to the ER to get it glued or stitched.

He stood up, using the wall for support. His legs wobbling like two wet noodles. Before, he had refrained from calling for help, because he had no idea who was on the chief's side. Now, things had turned desperate. He removed his radio from his belt and issued a call out to dispatch. He only hoped that this decision was not too late.

Dispatch did not respond. He radioed again, but no connection was made. The radio was silent except for an odd crackling static.

He pulled out his cell phone, but there was no juice. The battery should have been at full charge.

He saw a landline phone at the opposite end of the hallway sitting on a little wooden shelf next to the chief's bedroom. He hobbled over to it and picked up the receiver. The line was dead.

No, not quite dead. He heard the same crackling static he heard on his radio. He listened closely and heard more.

It was the sound of many voices. They were laughing and cursing simultaneously.

Hearing those voices made his skin crawl. "Hello," he managed. "Hello, is anyone there?"

"Hello, is anyone there?" the voices repeated in a mocking tone before reverting back to the laughing, cursing combo.

"Hello?"

The voices vanished. The line went silent. He hung up the receiver and spun around. Somebody was screaming, and it was not the banshees from his nightmare.

He ran back to where he had fallen and retrieved his Beretta. It seemed strange the chief had not taken that weapon away. Then again, he probably thought Simon was dead.

Retrieving the weapon made him dizzy. He staggered and leaned against the hallway wall until his vertigo subsided. He had certainly put his body through a lot. He needed to conserve whatever strength remained for what still lied ahead.

In his condition, he would have to grab any advantage he could. He would have to maintain the element of surprise.

That should not be too difficult as long as the screaming continued. The noise would cover any sounds of his approach.

He descended the stairs slowly.

He refrained from going any faster and fought the urge to simply burst onto the scene like some comic book superhero. He was no superhero. He knew this. He was just Officer Simon Birch (aka Enos Strate/Barney Fife).

He cared for Reverend Hernandez and Sasha. He had no idea what the screaming meant but feared the worst.

He descended the stairs and entered the dining room. His heart nearly stopped because at that moment, Sasha went silent.

Chapter 42

Within the abyss, Legion's many mouths grinned. It knew the prisoners in the house above would not be able to alert anyone outside of its imprisonment. It heard one of them try to call out, but Legion disabled all modes of communication. Doing such a task had once again depleted their reserve, but it was worth it.

"Soon," it said to its selves. "Soon the pets will be ours, and we can take their energy for our own."

Chapter 43

A feeling of giddiness was growing within the chief. This always occurred when it was playtime. His excitement had been dampened. In the past, his little home-spun version of Twister always culminated in the death of the players, but this time he would have to refrain from completing the killing round.

He thought on that. Perhaps, one of them was expendable. Maybe he could get away with murdering the reverend. He tried hard to recollect the rules of these prisoners. Sasha, for sure, had been reserved for Legion. She had to live. But he could not recall if the reverend was up for grabs.

He retrieved the game from the living room behind the couch. He held it in his arms and smiled. It would be a challenge playing the game without losing too much control, without enacting lethal doses of current.

The game was simple. There was the familiar game sheet with red, blue, yellow, and green dots. And, of course, there was the spinner.

The sheet and the spinner had come in the original store-bought box, but that's where the Milton Bradley factory parts ended and his began. Meticulously, he began to remove the many wires and battery packs. He had designed these components to deliver amps through living flesh in lethal levels. He also pulled forth the sponge electrodes along with a large bottle of saline solution. He preferred to soak the sponges in saline as it worked better than water to reduce resistance of electrical current.

With his mind firmly on the game, he felt his heart flutter with excitement. The chief always controlled the spinner. With every spin, the participants would have to obey the spinner under pain of being shot dead. With every spin, the current to the saline-soaked sponges which were on the colored spots would increase. If a player fell, they were executed. If they refused to fall, the voltage would eventually fry them like an egg.

The chief chuckled to himself because, in the end, there was only one winner, the one who controlled the spinner. He cherished the control he had over the players. That control combined with the torture and smell of burning flesh was a real turn-on.

What he did to his victims during this game was no different than what the bullies had done to him in his youth. But this was not bullying. This was revenge. This was payback for all the times he had been on the losing end of the game, being tortured by those who metaphorically controlled and spun the dial.

As he gathered his things, he could hear Sasha screaming. He grinned because he heard the sound of a mind on the edge of breaking in her voice.

Honestly, he had done her a service by crushing her hope of a rescue. It was the truth. She had only one destiny; she would become Legion's, and she would parish.

Her screams stopped, and he paused.

Had she screamed herself out? he wondered. *Had she died of fright?* For his own sake, he hoped she had not.

Quickly, he began to gather the wires and other things needed for the game. It was a lot to juggle, but he would manage it all in one trip.

For a brief moment, he wondered if Clay had done something foolish to silence Sasha. Then he remembered this was not possible. Clay would do nothing without his permission. In fact, the golem probably lost all awareness very soon after he left the room.

Why had the screaming stopped?

Chapter 44

A ghost entered the room and Sasha stopped screaming. She didn't believe in ghosts, but no other explanation presented itself.

The apparition descended the stairs and entered the dining room, standing there with shotgun in hand and caked with dried blood.

Phantom Officer Birch stood directly in front of Clay. Clay didn't react. This made her think; perhaps only she could see him. Maybe that was the way it was with ghosts.

***

Simon stepped into the dining room. The hairs on his neck rose to attention. He found himself staring eye-to-eye with Clay.

So much for the element of surprise.

The man held Sasha by the wrist with one of his massive hands. With the other, he secured the reverend. He demonstrated no reaction whatsoever. At first Simon thought this was the result of an overconfident enemy. The lack of fear in Clay's eyes supported that theory. But more than fear was missing from those terrible peepers. They were blank as if the brain inside had closed up shop for the weekend. Simon took a step closer, bringing the barrel of his shotgun up, jamming it into the underside of Clay's jaw. Still no reaction.

He was so close to this man he could smell him, but he didn't smell as a man should. He smelled like a freshly tilled field.

The man's eyes looked fake, like marbles, as if the one behind the stare was not actually a living thing but only something an artist had made to mimic life.

He pressed against the man, jamming the barrel of the Beretta harder into that jaw. He expected to feel the man's chest rise and fall as he inhaled and exhaled, but he felt nothing.

Out of his peripheral vision, he could see the basic outline of Sasha and Xavier who were both trembling. Clay however remained steady as stone. He felt the terror rising, but he pushed past it. He needed to prove to himself that he was no Enos or Barney but a real cop.

He hated what he felt inclined to do. Still he had to do it. With a trembling hand, he reached out and touched Clay's throat where the jugular vein was. There was no reaction, and he felt no pulse.

The man's skin felt cold and unnatural. He pulled his hand away.

Simon rubbed his fingers together. A dusty residue coated his fingers where they had made contact with Clay.

His thoughts screamed, trying to organize themselves, trying to derive logic from that which was illogical. Pulling himself out of his delirium, he noticed that the reverend and Sasha were trying to get his attention, but the confusion had settled. He could not hear their voices, though it seemed by their expressions, they were saying something to him in a frantic volume.

He stared at their lips and made the interpretation. "Run!" they were telling him. *"Run!"*

But it was too late. He felt something cold press against the back of his head. "Drop your weapons," came a familiar voice.

"No, you drop them," Simon responded. "Or your buddy here is a goner."

"Pull the trigger. I am sure you have guessed by now that bullets won't hurt him anyway.

Simon hesitated.

"Don't test me, Simon, unless you want to see what a 410 can do to your skull."

Without options, he lowered the Berretta and laid it on the ground.

"And your sidearm."

He pulled his sidearm from its holster and put it beside the shotgun. Everything felt like a bad dream. He looked down at his discarded weapons and lamented the fact he was nothing more than the combined incarnation of Barney Fife and Enos Strate, more of a liability than asset.

***

The chief had been given a surprise. And, that was saying something, because not a lot surprised him in these post-Legion days.

"I see you finally took my advice and started wearing your Kevlar," he said as he kicked Simon's shotgun and sidearm away to the far corner of the room. "That's good. Even out here in the sticks of Iowa you might run into a hairy situation now and again. Don't you agree?"

Simon didn't verbally respond but put his hands in the air. His shivers reverberated through the barrel of The Judge which pressed against the back of his head. The man was scared, and the chief loved it.

"Of course, Kevlar doesn't do much to stop point-blank shots to the old noggin," he gave Simon a solid nudge with the end of the gun's barrel to drive his point home.

The chief looked at his golem who was slowly rising from his comatose existence. He flinched minutely as a look of mild surprise engulfed his face.

"Very slowly, I want you to remove that vest, and I want you to keep crystal clear in that dim grey matter of yours that I will blow your brains out without hesitation if you cross me in any way. Do we understand each other?"

Officer Birch did not answer which irked the chief a little. Still he complied with the command, and that was what really counted at this point in the game.

Soon the Kevlar was on the ground . The chief kicked it over by the shotgun and sidearm.

He then grabbed Simon's walkie-talkie, placed it to his ear and listened.

With a grin, he put it back in its place on Officer Birch's belt. He didn't care if the man kept it. It was useless. The chief knew this fact the moment he listened to the static-ridden conglomeration of Legion's many voices.

"Why are you doing this?" Simon asked in a quiet but steady voice.

"Really, you are going to try your standard 'keep a dialog going with the bad guy' bit? Oh, man, Simon, this is right out of your training manual isn't it?"

Simon said nothing.

"Okay, I'll play along for now. Let's keep the lines of communication open. Although, I do give you fair warning, I don't think it will change the outcome today."

"You never answered my question," Simon's voice was monotone. The chief assumed this was his way of keeping panic at bay.

"Refresh my memory please. What was the question?"

"Why are you doing this?"

The chief replied, "You're going to need to be more specific."

Simon remained silent.

The chief let out a forced breath. "Geez, Simon. You need to work with me here. Your question is too ambiguous. I mean do you want me to tell you why I have you here today? Or were you more interested in the big picture of why I have become what I am and why do I do what I do?"

Simon shrugged.

"Leaving it up to me, huh? Okay, let's talk about the latter."

"I believe you know my mother passed away when I was ten years old."

Simon nodded.

"Well, I don't believe I told you this part, but my father and me never really got along. You see, he didn't want me around if my mom was out of the picture. I can tell you it sucks being unwanted by a dad who somehow blames you for your mom's death."

"That must have been hard," came the voice of the reverend.

The chief ignored that input from the peanut gallery but was glad the reverend had spoken. It reminded him he was there.

Honestly, the chief was more wary of the reverend than he was of Simon. Simon was just a man of the law, but the reverend had the potential to be so much more. The reverend had within him God's knowledge. Such men could be treacherous, especially to followers of Legion.

The chief continued. "With all the baggage I had to carry around, you would be correct in saying that I was troubled. You would think people would be kind to kids like me after all I had been through, but no. I learned that people are not capable of kindness. I was bullied. I was rejected. I was left without a friend!"

Unintentionally, he shouted the last sentence. He took a deep breath, a calming breath. Losing his temper was the last thing he wanted to do. He did not want to go down in the history books as a tantrum thrower.

Lowering his voice, he continued. "I have no problem testifying as to the garbage that my life was. The pain was terrific. I can tell you first-hand that mental pain is not like the physical. You can't heal it with ointment or hide it under a bandage.

"That's not to say that you can't remedy it. I discovered that creating pain in others dulled that of my own. But you already know that, don't you?"

He looked at the trio of captives, letting his last statement sink into their skulls. They all acted as if they had no idea what he was referring to.

"Oh, don't play stupid. I know you were in my room, and I know you saw my little collection in the closet."

Simon shifted minutely, but it was enough for the chief to notice. "Yes, I know you were in my room. By the way, did you like the décor on the walls? You did dare to turn off the lights did you not?"

Again, a shift from Simon. "Maybe I should go into interior decorating. What do you think, Simon?"

"Where did the skulls come from?" Simon asked, ignoring the last question.

The chief didn't mind divulging. That collection was his pride and joy after all. "When I had the life of some poor animal in my hands, I felt so powerful. That power would mask my pain. Some were pets. Some came to me by chance over the years. Have you ever killed anything Simon?"

Simon shook his head.

The chief scoffed. "Why am I not surprised? Anyway, when you take a life, not for food or in self-defense but simply for the purpose of causing pain and playing god, the feeling is like no other. It's glorious. There is no other word to explain it. Simply glorious."

The reverend spoke again. "Even with all of these wrongs you have committed, there can be forgiveness. You can get help for this--"

"Ha!" the chief interrupted. "Forgiveness for what? For killing animals? For the moment when I took that leap from animals to humans?"

"Yes, for all of it."

"I am not forgiven!"

"You can be," the reverend said, barely above a whisper.

"Wrong! You need to be penitent to receive forgiveness. Isn't that what your God teaches? Repent and be saved and all of that garbage! I am not sorry for what I have done, ergo I am not forgiven."

He waited for a rebuttal, but the reverend remained silent which suited the chief fine. There was strength in words. In the past, he had been lured by smooth-talking Christians but had learned from their forked-tongue words. He would not fall for their schemes again.

"You don't know the gods like I do, reverend," the chief spat. "I have Legion under my control!"

At Legion's name, it became the reverend's turn to shift. "If you think that you control Legion than you are living an illusion," he said to the chief. "It cannot be controlled by men. It only wants you to think that so it can control you."

"Shut up!" The chief was finding it more and more difficult to keep calm with this man of Christ blabbing on and on. "It's you who's living an illusion, choosing to believe in fairytales about a forgiving God that doesn't care what you've done as long as you believe in Him. My gods promote real truths like self-gratification and vengeance without mercy."

"Vengeance is mine, sayeth the Lord." The reverend's words pushed the chief past restraint.

"Clay, squeeze your left hand."

Clay squeezed. The reverend let out a howl and fell to his knees.

"Go on, break it."

It was hard to make out over the ruckus from the squealing reverend, but he heard it nonetheless, a most satisfying crunch.

The chief stood over the red-faced, crying preacher man. "Now, do you see the power you are facing? Do you not see I am in control and the demons do my bidding?"

The reverend didn't answer which was fine. The chief grew tired of this man's comments anyway.

"Clay."

"Yes, Chief?"

"Release your grip."

The golem let go and the reverend fell into a fetal position cradling his arm and sobbing like a spanked child.

He leaned down, pointing The Judge at him. "Do you still question who has the control?"

The reverend did not answer.

"Do you still think vengeance is your Lord's only?"

Still, no response. In fact, the reverend didn't even look up from his cradled arm. The chief wondered if the reverend was even listening or if the pain overrode everything else. He could certainly relate to that.

"And where was your God just now? Why didn't he protect you? Hmm?"

Nothing from the reverend.

The chief looked down at him and scoffed.

***

Sasha's life had become one horrible rollercoaster ride—her spirits picking up when she saw that Officer Simon had escaped death—but taking a nosedive shortly thereafter. Her heart went out to Xavier. His only crime had been helping her. He was now paying a high price for this single act of mercy.

She knew the reverend was a compassionate soul. He tried to empathize with the enemy. She had no idea if this was genuine empathy or if it was just a tactic to gain the upper hand. If it was the later, his strategy failed.

She looked down at him as he curled up on the floor protecting his hand as best he could. Her attention returned to the chief, fear rekindling.

The chief glared at her, his smile revealing gritted teeth. "Let the games begin," he said. "Let the games begin."

***

The pain from his crushed wrist brought Xavier to the brink of unconsciousness. The fact he held onto consciousness was nothing short of a force of will. He simply could not pass out.

He feared but did not hate the chief. In that man, he saw a tortured and confused soul. Jesus himself came not for the righteous but for the sick. Xavier had to do the same, to try and save that which was lost.

He looked up as the chief glared at Sasha, then sneered like a madman. He was definitely one of the lost. The battle that was coming would be difficult. He prepared for it as best as he could.

*****

From watching and relishing the reverend's pain, the chief attained a state of nirvana. He was confident that the reverend wouldn't try to escape, not in his condition. As such, his attention turned to Officer Simon. He directed Clay to restrain Simon. Clay complied with the free hand that had so recently crushed a man's wrist.

With Clay restraining both Sasha and Simon, and with the reverend unable to flee, the chief could concentrate on the assembly of his home-grown version of Twister. He laid out the mat. He connected the leads to the large battery packs. He picked up the large bottle labeled "Saline" and realized it was nearly empty.

"Now, don't go anywhere," he announced as he departed the room. He had extra bottles and would only need a moment to retrieve one.

He hurried to the kitchen, going directly to the cupboard under the sink. He obtained the extra saline bottle he kept there and then returned to his quarry.

Once again, Clay blinked as if waking from a little siesta. "Oh, boy!" he said as he looked at the bottle.

The chief smiled. Clay always got excited when it was Twister time. Who wouldn't? This game was positively electrifying.

He looked the game over and smiled. This was one of his favorite instruments of revenge.

He moistened the sponges with the saline, careful not to get them so wet as to puddle. He only wanted them damp enough to eliminate electrical resistance.

He went over the rules out loud more as a means to torture the captives than for any other reason. "I spin the spinner. The players obey the spinner under pain of being shot. For every round, the electrical current will be increased slightly. Upon the first one falling, the current maxes, and it is game over."

Honestly, he rarely gave the losers the luxury of death in the first round. He designed it that way. It's not the voltage that kills in electrocution. It's the current. Sure, the game is able to produce lethal current, but he only ever delivers that lethal amount when the fun is done. He had even gone so far as to resuscitate the players with a defibrillator he kept handy for just such a purpose. That's how he got maximum satisfaction from them. That's how he got maximum masking of his own pain.

Eventually, they would die. It would not be a total act of revenge if his victims did not eventually die. After said deaths, he would always feel a deep sense of euphoria similar to the feeling after getting a good night's sleep and eating a good breakfast. Usually while in such a state, he would go into town and watch those who had been affected by his murders. It was like basking in the sun to watch those who had bullied him as a child feel pain equal to his.

What a rush.

Sometimes the high would stick with him for days. Other times it would take weeks for the glorious feeling to fade. Eventually, it would fade away as all good things do over time.

When that feeling was gone and he found himself wanting, he would start preparing to repeat the process. He needed to requisition new players. Then the games commenced once again. New victims would die. A renewed high would be obtained. And his little version of The Circle of Life would start anew.

"I'll be honest," the chief remarked. "This is a rare event. I don't think I have ever had two game players and a spectator, other than Clay. Sasha, I think you and I are going to really enjoy ourselves as we watch. Heck, I may even let you flick the spinner a few times. I hope I don't have to tell you what an honor that would be.

He wasn't insulted by the look of disgust on her face. It was expected. In fact, it excited him.

"Of course, you are worth many spins, my girl."

Silence from Sasha.

"Seriously, I don't think you realize how special you really are."

Still nothing but silence and that perpetual look of repulsion.

"You are in an elite club, destined to be Legion's personal pet." He watched the look on Sasha's face intensify. "I'm afraid your friends didn't make such a player's club upgrade."

He saw tears form in the corners of her eyes. He was pushing all the right buttons.

"Let's call these two the "B" team." He smiled, indicating Simon and the reverend.

Sasha however did not smile, not in the least.

Chapter 45

Legion grew impatient. It had no pets, and Shedeem failed to provide a status report. The demons lamented having to send that cat to do their dirty work. Felines are a distractible breed, but they had no choice given their current restrictions.

Legion conferred with their many selves. "Where is the pet?" it griped.

"We don't know," it answered to themselves.

"The chief does not properly give us our dues."

"We speak the truth."

"Where are our pets?"

They repeated this among themselves, further escalating the agitation within the great abyss. Of course they knew that their relationship with the chief was a finite thing.

The chief had been an enigma lasting longer than any of Legion's other slaves. His secret to longevity? Loyalty. He was so obsessed with his self-serving list of revenge he would do anything Legion wanted–anything.

Still, the time approached when it would tire of this slave. On that day, Legion would toss him aside like the refuse he was. The only thing stopping it from doing this now was the fact that no suitable replacement had yet presented itself to them. Someday, that would all change, and the chief's eyes would be truly opened.

When that moment of truth arrived, it would be too late for its poor slave. Being surrounded by the bars of his prison there will be no escape.

Legion's many selves licked its demonic chops as it fantasized on this future. "One step at a time," one of the many selves shouted to the rest. "Let's keep our collective mind on the present goal. We need our pet!"

Just like that, Legion's frustrations rose. It was unable to go up to the surface physically, but that did not mean it didn't have influence.

Using as little energy as possible, it called out through the medium it was most comfortable with, that direct line to the chief. It called and waited for him to answer.

While it waited, a most peculiar smell caught in its many nostrils: barbeque.

Chapter 46

The chief moved the table up against the wall in order to make more space for the Twister mat. To his delight, everything fit.

Clay placed Simon before the mat, and with some persuasion from The Judge, the reverend joined him. The chief stood back and looked over his two game contestants. "Well, I think we are ready to begin."

Neither of the game players showed any response. The chief tried to ignore their placidity.

"Oh, come on, why the long faces? This will be fun, and given your disability," he said indicating the reverend's arm, "We will start at the novice level."

Still no reaction. The chief certainly hoped the party would liven up once it got going. A rip-roaring celebration was always more fun. He wasn't too worried. This game always livened things up a notch or two.

"My dear, Ms. James," he said, glancing sweetly at Sasha. "Would you do me the honor of taking the first spin?"

The chief held out the spinner to her. She looked down at it momentarily but did not reach for it. The chief was not daunted. He had become used to rude guests. "Oh, come on," he said. "I won't bite."

She stared at him, anger filling her eyes. Such an emotion was a serious faux pas, but again, not uncommon at his get-togethers.

After a second or two, he retracted his offer. "So, I guess I will do the opening spin but once you see how much fun it is, I am sure you will be more participatory."

He spun. The spinner glided along slightly scraping the color-coded cardboard. "Round and round and round it goes. Where it stops no one knows."

The chief stopped the spinner with his finger. He had to stay on schedule knowing Legion would not be kept waiting indefinitely.

With the spinner still, silence reigned. Within that silence, a sound emerged, a tapping sound. This was Legion's ringtone.

The chief did not want to stop the fun. It was just getting started, but it was best not to keep Legion waiting. Slowly, he approached the dining room table, preparing to answer the call.

***

Sasha couldn't have spun that spinner even if she wanted to. The mixture of fear and anger made such actions simply beyond her.

In horror, she anticipated retaliation for her insolence. Nothing of the sort happened.

This only confirmed what the chief told her. She was in an elite club, reserved to be Legion's pet. She had no idea what that meant. It was a bad thing though. It had to be.

***

The chief stared at the damaged Ouija board. Looking at it rekindled his anger toward those who dared commit such an act of vandalism.

"I know you did this, Reverend. Only a closed-minded idiot such as you would have the guts to do something so heinous." His voice cracked as his rage swelled.

The reverend said nothing, but it didn't matter.

"I have tried to remain calm with you, sir," the chief continued. "I didn't get too angry when you tried to keep Sasha from me. I remained professional when you broke into my home. I restrained myself when you invaded my closet and defiled my collection. But this act of vandalism really pushes my buttons!"

Realizing he was shouting, he took a deep breath, a calming breath. He wanted to teach the reverend a thing or two about what happens to those who defile items sacred to Legion but such tasks would have to wait. The planchette was still tapping. Legion was calling, and Legion would not be kept waiting.

"Luckily for you, preacher man, the board still works," he said through gritted teeth. Then, he answered the call.

Chapter 47

Legion's anger had been aroused. The many curses and blasphemies which emanated from the abyss stood testament to that fact.

It was taking too long for its servant to answer. The speaking board through which it was forced to communicate was tedious to say the least. The planchette had to be maneuvered about, spelling out messages one letter at a time. Letter by letter, word by word, sentence by sentence; Legion spelled out its frustration.

"Where are you?" Legion asked the chief.

It waited as the board spelled out the question hoping the chief was nearby the board. It had no way of knowing for sure, but this was its only option.

Slowly, the answer came to it from the board. "In the djnning room."

The spelling error irked Legion. It showed the incompetence of its associate. It also showed weakness on its part—a painful reminder that they were prisoners of the abyss and forced to rely on corrupted humans to carry out their deeds.

"Do you have Sasha James?" Legion inquired.

"Yes."

Legion liked "yes" or "no" questions because the words "yes" and "no" were on the board and those responses came quicker. However, the answer to this particular question only aggravated them further. Their servant had the pet in custody and yet the delivery had not been completed? That was a real slap in the face.

The heat within the abyss rose, now a fiery furnace. "Why then have you not made good on your promised delivery?"

"I was just having some fun with the other two."

"You will bring all three to us now!"

Legion waited for the response but nothing came back. Not even a simple "yes" or "no."

"Bring all of them to us now!" Legion iterated as the abyss flared blisteringly hot.

"But I get the other two. You said so. Sasha is yours, but the others are for me," came the response. It came very quickly considering the medium used.

Legion spontaneously combusted a line of expletives from its many lips, a wildfire of rage. "We are in no mood to debate! Bring all of them to us *now*! Do you understand?"

Legion waited. Finally the answer appeared.

"Yes."

Chapter 48

The chief pushed the Ouija board from him, thus disjointing the broken halves. Within him brewed a volatile mixture of anger, pain, and frustration—the sort he normally medicated with murder. This time, it appeared Legion had denied him said medication.

"What did the board say?" Clay asked.

The chief stood and turned to his golem, trying hard to keep his true feelings from bursting forth. He opened his mouth, but nothing came out.

Legion's demand was an insult. Legion needed him! Without him, it was nothing but a prisoner of the abyss and could do nothing beyond a few parlor tricks. It had no right to treat him this way!

On the other side of the coin, he needed the demons as much as they needed him. Without Clay and Legion's spell upon the town, his agenda of revenge would be much more difficult to complete, impossible even.

With that in mind, he began to pack up the Twister game. There really was no point in leaving it out now Legion had crashed his party.

He disconnected wires from batteries and wet sponges haphazardly, not caring if he damaged the game or not. He rolled up the mat pushing the whole mess into the space under the dining room table.

"Aren't we going to play?" Clay asked repeatedly as things were packed up.

The chief shook his head.

"Why not?"

"Because Legion wants them all," he uttered through gritted teeth. "Legion wants them all."

***

Legion wants them all. That statement summersaulted over and over again inside Xavier's mind.

Legion wants them all. It sounded so finite, like an executioner asking a death row inmate what he wanted for his last meal.

Legion wants them all. His terror increased exponentially with every repeat of that phrase.

Regardless of those festering fears, he felt a sense of peace wash over him. It made no sense, but the feeling persisted.

He knew the origins of this feeling. It grew from his faith. Even now as he stood with a throbbing wrist staring at one controlled by demons, he had faith that God was by his side. *I will never leave you or forsake you.*

Xavier was glad that what he was about to face he would not face alone. Jesus would be with him. *I can do all things through Christ who strengthens me.*

Clay still had Sasha in one hand. The chief instructed Clay to grab Simon in the other. That left Xavier untethered for the moment.

The chief now stared Xavier down, glaring at him eye to eye.

Xavier looked back, knowing he was staring into the windows of a soul. He stared into emptiness—the eyes of a slave—the whipping boy of demons.

Within those eyes glimmered ignorance. He had seen this many times before when confronting the lost. Such people don't see the chains that bind them. They choose instead to deny the chains exist, voluntarily selecting slavery in lieu of God's free gift of grace and mercy.

The reverend understood the lure of such traps. Demons, after all, are masters of lies, experts in manipulation, and adept in the arts which corrupt souls. They have skill to convince the weak-minded if only the right spells are chanted or the correct number of candles are lit at the right moment, then demons become Genies, available to grant wishes.

Xavier felt sorry for the chief because he was a fool. He rubbed the proverbial lamp believing Legion would grant his wishes. In reality, his future held only eternal damnation.

The chief was not the true enemy. He was only a stupid puppet of his masters. Xavier would try to help this lost man if he could. He would have to move covertly and at the right time. When would that time arrive? He had no idea.

***

Simon stood in Clay's clutches. Where their skin touched, a tingling of gooseflesh erupted. He had determined that Clay was not alive, at least not in the traditional sense. *So what was this creature?* he asked himself. Clay reminded him of Mary Shelley's creation. Still, even Frankenstein's monster had a beating heart. Clay had no pulse whatsoever.

The tingling continued on his hand. It grew from his wrist where Clay held him and extended to his fingers.

Could Clay be of the Bram Stoker persuasion? A vampire? If so, then the movies and books had woefully overestimated the sly intelligence usually attributed to that night breed.

He shook his head, forcing such irrational thoughts from him. Frankenstein and Dracula were fictional. This was reality, no matter how bazaar.

The tingling now encompassed all of his fingers. Unable to ignore that feeling another second, he looked down at his hand.

An earthworm startled him, dangling there. It emerged from a wormhole between Clay's thumb and forefinger.

He looked up into the characteristically soulless face. Clay smiled meekly. "Yup. I've got worms."

That statement left Simon speechless.

"Why aren't you laughing? The chief always laughs at me when I say that."

"It's not funny," Simon responded after a moment's pause.

"Yeah. I never got it either."

***

The chief led the way, keeping The Judge pressed against the reverend's back. Unlike the previous incident with Simon, there was no Kevlar to deflect the damage if the gun discharged. How he wanted to pull that trigger. The only thing stopping him was the fact that this one was now "pet status." He would have a little heart-to-heart with Legion on that issue.

***

Sasha brought up the rear, being guided by Clay who had her securely in one hand and Simon in the other. As they descended the stairs which led to the basement, her claustrophobia grew. This subterranean space felt like a one-way ticket to death, allowing entrance but banning escape.

She didn't struggle against the one who held her. Fighting against Clay was pointless. They ventured further into the basement; she witnessed her hope dissolving with every step.

With Clay in-between them, she had a hard time catching sight of Simon. She wanted to see him, hoping his presence would rekindle her hope but when she finally caught a glimpse, she saw nothing but a dead man walking.

In that absence of hope, her senses fine-tuned themselves. She could hear her own heart beating like a war-drum. She felt oxygen as it jumped from her lungs into her blood. She sensed the drain of her situation and knew her end must be near.

With this deep sorrow engulfing her, she began to sob. She tried to stifle them to no avail.

"What's the matter?" Clay inquired.

She didn't answer, tired of these cruel games.

The chief chuckled. "You'll have to forgive Clay. He is just a simple lump of dirt, mentally a mere child. Isn't that right, Clay?"

"If you say so, Chief."

Clay's voice had no hint of sarcasm, and it made Sasha wonder more than ever what in the world this mammoth creature was exactly. With nothing to lose, she ventured the question. "What are you?"

"Can we tell her, Chief?" Clay asked as if he were a school kid whose turn it was for show and tell.

"No need to keep any secrets I suppose. Go ahead, Clay."

On Clay's face, an ear to ear grin grew. "Oh, boy, I'm a gommer," he blurted.

The chief began to laugh. "Sorry, buddy, I call you that from time to time just to have a little fun. You are actually a golem."

Clay looked confused momentarily. Then his eyes brightened. "Yeah. That's what I meant. I am a golem."

The chief continued. "What's a golem you may ask?" He paused. "Well a golem is a mythical creature out of ancient Hebrew mysticism. Only they aren't mythical at all. They are as real as real can be. Isn't that right, Clay?"

Clay nodded with enthusiasm.

"In essence, they are simply mounds of dirt given life through their creator. The great thing about them is the fact they are so loyal to their master. In Clay's case, that would be me."

"You made him?" she asked.

The chief chuckled again. "Not me. God gets the credit for this one."

"God had nothing to do with this," Xavier uttered.

"Untrue, my dear reverend. Maybe your God isn't capable of such miracles but my Legion of gods certainly are."

"Your gods are nothing but demons." Xavier's voice was cold as stone.

They were now in the basement, walking down a hallway. To one side, an open door revealed a dark room.

Something was lying on the floor of that room. Sasha saw it as they passed by. At first she could not tell what it was exactly except it was dark and lying in a puddle of red.

After a moment she recognized it as the cat she had seen earlier, only it wasn't the whole cat. Its head was missing.

She felt vomit rise as her mind identified the body. Who would do such a thing and where was the head?

She looked away, swallowing hard to force the lump down. If the chief had seen the body, he didn't acknowledge it.

As they neared the far end of the basement, Sasha's fears escalated. *What would happen when they reached the far end? Would this be where death waited?*

Terror weighed her down making her feet sluggish, almost too heavy to lift. Clay tugged her along, overcoming her weakness and forcing her forward.

Xavier and the chief suddenly disappeared from her view. She closed her eyes and reopened them.

Nothing changed. They simply vanished!

It was then she noticed the hole in the basement floor. Xavier and the chief had not disappeared, they simply entered this hole.

Against her will Clay dragged her into the steep downward tunnel. Panic pulsed through her, prompting her to claw at the earthen walls of the tunnel. Such action did not slow her progression.

Dirt flaked off and coated her arms. This was the dirt of her grave, her final resting place. As she descended deeper into this gaping tomb, she gasped, panting, trying to breathe through her panic.

Chapter 49

In the distance, someone was crying, a sound pleasing to Legion. It meant that its pets were finally in route. Its many mouths shouted out in triumph redirecting their sadness and anger temporarily. Legion had plans for Sasha James, horrible, nasty, wonderful plans.

Almost as much as Legion relished the idea of having its way with Ms. James, it was also excited at the prospect of stealing away what it sensed the chief still perceived to be his finder's fee.

Of course the chief's thinking was flawed and Legion loathed him for it. Its servant was delusional actually believing he had the ability to control an abyss crammed with demons.

Legion shook their many heads and wagged their many fingers thinking about the chief's stupidity. The idea of mere mortals controlling demons was laughable.

This man's destruction was just around the corner. He just didn't know it yet.

"Soon," Legion hissed to his many selves. "Have patience," they encouraged one another.

It was bad form to toss a slave aside before a suitable replacement could be garnered. That was the thing which kept the chief safe for so long. But Legion had its many eyes on a new candidate.

The recruit was green but showed promise, having both a chip on his shoulder as well as a void in his life. This human had an unholy agenda similar to the chief's, thus opening a need for what Legion offered.

Having this new one in their sights, Legion wanted nothing but to immediately destroy the chief. But it refrained because the recruit, although interested, had not yet signed on the dotted line. "Patience,"

Legion whispered among their many selves. "We must be patient. We must bide our time."

Legion inhaled and smiled. Although it could not see those lambs being led to the slaughter, it could smell the terror wafting from them. With forked tongues, it sampled the air, savoring every molecule of fear as if it were a fine wine.

It cupped gnarled demonic hands around its many ears to hear those glorious noises better. The anticipation built.

Despite all these wonderful things, something was throwing bitterness into the mix. One of the lambs was praying to the enemy!

Curse them!

At first, Legion tried to ignore the prayers and bring back the joy of the moment, but it was no use. The prayer was loud and sincere, silent yet booming in the demon's ears like an atomic bomb. It covered its ears in protest, but that grotesque noise bombarded it from beyond the sense of the auditory.

It hated the one who was doing this and promised vengeance. The praying one would pay most severely.

In a rage, Legion pounded the walls of its prison, shaking the abyss. "You will pay, man of the most high God! Do you hear us? You will pay!"

Despite its tantrum, the praying continued. Pure torture.

***

Sasha felt the tremor and used the side of the tunnel for balance. She thought she heard a voice say, "You will pay." *What in the world are we approaching?* she thought as a shiver escaped.

Terror spiked and spiraled out of control. Weakness overtook her knees, buckling with every step. But there would be no rest. Clay forced her onward.

Ahead, she saw the chief with Xavier. The reverend cradled his broken wrist, moaning every time the chief shoved him and it bumped against the side of the tunnel.

It was not dark here. From behind her, the light from the basement cast a cold glow. In addition, strings of Christmas lights dangled above, twinkling with out-of-place festiveness.

The tunnel ended and she found herself being guided through a cavern. No more Christmas lights dangled, yet her surroundings grew progressively brighter.

Ahead she saw a strange radiance. She could not place the origin of this glowing. It was unlike anything caused by fire. It was unlike anything caused by man.

This strangle light created additional uneasiness within her. It did more than illuminate. Under its glow, she felt exposed.

She wondered if Xavier felt it as well. She wondered and grimaced, realizing she must be teetering on the edge of insanity.

***

Despite the terror before him, Xavier put on a brave face while continuing his silent prayers. He needed God's help to keep the others strong. Inwardly, he struggled. He wanted to believe God was here with them, yet he struggled with thoughts God had forsaken him.

He had no doubts his God was mighty. He knew that his fear grew from the idea of what demons were capable of doing to his body. He kept in mind the scriptures. *Do not be afraid of those who kill the body but cannot kill the soul.* Regardless, his mind gravitated toward dark thoughts. His terror persisted and festered.

He repeated the verse over and over forcing it into his permanent memory through repetition. He wanted it to remain there no matter what the future held. *Do not be afraid of those who kill the body but cannot kill the soul.*

As he continued forward, the stench of Sulphur became strong. The stench of Hell.

Do not be afraid of those who kill the body but cannot kill the soul!

The chief guided him across a vast cavern toward a glowing red light. *Do not be afraid of those who kill the body but cannot kill the soul! Do not be afraid of those who kill the body but cannot kill the soul! Do not be afraid of those who kill the body but cannot kill the soul!!!*

Over and over again, he cycled his mantra, trying with all his might to force the dark thoughts away. *Do not be afraid of those who kill the body but cannot kill the soul!*

The light was now everywhere, repulsing him. It seemed to penetrate his skin and sully his soul.

He found himself standing before a great abyss. It was from here the cursed light emanated. His scripture-recital ceased as he began to tremble.

***

Legion peeked out over the ridge of the abyss and glared at those approaching. Finally, the long-anticipated arrival. Its many mouths salivated. The wait had been long, too long given its caliber and standing. For the delay, it would claim their reward with interest.

Its many eyes zeroed in on the praying man. Of the group, it hated this one the most. It glared at him, a seething rage boiling within its many selves. This one had within him the spirit of Legion's greatest enemy.

In disgust, it looked past the reverend as well as the chief. Behind them were the others.

The golem led two prisoners. In Clay's one hand was the man with the badge, and the other hand held the most coveted of them all.

Legion grinned through its many mouths. "Sasha James, we presume."

Sasha looked up at the mention of her name. Fear filled her eyes—beautiful, glorious fear.

Its grins grew wider. The prisoners were being led like lambs to the slaughter. "Welcome," they uttered with the chorused voices of its many selves. "Bring them closer, my good and faithful golem."

It glanced at the chief, noticing a hint of anger welling up in his eyes. They knew why he was angry. He always thought himself to be the sole master of the golem. No doubt the fact they commanded his servant was irksome to say the least.

The chief now followed the others—nudging his prisoner forward with a jab from the gun—enticing a moan from the man of God as he cradled his injured arm tighter.

At that moment, a stench hit Legion's nostrils. The man of the cloth began praying again.

The chief prodded the praying one to the edge of the abyss so the prisoner's toes extended over the edge.

With slow precision, Legion crept its kraken-like tentacles up out of the crevasse and caressed those feet, desiring nothing more than to simply throw this one into the abyss and watch him squirm under their various methods of torture.

What it wanted and what it was allowed were two separate things. The man was praying. A praying man could not succumb to the abyss as the abyss could not accept a man praying to the true God.

Legion would have to cure this man of his prayer addiction. For this, there was no 12 step process. Slowly, it slid those tentacles up the man's pants and coiled around his legs, flexing their demonic muscles.

Legion knew the repulsion it was giving this man of prayer. Legion's many mouths grinned wildly because the spiritual showdown had begun.

***

Xavier Hernandez stood at the brink of the great abyss. *Lord, take this cup from me.*

The prayer was not his own. Jesus Christ had prayed it, or something nearly like it, just before being led to die for the sins of the world.

Lord, take this cup from me, he prayed again as he felt the demons touching his feet.

He knew he was leaving out some of the verbiage his savior had said back on that fateful day. Xavier, however, could not utter those exact words, he just couldn't.

"Take this cup from me," he whimpered as he felt the touch of the demons rise from his feet to his legs.

Their touch incited shivering. Those tentacles were cold beyond cold which surprised Xavier considering the fact that the abyss put off such heat. It was a coldness which penetrated deeper than skin, deeper than flesh and bone. It chilled his very soul.

The repulsion made praying difficult. He continued regardless. "Take away this cup!" he demanded.

"Take away this cup. Take away this cup. Take away this cup." He heard the many demons taunting him through repetition of his own words.

He gagged as they coiled their awful appendages around his legs. He could feel the throbbing, pulsating, vibrating hideousness of their power.

Xavier sensed they were scouting his defenses, looking for a weakness to exploit, an entry through which to access his soul. With all that he had he shouted, "You have no power over me!"

He knew this to be true. As long as he continued praying to his Lord, it would be true.

The problem was his prayers were not coming easily. The pressure of the demons was a distraction clouding his spiritual eyes, fighting to blind him from the truth.

He continued praying, despite the thought that they were going unheard. He knew his prayers were left wanting and knew what the missing element was. Yet he could not bring himself to amend his ways.

Under his shirt, the demons progressed. Perhaps, they were even under his skin. Their touch was so cold he couldn't tell.

"Let go of your agenda, man of God," they shouted. "Quit demanding that your God save you, for he cannot. He has no power here!"

"He can save," Xavier answered, but his voice lacked conviction. Would God save him?

"Your voice betrays you, praying man. You sound so unsure and rightly so. For you are relying on lies."

Xavier pushed back with everything he had. "No! It is you that lie. You belong to Satan, and Satan is the master of lies. You are his children, and you act just the same!"

"You stand here at our doorstep and dare speak to us this way? We are Legion, for we are many."

Something clicked inside of Xavier at that moment. Strangely, Legion had helped him to overcome the obstacle he was up against. Within Legion's lies, were bits of truth. It was right. He needed to let go of his agenda. He needed to stop praying demands to God, for he was but a man and not one to make demands of his savior.

"Dear God, please take this cup from me. Yet not as my will, but yours be done."

Finally, he uttered that additional phrase. He gave up control and handed it completely over to Jesus.

Despite the invasion on his body, he smiled. He smiled because he realized he had never been in control. Everything was in God's hands as it had always been and as it always would be.

He glared down into the abyss and for the first time beheld the wretched creatures who resided there. The seething mass was quite a sight to behold. Yet, there was something to be pitied here. For these demons had been angels once upon a time, but chose to align themselves with Satan, and God cast them from his presence.

If they had not been who they were, Xavier would have even felt compassion for them and prayed for their healing. Of course they were what they were: demons. There could be no healing and no salvation for these Hell-dwellers.

Xavier watched them as they congregated in slimy masses. They stared up at him with lust, and he knew they coveted what they could not possess.

He stood tall, knowing his soul was beyond their limits. He belonged to Jesus and no other could claim squatter's rights.

Being freed, his concern turned to Simon and Sasha. Sure Simon attended church, but that did not guarantee salvation. Only God knew Simon's heart. As for Sasha, he knew virtually nothing about her walk with God as he had only recently met her. He prayed for them both. He prayed hard.

***

It tried to resist the urge to let go, coiling its tentacles over his flesh but in the end, it had no choice. Repulsed, Legion gave up their hold on the preacher.

It angered Legion that the preacher was beyond its reach. Its only chance at him now would be to chip away at his faith and slowly gain ground.

Legion commanded Clay, "Hold the man of God out over the abyss!"

Letting go of Sasha and the officer, Clay took charge of the praying one. Upon release, neither of the sick and weak ran. Legion suspected terror kept them planted. Plus, where would they go? They had little option for escape here in the cavern.

Clay held the man out over the abyss. Legion marveled at the strength of its creation. The golem held the man as if he weighed nothing.

The demon's hopes rose. Despite the continued prayers, it sensed fear from the one who dangled just above Hell's chimney.

What really intrigued Legion were the waves of terror that wafted from the two weaker ones.

"Bring the others over to me," Legion bellowed to the chief.

The chief obeyed, using The Judge to nudge Simon and Sasha forward. Legion grinned through its many mouths as the sacrifices came closer. Again, there was no prayer from these two, only terror!

***

The chief didn't like how things were unfurling. Legion overstepped its bounds. He felt the need to show his value to the demons. After all, without him there would be no pets.

In the end, he remained silent on the matter. Challenging demons was a risky business, like hitting explosives with a hammer. You might get away with it but eventually you'll blow your face off.

He looked at the dangling preacher man. It concerned him his golem had been so quick to comply with Legions' command. His concern bordered on fear.

Agreements had been violated. The reverend was not to be Legion's pet. Neither was Simon. No, these two were to be his payment in exchange for the apprehension and delivery of Sasha James.

The voices of Legion brought him from his thoughts. "What do you think, Chief? What should we do with this worm we have dangling over the shark tank?"

The chief didn't answer.

Legion commanded Clay to dangle the reverend more freely. Clay obeyed, flipping the reverend around, holding him only by his heels, swinging him back and forth like a slow-moving pendulum.

"What's the matter? Cat got your tongue?" Legion taunted.

The chief could hear the man moan as he dangled. The moans mingled with words of prayer.

At this, the chief could not help but smile, because he knew how repulsive prayers of this nature were to the abyss-dwellers. Plus, he knew what it meant. One praying to Jesus was exempt from Legion's control.

Knowing that prayer was a distraction to Legion, the chief took his opportunity. With one quick movement, he yanked Sasha to him.

He could feel her body trembling as he pressed against her, a most satisfying trembling. He held her from behind reaching The Judge around, jamming it into her throat.

The light from the abyss intensified, a sure sign that Legion did not approve of this challenge, but the chief didn't care anymore. He was calling their bluff. "Fine, you can have the reverend. I'll take back your pet and everything will be even."

He jammed the gun into her chin hard enough to force her face up. He wanted Legion to have a good look at the merchandise to fully consider what was on the bartering table.

The chief waited as their little game of chicken ensued. He found the status quo to be crushing. "Look," he finally said. "I know that you would rather have Sasha James. Quite frankly, that's fine with me, but let's not get greedy. I want the reverend and the officer for myself."

The chief paused and waited, but the demons held their tongues.

"What do you say?" he continued as calmly as possible. "Can we strike a deal?"

Legion answered at last. "Come closer."

The chief did not like this situation. There was no reason he needed to go closer. "You know me well enough, Legion. You know I have sworn off being bullied and that includes being bullied from the likes of you."

"Come closer," Legion repeated, this time with greater intensity.

The chief considered Legion's demand. After a moment, he decided to obey for now to move the bartering process forward.

Keeping Sasha in between himself and the abyss, he edged forward. He forced his movements to remain steady because he knew Legion pounced on weakness. "Simon, stay with me," he barked to Officer Birch.

Simon stayed where he was.

"Simon, I suggest you do as I say. You know how itchy my trigger finger can get when I am not obeyed. We don't want anything to happen to Sasha now do we?"

Simon moved to the chief's side. That was good. He wanted to control all of the pawns in this high-stakes game of chess.

"Do we have a deal, Legion? Can we strike a trade?"

Again, only silence came from the abyss, a suffocating silence.

"Answer me!" The chief demanded. He was done playing games.

"We have considered your proposal," the many voices finally responded.

The chief held his breath. This was the moment of truth, the crescendo of the opera, the pinnacle from which he could fly to new heights or crash into the depths in a burning ball of flames.

"We accept your offer."

The chief exhaled. "I am glad to hear you have come to your senses, Legion."

From the abyss, Legion's many voices began to laugh. It started low and grew into a deafening chorus.

The laughter continued. *Why were they laughing? Are they laughing at me?* It was all a little too reminiscent of his youth. "*Stop!*" he screamed.

The laughter ceased.

"Don't ever laugh at me again!" the chief shouted. He won the showdown and earned the right to be taken seriously. "You accepted my offer, so let's make the switch and be done with it."

"We made no such offer with you."

Sweat began to bead on his brow. "But you did."

"Did not, did not, did not," came Legion's reply with a hint of mockery in their many voices. "The deal we made was with another."

The chief tried to make sense out of the conversation but before he succeeded, a sharp pain overwhelmed him. Something red and shiny emerged from the front of his throat, reminding him of the chest-bursting scene from *Alien*. An unexpected scent entered his nostrils.

Barbeque.

He tried to discharge The Judge, but his fingers seemed unwilling to obey his brain's command. Instead, the weapon fell from his hands, clattering to the floor.

He looked down at the red shiny blade which still protruded from the front of his neck. How ironic. Despite his previous precautions of helmets and Kevlar vests and shields, his throat was completely unprotected. That one vulnerability had been exploited.

His last memory was the realization the gushing blood was his own. There was so much of it, spurting from him like a crimson geyser. His thoughts faded as a general malaise settled in.

Then, nothing—only intense darkness.

***

He awoke confused, bewildered. He remembered intense pain. He remembered the blade protruding from his neck. It reminded him of the chest-bursting scene from the movie *Alien*. He remembered the blood, his blood. It covered everything.

Who dared do such a thing, a walking barbeque? He opened his eyes and pure terror overtook him. He was in the abyss. Legion surrounded him!

The pain of that blade stabbing through his throat paled in comparison to the pain he now endured. He screamed in agony as the many voices of Legion taunted and laughed. He knew he had chosen the wrong gods.

The knowledge came too late.

Chapter 50

Sasha was confused. She felt the chief's grip suddenly tighten as he gurgled like a drain backing up. Then, his hold weakened. His gun drifted from her throat.

He tried to stay upright, using her for leverage. She felt warm wherever he had contact with her. He fought his battle against gravity, slowly losing ground, sliding down her back and legs. Finally, he crumpled in a heap upon the cavern floor, defeated.

She inhaled and caught a strange scent. *Barbeque?* She didn't dare turn around, fearing it was all just some sadistic trick. Instead, she focused on the reverend who hung upside down over the abyss.

"Who are you?" she heard Simon inquire.

Curiosity overrode her apprehension. She turned and looked. What she saw shocked her.

A concentric circle of blood was expanding upon the floor, flowing from the filleted neck of the chief. The flow was only a trickle and an indication his heart no longer pumped.

She wanted to look away, but she found the scene strangely mesmerizing. With effort, she broke from her trance and glanced at Simon, but he wasn't looking back at her. His focus was elsewhere.

She followed his gaze and shock hit her like a tidal wave. The creature's flesh was a mottled red and black, naked except for a gold chain around its neck. On the chain was a brass key which shone brightly against the darkened backdrop of its chest. Not one follicle of hair could be seen on this creature. It shifted slightly and the visible movement of tendons and muscle-fibers confirmed that skin was absent.

Two eyes peered out at her from deep sockets. Muscle, sinew, and in some places bone was visible. The thing grinned at her with a lipless, skullish grin.

In her shock, her lungs chugged into overdrive and with every inhalation, she caught more of the barbeque smell that wafted from this being. The smell made her stomach turn.

Within the repulsion she felt another sense stirred within her, the sense of familiarity.

It stood there shivering, the bloody knife used to impale the chief's neck still in its gnarled grip.

Everything seemed to freeze in time and space as she searched her mind for the source of her *Deja Vu*.

The creature took in a deep, labored breath and then rattled out the exhale which ended in a cough. A mist of blood protruded from its skeletal mouth as the cough ensued.

A blackened tongue licked those pearly whites and washed away the red flecks.

There was something on that face. She stared closer. The thing was wearing glasses. *How odd*.

The sight of those wire-rims contributed to her memories. Where had she seen those glasses before? *Think!*

Then, it clicked. "Mr. Kahler?" she asked.

The thing nodded trying to speak, but only succeeding in a labored moan. He tried to move toward her but collapsed on the way, tripping over the lifeless form of the chief.

He struggled to regain his footing but could not. Defeated, the thing let out a deranged howl, a cry of agony.

Not knowing what to do Sasha knelt down beside what remained of Mr. Kahler. Pity welled up within her.

***

Simon watched the creature writhe upon the floor with Sasha by his side. *Who or what was this creature? Where did he come from? Why was he in such a condition? And, how in the world did Sasha know him, this Mr. Kahler?*

He pushed these questions away. More pressing matters needed his attention.

He approached Clay with caution, knowing this one had the power to release Reverend Hernandez into the abyss at any moment. All was silent except for the constant mumblings of prayer issued from the preacher.

Simon's voice waivered. "Clay, don't do anything rash. It's over. So, let's put the reverend down nice and gentle on the ground. What do you say?"

Clay didn't respond.

Simon took a tentative step closer praying that the worst case scenario would not play out. His best chance, he figured, was through hostage negotiation, a skill he had not used since his days at the academy.

Clay had yet to acknowledge Simon's presence. No matter how hard he thought, the only image that flashed before him was of the reverend falling down into the pit.

"Clay, don't make things worse for yourself. Put the reverend down safely. I promise I will do everything in my power to get you a fair trial."

Silence from Clay.

"I know you weren't the one calling the shots."

Still nothing.

"You were just following orders. You know the courts will look favorably on that."

What he said was true. Especially considering Clay's apparent intelligence level, there would be a chance to convince the judge he was only a pawn in a game out of his control. The fact that Clay was not human did change things slightly. He had no idea what that fact would do to the whole scenario and for now, it really didn't matter. The only thing that did matter at that moment was the reverend's safety.

Simon had been edging nearer as he spoke. Clay was only just out of his reach and the reverend only a smidge further.

He glanced briefly at the reverend whose hair was standing straight out under the power of gravity. With his face reddened by all the blood rushing to it, he resembled a lobster about to be thrown into the boiling pot.

"I think it's just like earlier," the reverend said, interrupted his own prayer.

Simon didn't answer. He worried what effect his answer could do to the precarious predicament.

"I can see his eyes, and I don't think anyone's home in there."

Memories of staring into Clay's eyes back in the dining room came to mind. He didn't understand this comatose state but was thankful it hadn't resulted in the loosening of his grip on Xavier. Slowly, he skirted the situation creeping around to get a better glimpse of Clay's face. Sure enough, it appeared whoever lived there, had departed, and turned out all the lights.

This seemed more profound than before. Clay's face had that complete vacant look, as if the spark of life had not simply fallen asleep but had died.

A fine dust flittered off Clay's extended arms as the reverend swayed slightly.

"Try not to move," Simon hissed.

A sinking feeling grew within him as he noticed tiny fissures erupting all over the surface of Clay's body, the sort that appeared on sandcastles just before collapsing.

"Don't move a muscle."

Simon reached out one of his arms toward the dangling one, grappling Clay's legs for support with the other. A sickening feeling grew within him. For those legs were cold. Bits flaked free as Simon put more of his weight against them.

He extended over the edge of the abyss. Instinctively, he looked down. The crevasse appeared infinite. He could not tell if this was reality or simply an act of illusion since the reddish glow had retreated deep into the depths.

Mesmerized by this phenomenon, he stared, his eyes adjusting to new levels of dimness. Far down, he saw flickering. They looked like firefly couples. No! They were eyes! They flickered as they blinked angrily, glaring up at him from the distant reaches.

Vertigo struck just as he remembered one should never stare down when at such a height. He felt his hand slipping as Clay's legs disintegrated further. Below, the owners of the eyes called to him, using a seductive voice.

His hand slipped further, leaving a trail of moisture against the powdery dryness of Clay's legs. The voices continued flirting, enticing him to let go.

"Don't look down there, Simon. Don't pay attention to what they say. All that lives down there is evil and anything they say is lies." The reverend's voice came to him as if one calling from a far way off, barely perceptible.

Simon shook his head in an effort to rid himself of the temptations. He looked up from those depths and saw the reverend reaching out to him with his good arm.

Officer Birch reached for him, their fingers touching, but was unable to secure a hold. He tried to edge further out but stopped. His grasp upon Clay's legs was precarious at best. If he stretched himself any further, he would risk losing it.

Again he heard the voices calling to him from below, pleading with him to join them. He wanted to cover his ears and block them out, but there was no way for him to do so not without letting go of the only thing keeping him from plummeting into the hole.

The reverend began to sway toward Simon's outstretched hands. They only needed an inch, just one inch.

Those below were now shouting their promises of wealth and majesty and honor only if he would take the dive.

Simon looked down again, watching the flickering eyes of those who coveted him. As he was about to give in, he felt Xavier's hand grasp his, the contact bringing him back to his senses.

A second later, the hands that held the reverend by his ankles broke free and fell into the abyss. Moments later, the rest of Clay disassembled.

Instinctively, Simon dropped to his stomach to create as much friction on the ground as possible. It wasn't enough! The momentum of the reverend's body was pulling them both down.

For a fraction of a second, he considered letting go to save himself, but their eyes locked and he knew he would die trying to save this man. He would play the Enos-Barney character no longer.

"No!" he heard Sasha's voice shriek as he felt her grab his legs.

Her added weight was enough. They stopped their progression into the abyss.

The voices below were no longer sweet and seductive but full of curses and rage. This time, though, he refused to look down past the dangling reverend. He would not be tempted again.

In a joint effort, Simon and Sasha edged Xavier out of the abyss. Together, they rolled onto the cavern floor, panting and gasping.

He looked at the pile of rubble that had been Clay. Before his eyes, that rubble degenerated further into nothing but dust caught in the updraft from the abyss. He was airborne, and what remained of him departed.

He could no longer hear the voices from those within the hole but knew they were there and felt their rage in the vibrations which now rocked the cavern floor.

Regardless of the tremors, Simon wanted nothing more than to lie there soaking in the fact he still lived. Now was not the time. There was more to be done, so much more.

Using each other for leverage, they helped each other to their feet and then staggered over to where Mr. Kahler laid, writhing in obvious agony. The smell of him wafted into Simon's nostrils, and he knew without any doubt he would never be able to enjoy barbeque again.

Raising his arm, Mr. Kahler motioned to Sasha. "Come close," he hissed.

She leaned down close and Simon heard whispering. She looked up from him and stared Simon in the eyes. "Mr. Kahler has something to tell."

"Later," Simon replied. "Right now, we need to get him to a hospital."

Mr. Kahler shook his head. "No. It's too late for hospitals. I must say my piece now."

Deep down, Simon knew that the barbeque man was right. He had never heard of one surviving such extreme injuries. Even if he survived the next 24 hours, the potential for infection was astronomical.

Labored, Mr. Kahler began to talk. What he told was bazaar beyond belief. Yet, his very existence stood out as testimony that every word was truth.

***

"I was in the chief's employ. It shames me to say it, but it's true. Every child I provided records on became a face on a milk carton soon after. The idea made me sick. I confronted the chief a few times, but he said I could be rich, or I could be in prison. The weird thing was we never got caught. As far as I know, we never even raised suspicion. The last time I was at his place, I voiced my concerns of what would happen if we were caught. He gave me this key and told me always to wear it around my neck. He said it fit a hidden lock in a secret door at the back of the house that existed behind a fake bookcase. He told me if I was ever in any trouble to come to the house using that door and lay low for a while. Well, he shows up at my place, wanting info on you, Sasha. I told him I was done doing his dirty work. He torched my house fully expecting me to go up in flames with it. I should have died in that blaze. I should be dead right now. I think the only reason I am still here is because of my promise of revenge. Now, it's been done."

In silence, Sasha stared at him. Mr. Kahler's trauma was extensive both physically and mentally. *He is right in saying he should be dead*, she observed. He was little more than charred bones and scorched flesh. "We need to get you to a hospital."

He did not answer her. The cavern grew eerily dark, the glow from the abyss uncharacteristically dim. His blackened body blended into the darkness. She could only see his exposed teeth and bulging eyes. Those eyes were unmoving and had no lids to blink. His only sign of life was the rasping breaths she heard.

"We'll get you help," Simon said.

He tried his radio again without success. It was either broken or had a dead battery.

Mr. Kahler let out a laugh that evidenced more pain than humor. "It's okay. I wouldn't expect Legion to allow you to call for help anyway." He inhaled laboriously. "I know now my purpose in life. I know now that everything will be fine."

Sasha stared at what remained of the man who only yesterday had been sitting with her in the teacher's lounge, in his right mind and casually reading the newspaper. Looking at him now, she knew he was delusional, because there was no way that things could be "just fine."

The reverend spoke. "Do you know Jesus?"

Mr. Kahler stared at him with those sunken, unblinking, eyes.

The reverend continued. "Jesus doesn't care what you have done in your life. He only asks that you repent and come to him. The Bible says to cast your anxiety upon the Lord because he cares for you."

"I don't deserve to have your God care for me. Not after what I've done," Mr. Kahler wheezed.

"We all fall short of righteousness, and you are right in saying you don't deserve forgiveness. But it is being offered to you just the same. It's free for the taking. All you have to do is believe Jesus took all your sins away by dying on the cross."

Mr. Kahler said nothing but looked away.

"You may not be in this world much longer. Trust me, you will want to be right with your maker."

Mr. Kahler turned back toward them once more, his lipless teeth glimmering in the faint glow which emanated out from deep within the abyss. "I've already been redeemed," he said with little more than a whisper.

"Only Jesus can save. You must believe that Jesus can save you. Salvation comes in no other form."

Mr. Kahler let out another pained laugh. "When I came here today, I had one goal. I wanted to kill the chief. Then, with the mission complete, I would kill myself. It was a simple plan. I snuck in through the secret door. Having never used it before, I had some difficulty finding it but in the end I succeeded in locating it behind a thick row of shrubs at the back of the house. Once inside, I found this little cat and mouse game going on. Everyone was so consumed with hunting or escaping I was able to get to the basement unnoticed, well almost unnoticed."

Sasha's unsettlement was growing with every word that Mr. Kahler said.

He continued. "They say curiosity killed the cat. Well, Shedeem was just a little too curious for his own good."

Sasha had no idea who Shedeem was. Regardless, she felt confident this person was now among the long list of victims.

"I watched Shedeem come up from the hole in the basement. Having never been there before, I had no idea this cavern existed let alone the abyss. Before then, I always thought the chief did not want me in the basement because that was where he did his murdering. I had no idea what he truly hid down here.

"Anyway, I decapitated little Shedeem, simply because the chief had a fondness for him. I knew the chief was somewhere in the floors up above hunting but having been warned never to go into the basement, I knew that this was a special place. I knew he would return there. I waited for him. Besides this, there was another reason I descended the tunnel. Once having killed Shedeem, I felt a strange power pulling me to this location. I didn't understand it at the time, but I felt simply that the answer to my situation would be revealed if I allowed myself to be pulled along."

"What situation?" the reverend interrupted.

Mr. Kahler laughed until a choking wheeze silenced him. "Why, my situation of course. I knew I should have died in that fire. Geez, I should be dead now. I knew some power was keeping me alive, and it was more than sheer willpower or my desire for revenge."

The reverend looked as if he wanted to argue but no words came out. Sasha felt a twinge of fear.

"Once down here, I met Legion. It explained to me the situation. It explained it could take away all of my pain if I destroyed the chief."

"No," Sasha whispered.

Mr. Kahler nodded, staring at her with that lipless grin.

"These demons," the reverend said, gesturing toward the abyss. "They cannot save you. The proof is in your pain. I see your pain. The demons have not taken it away. They have not kept their promises."

Mr. Kahler remained silent.

"The only salvation for you is found in Jesus Christ!" the reverend added.

"Untrue," Mr. Kahler said calmly. "Legion has promised to heal me. I only have to do one more thing."

"Whatever it is, I beg you not to do it. There is still hope. You don't have to satisfy the demands of demons. You can still turn to Jesus!" the reverend shouted.

"I must deliver Sasha James. She is the price for my healing."

As Mr. Kahler spoke, he grabbed The Judge from the ground, took aim, and shot the reverend.

Chapter 51

Everything seemed to transpire in slow-motion. Simon dove onto the barbeque man just as the shotgun discharged, the reverend collapsed, and Sasha screamed. The gunman laughed, his skullish teeth chattering like one of those cheesy novelty store gag items.

Simon wrestled with Mr. Kahler needing control of the weapon, because whoever controlled the weapon controlled the situation. The gun discharged again, leaving his ears ringing and his hair unnaturally parted by speeding pellets.

In his peripheral vision, a light flashed. The abyss now flared with blinding brilliance.

Officer Birch had one hand secured around the barrel of the shotgun in an attempt to control its trajectory. That barrel was hot to the touch, but he fought the urge to let go. He could not let go!

His other hand pushed up against Mr. Kahler's wet and sticky chin. Simon could feel exposed bone, sinew and tendon and pushed harder. His goal to use his enemy's weakness against him. Despite the nastiness of it all, Simon went one step further jamming his thumb into the underside of that jaw, submerging his appendage all the way to the second knuckle. Mr. Kahler howled and gnashed his teeth but refused submission.

Out of the corner of his eye, Simon spied movement from Sasha. "Stay back," he shouted in between gasps. He wanted her to be safe.

The light erupted brighter and brighter from the abyss as if those within had a large bellows. In that throbbing glow, Mr. Kahler looked positively demonic. Burnt flesh shimmered in the eerie light glimmering as if smoldering embers had embedded themselves into his scorched flesh.

The voices came with the increased light. The demons cheered for their champion. "Fight him! Conquer him! *Kill him!*" they shrieked.

Simon's ears were still ringing from the report of the gun, yet those voices transcended the auditory "Kill him! Kill him! *Kill him!*"

Those voices pounded him like bags of rocks. Pushing past this bombardment, Simon flexed his thumb, hooking the jawbone of the other and pulling. He twisted it in his grip and a gurgling howl erupted from his opponent. Encouraged, Simon yanked.

"Kill him, and I will heal you. Your burnt flesh can be made new. Your sorrow will turn to joy. Just kill him and bring us our pet!"

Just as the voices weakened Simon, they appeared to strengthen Mr. Kahler. Like a dog trying to kill a squirrel, he shook his head from side to side until Simon's thumb slipped free of the mandible.

Beneath him, Simon could feel Mr. Kahler quivering as if he were being recharged. His teeth bared. His ghoulish eyes bulged. His breathing quickened.

All sounds were now muted in Simon's ears save the shrieks from the abyss: "*Kill, kill, kill!*"

With a scream, Mr. Kahler rallied and rolled Simon to the bottom of the pile. Above Simon, he fought with unbridled fury. Those skeletal teeth gnashed at him, snapping together just inches from his face and splattering blood particles from the dripping thumbhole under the mandible. Simon dodged this attack as best he could while keeping a hold on the shotgun. He had to keep hold of that shotgun!

Beside him, the chief's was a lifeless corpse, his blood sticky and coating the back of Simon's head. The chief's cold lips grazed Simon's cheek as he struggled. Repulsed by this kiss of death, he dug deep to keep fighting.

"*Kill, kill, kill!*" Legion's chanting continued climbing in volume and pitch disturbing him to the point of insanity.

In the pauses between Legion's shrieks, he heard or perhaps felt something else. It bubbled from a deep space within, deeper than the demon's penetration.

"*Yes! Shoot him! Shoot him dead and your healing can begin!*" the abyss-dwellers boomed.

The bottom of a fight was always the most exertive and Simon was nearly spent. Above him, Mr. Kahler crushed down with a weight beyond what appeared possible.

Heat from the abyss undulated above him, draining his reserves. He glanced that direction, his skin near blistering with the torrent of hellfire roiling from its brim.

He noticed how close to the abyss their fight migrated. The demons screamed to him louder than ever, spiking his terror and exhaustion to new heights. His grip on the gun's barrel continued to slip, the wrong end progressing toward his face.

Laughter from the abyss virtually paralyzed him with fear. Mr. Kahler joined, those skeletal teeth clattering with every guffaw. That barrel continued to realign itself.

Despite the noise, the quieter sound from before intensified. It was a voice. "Simon..."

"*He is mine!*" Legion interrupted the quieter voice.

Simon listened hard for the quieter voice. "Simon, just ask for help. Ask me for help."

"Who are you?" Simon vocalized.

"*He is nothing! Kill him now, Kahler! I will heal, but you must kill him now!*"

The barrel moved within inches of Simon's face. If it fired now, he would catch some of the shot. It might kill him. It might not. Either way, it would be less than pleasant.

"Simon," came the quieter voice again. "Simon, listen."

"Shut up! You have no power here! There is no herd of pigs this time! You cannot banish us again! We are already banished to the Abyss, remember? Do you remember?"

"I remember," the quiet voice replied to those within the abyss.

Simon found himself wanting to listen to this new voice. It was so calm, yet so powerful.

"Kill him now! I will heal you, but it must be now."

Trembling from exhaustion, Simon grabbed the key around Mr. Kahler's neck with his free hand and twisted the chain tight enough to stifle the other's air supply.

The ringing in Simon's ears began to diminish. He could hear the reverend from somewhere outside of his focus. "Listen to that soft voice. Do what he says. Ask him for help."

Simon was shocked. The voice was clearly coming from some space within him, yet the reverend could hear it, too? "Who is he?"

"Do you have to ask?" the reverend replied. "He is the enemy of the demons fighting you and you have to ask who he is?"

Then, Simon understood. He prayed to the owner of the voice. He asked for help. Then he gave up his hold on the barrel.

Mr. Kahler used the opportunity, pressed the gun hard against Simon's face. The triumph in those ghoulish bulging eyes and skeletal grin said it all.

Simon continued to pray, and everything seemed to fade out of his head, including the voices from the abyss. He closed his eyes and prayed in earnest. In the silence, only one sound came to him. It was the sound of a trigger being pulled.

Chapter 52

The Judge jammed. With no intention of throwing away a miracle, Sasha slammed into Mr. Kahler with all that was in her.

The contact was disgusting; her healthy flesh connecting with skinless, half-cooked meat. He teetered, trying to maintain his hold on Simon, but his slippery grip eventually failed and he plummeted head-first into the abyss.

His scream lasted only a moment, followed by an eerie silence. The brilliance from the abyss flared and ebbed as if digesting a fine meal.

***

With difficulty, Xavier staggered to his feet. If it wasn't for Simon deflecting the gun at the last second, he would be dead. The way it was, pellets still riddled his body from the periphery of the gun's shot-pattern. He looked down at the growing blood stain on his shirt. *This is not good.*

"Leave now!" the quiet voice said from somewhere deep within him.

He took only one step before wobbling and falling to his knees. Sasha and Simon ran to his aid. "We have to get out of here. We have to get out now!" he said with a voice too quiet for the effort it took.

"I know," Sasha said. "I hear the voice too."

A deep rumble rose from the abyss. The chief and Mr. Kahler might have been destroyed, but the real enemy still thrived, undefeated.

***

There was no reason for the gun to jam, and Simon knew it. Every other time, it had operated correctly, and he knew the chief well enough to know the man would not keep his weaponry in anything less than pristine condition.

Why had it failed?

There was only one plausible answer. God himself prevented the gun from working.

That quiet voice commanded, *Get out of the house now.*

The rumbling beneath their feet intensified as they moved away from the abyss. The reverend moaned as they proceeded, clearly in pain from his injuries. Regardless, Sasha and the reverend dragged him along as quickly as possible, obeying the voice of God.

The rumbling increased. Chunks from the cavern ceiling began to fall, exploding into piles of rubble upon impact.

They pushed forward.

The light from behind them surged and with it a tidal wave of heat bombarded them. Against that light, their shadows were cast in high-level definition. Those shadows ran before their living counterparts as if they were scouts running ahead of the retreating forces.

At the entrance to the tunnel, Sasha began to scream. She was staring back. Simon followed her gaze, and what he saw elicited a scream of his own.

Fissures erupted from the main abyss. They progressed closer and closer to the escapees with every tremor that shook the cavern like hellish fingers reaching out to them.

The nearest of these fingers advanced to within a few feet and continued closer still. From within this gap, angry voices called, "You will not escape us! *You will not!*"

"Come on!" Simon screamed as he shoved Sasha and the reverend ahead of him.

"You cannot escape us!" the many voices echoed.

Within the narrow tunnel, they were only as fast as their slowest member. It was agonizing being behind the reverend. Time and time again, Xavier leaned against the tunnel for support, leaving crimson smudges on the earthen walls.

They stumbled into the basement just as the tunnel collapsed upon itself. They stood there panting and staring at the place where the tunnel had once been. Now nothing but dirt and debris remained. The rumbling subsided. In the silence Simon heard a new noise. He turned just as the reverend moaned and collapsed to the floor.

***

In the back of her mind, Sasha still heard the quiet voice telling her it was time to get out of the house. However, she ignored it for the moment, choosing instead to attend to the fallen.

The reverend was conscious, which seemed miraculous considering his appearance. His right side was emblazoned in dirt-flecked crimson. His blood was so dark. His face was so pale. The contrast between them caused her stomach to turn.

"I can get up in a moment," he said, managing something akin to a smile.

With Simon's help, he staggered to his feet, looking about as steady as a newborn fawn.

"You should just rest here while we go and get help," Simon said.

Sasha was about to volunteer to stay with Xavier until help arrived but before she could communicate this, the reverend said, "Haven't you been listening to the voice? It's still calling. There is no time to wait around for help. We must leave now!"

Sasha looked at Simon and Simon looked back. True, she had stopped listening to the voice the moment the tunnel collapsed.

"Get out of the house now!" the quiet voice came to her, clear as crystal.

***

Adrenaline overrode Simon's exhaustion, boosting him to action as the earthquake began. The quake was rhythmic as if the mass of demons were using a battering ram in order to smash through from the realm below to the world above. A noise boomed as the floor under their feet split, running a fissure the length of the basement about an inch wide and glowing with the same light as from the abyss.

Tapping into some unknown reserve, Simon found the strength to hoist Xavier over his shoulder. He heard a weak whine and hoped more damage wasn't being done to the poor guy, but there was no time for such considerations. The bottom line was, they should not have stopped. They should not have ignored the quiet voice of God.

Time had run out.

Sasha led the way and made it to the stairs when the lights flickered and went out. In the darkness, with the steps swaying in rhythm to that unseen battering ram, they ascended.

"Whatever you do, don't look back," he heard the reverend mumble.

***

From Xavier's position, being lugged over Simon's shoulder, he had a clear view of what they were running from. Even from the stairs, he could see the buried tunnel from the far end of the basement. Although still sealed off, the rubble that filled that tunnel was glowing crimson as if it were morphing into molten lava.

They stepped into the dining room just as the stairs disintegrated, falling into the depths of that lower level. Despite the noise and the layer of earth separating them, the screaming demons could be heard. "You cannot escape us. *You will not escape us!*"

"Focus on the quiet voice of God," the reverend shouted. "Pay no attention to the enemy."

"There is no God for you anymore," the enemy rebutted. "We are the only gods here. There are no others! *There are no others!*"

Xavier knew such temptations could be swaying. He prayed for strength. He prayed for safety. He prayed for the demon's screams to stop, yet they continued all the louder.

***

Sasha took the reverend's advice, desperately focusing in on that still, quiet voice. All she could hear were the screams of demons.

With the absence of that quiet voice, she stuck to their last instructions. They had to get out!

From the dining room to the kitchen, she ran, the tremors making straight-line escapes impossible. A large piece of plaster fell, hitting her squarely on the head. She shook off the pain and continued.

More plaster followed. The house was coming undone and would soon be inescapable.

The demons no longer used words against them. Their language devolved into shrieks and cackles—loud and lingering— reverberating throughout the house as well as through the marrow in Sasha's bones.

In the living room, the coat rack toppled toward her as if it had been waiting in ambush. The hat and hair combo resting on it wrapped around her face in an act of sabotage. She flung it from her with difficulty, her fingers intertwining with the long strands.

Oddly, the cat clock continued to cling to its spot on the wall as if it was somehow crucial to the integrity of the house's structure. Tick-tock, tick-tock, the eyes and tail wagged to the movement of time as if nothing unusual occurred.

They arrived at the door which led to the garage. Kicking aside the debris that had congregated there, she slammed into the door, but the padlocks still held. She stumbled into the windowed rooms, but the polycarbonate glass remained intact.

With sounds of the demonic reverberating around and within her, a feeling of hopelessness took over. They were no less the prisoners here than they were down below. Either way, a cage surrounded them and was on the verge of implosion.

***

Simon's last ounce of hope crumbled as they reached the locked door. There was no time to break those locks (not that he would be able to anyway with the house shaking as it was).

Indeed, the house was falling to pieces. Chunks of plaster were missing from the ceiling, exposing rafters bowing from strain.

Above the din created by the demolition, laughter echoed.

There was another sound. He didn't know what it was and found it difficult to discern from the rest of the ruckus.

He focused on this new noise. It came from the reverend. He was shouting. From the hoarseness in his voice, Simon conjectured he had been doing it for a while.

"Am I the only one listening to the quiet voice of God around here? Am I the only one who can hear His instructions?"

"All I can hear are the demons!" Simon retorted.

"God says to look in your hand Simon! What do you have in your hand?"

Simon opened his hand and looked at what sat in his palm. He must have grabbed the item from before, during his fight with Mr. Kahler. He could not remember, but its presence rekindled his hope.

***

Sasha shouted for joy as Simon showed her the key in his palm. It was the key Mr. Kahler wore around his neck. Simon must have grabbed it and ripped it free from its chain as Mr. Kahler toppled into the abyss.

They ran to the door and tried the key in one of the padlocks. It was not a match. Then, Sasha remembered what Mr. Kahler said about needing to get to the back of the house and find the secret door.

She didn't know exactly where to look; Mr. Kahler had not been specific. He only said the door was hidden behind a bookcase along the back wall of the house.

They reentered the living room when a particularly violent tremor shook them. The floor from the hallway they just exited fell away. A second slower and they would have fallen with it.

The hole mesmerized her. It was deeper than a basement should have been. In fact, there was no basement. There was only the churning red lava expanse of the great abyss.

Through that gaping hole in the floor, the demon's voices called out louder than ever. "You will not escape! *This will be your tomb!*"

"Ignore them!" she heard the reverend shout from where he dangled over Simon's back. "The threats of demons are empty as long as you keep your focus on God."

Sasha believed—too many things happened in their favor to be considered coincidence. The bobcat in the tree, the unforeseen killing of the chief, the gun in Mr. Kahler's hand jamming at just the right moment: These incidents were nothing less than evidence of the hand of God.

They weaved their way toward the back portion of the home. They passed two doors. One led upstairs and the other to Hell.

She tried to keep her gaze from wandering toward that direction but something pulled at her, enticing her to look. She looked. The door itself was gone. The stairs were gone. The red glow from below radiated through that opening with unholy power.

She turned away, fighting the urge to stop and stare. At the back of the dining room was a door which she had not noticed before. They opened the door and entered a new part of the house.

Chapter 53

Legion was furious. The chief failed. Its new recruit failed. It didn't have any pets and found itself wanting.

Its only consolation rested with the fact that Hell was less lonely since both of their former servants joined them as permanent residents. It would torture the chief as well as Kahler for all eternity and would glean enjoyment from doing so. Still, that did not solve the current dilemma.

A renewed energy coursed through Legion, reinvigorated by the demise of Kahler and the chief. So, that was in its favor at least. In its rage, it shook the earth wanting to destroy the house and those within it but didn't.

Sure, Legion could knock the house free of its foundation easily enough and be done with it in less than a second. They knew, however, that killing these three in their current state would be wasted effort.

Dead Christians are useless to demons because they are beyond their reach. So, Legion made a two-step agenda. The first step was to destroy the prisoners' faith. Then they could harvest the souls.

So, it shook the house, screamed, taunted, and laughed all in an effort to take their focus away from the voice of God which Legion knew had been speaking. Such tactics worked in the past. Even Saint Peter, once he left the boat to walk on the waters, succumbed to the waves and the wind. He would have done well to keep his focus on Jesus, but the tantrums of demons provided sufficient distraction. Jesus reached out that day and kept Peter from sinking. Today things would be different. They would keep the distraction going so that the prisoners above would be blinded to the extended hand of their would-be savior.

"You are all doomed!" they shouted up from the widening abyss. "You will not escape!"

Legion smiled because it sensed a terror growing in them. Fear was the greatest distraction. As long as it could scare them, God's hand–which was reaching out to pull them from the churning sea–would remain ignored.

***

Demonic laughter was everywhere, coming from the walls, the ceiling, the floor and below. This new room disturbed but due to the desensitization Xavier experienced that day it barely raised his pulse.

As he dangled upside down from Simon's shoulder, it looked even more macabre. This was a room dedicated to the chief's pagan faith. Upon the walls hung cloaks smeared with red stains. Countless necklaces hung on a hook adorned with pentagrams, inverted crosses, and other symbols of darkness. The carpet under them was black as the walls. The ceiling had been painted a glossy red, mimicking fresh blood. Against this red, in white paint, the words "Hail Legion" were smeared. The room reeked of things dead and Xavier had no doubt sacrifices had been conducted on the very spot he now stood.

Xavier was aware of his blood loss. The pain in his side, which had previously been intense, was now only a dull ache. If he turned his head too quickly, he saw spots. So, he tried to remain as still as possible.

Two things were keeping him conscious: adrenaline and a promise. His shivers utilized the adrenaline. His actions sanctified the promise. It was a promise made to God that he would keep Sasha and Simon faithful.

"Ignore all of this," he said as they stood in the new room. "Just trust in God and listen for his voice." He spoke, having trouble producing volume. He prayed he was heard over Legion's ruckus.

He no longer heard the quiet voice which had been speaking earlier. Still, he knew he was not alone. *Lo, I am with you always even to the very end of the age.* Such scriptures motivated him at that moment to keep acting as a light in the darkness. God was perfect. In that perfection, there had to be a reason for the silence. Perhaps He didn't need to say anything else.

Legion's laughter grew louder and a feeling sprouted within Xavier that a tidal wave rose above them and was about to come crashing down. He prepared for the onslaught with a defense of intense prayer.

***

Simon had to tell himself to keep going. As a police officer, he made it a point to keep in decent physical condition, but he hadn't trained for the rigors the last 24 hours dealt him.

He stood in this new room, fatigue ransacking every cell. The chief's obsession with the occult baffled him. It was strange to think of all the years he worked under this man's guidance. All those years, the chief seemed so normal. Who knew the normalcy was only skin-deep, a mask worn to hide the psychosis brewing beneath.

Despite what he now knew—or perhaps because of that knowledge—he felt sorry for his one-time mentor. It was hard for him, being bullied and feeling friendless. He could only imagine the desperation within that predisposed him to the whim of demons.

Still the chief's choices were his own. He chose vengeance over forgiveness. He chose demons over angels. He chose Satan over Christ. Now, it was too late for him to change. Death had solidified his loyalties for all time.

As for himself, Simon knew where his allegiances fell. If before he was a lukewarm Christian, then going forward, he would be scalding hot. He would do everything possible to stop others from going down the chief's path.

Of course, there would be no going forward if they didn't survive the day. Legion's tantrum had been so loud but now as he prayed, he barely heard their taunts. In the lull, he once again heard the quiet voice: "The bookshelf is the door, and you have the key."

The voice calmed Simon far more than what he thought possible considering the chaos ensuing all around him. He lifted his eyes to the bookshelf–which was on the back exterior wall of the room–and staggered to it.

A haphazard pile of books laid in front of the shelf, knocked loose by the continuing quake. He reached out for the shelf and the tremors increased. Apparently, this was not what the demons wanted. In defiance of them, he forced his hand toward it.

***

Legion was livid. It sensed its victims had reached the sacred room and were defiling it with their deplorable acts of prayer. Now that they reached that room, what prevented them from escaping through the secret door? They shook the house with all of their might and cursed with all of their strength, careful not to kill them, at least not yet, not while their souls belonged to the enemy.

Once the escape had been thwarted, then Legion would have time to pick and pull apart their faith. "One step at a time," it said to its many selves. "One step at a time."

***

Sasha stumbled over the mess of books piled in front of the shelf. "Use the key!" she screamed to be heard. "Use the key!"

"How?" Simon replied. "Where's the keyhole?"

Sasha didn't know. In fact, she hadn't thought about it until that moment. They had the key. They knew the shelf was the door. What they did not know was how to unlock it.

***

Despite Xavier's adrenalin overdose, a general malaise washed over him and seemed to grow stronger by the minute. He looked down at the shiny redness soaking his shirt and wondered if any blood still remained within his veins.

He could still hear the quiet voice of God over the ruckus, but the words spoken to him sounded garbled in his ears. He knew confusion was a common symptom of low blood pressure and yet, he felt only mild levels of alarm as sleepiness took over.

"Put me down," he tried to shout knowing their quest to find the keyhole was hampered by his weight upon Simon. Sadly, his words were nothing more than a slurred mumble.

"Not a chance," Simon's said, his voice sounding oddly distant in Xavier's ears. "When I get this door unlocked, I want you on my shoulder so that we can get out of here as quickly as possible."

"You can find the keyhole faster if you use both hands to look."

Silence from Simon.

"You know I'm right."

Simon paused.

"There's no time to waste thinking about this and you know it."

With a sigh, Simon laid Xavier down on the floor, a few feet from the shelf. Lying flat on his back, he felt strangely light, as if he were floating on a pillow of air. Despite Legion's threats, he began to pray. "God, please get us out of here. If it be your will, please deliver us."

"Look at the shelf," the quiet voice suddenly boomed.

Xavier stopped praying. He had never before heard God with such clarity.

"Up on the shelf...look," the voice came again.

He looked up. Legion's tantrum dislodged all the books from the shelf, all of them but one. Despite his blurring vision, he made out the gold-gilded print on the spine of that tome. It was more than the brightness of the letters which made it so easy to see. From Xavier's perspective, it virtually shone out at him with a celestial light.

"*Watermelon*," he mumbled. "What kind of title is that?" The author's name was below the title. He read the name and understood.

"Look at the book!" He yelled to Simon and Sasha as he pointed at *Watermelon*.

He wanted to shout it again to make sure he had been heard, but he found himself unable. Instead, he closed his eyes and let unconsciousness intrude.

***

Sasha turned to Xavier. He said something, but she couldn't make out what it was, something about a book.

He was so still, so lifeless. Her heart skipped a beat. *Was he dead?*

"One down, two to go!" the Demon's voices taunted.

She caught sight of him just as his pointing hand went limp. It had pointed up at the shelf. She looked. There was only one book still on that space. All the others had fallen.

She knew that book and wondered what business that chick-lit novel had within the collection of satanic writings. She stared at it for a moment longer before the lightbulb flickered on in her brain. "That book is the keyhole!" she shouted to Simon.

He looked first at her and then at the book. She desperately hoped he understood because there was no time left for explanations.

***

Simon had never read a novel by that author before, but still that name had immediate significance. He grabbed *Watermelon* by Marian Keyes and pulled, but it would not come out, at least not completely. It seemed to be on a sort of track, allowing it to extend from the shelf about half of the book's length. On the underside of the exposed portion was a keyhole.

***

Legion, now connected to the house, sensed they were at the door and let out a most fearsome shriek. *"You will not escape us!"*

Its plan was failing. The best the demons could hope for would be to stop them from leaving the house alive. As much as it pained it to think of killing them only to see them enter their God's embrace, it would be much worse if they were allowed to live and tell their story. If they told others, then others might avoid the pitfalls which the chief and so many others over the millennia had fallen into.

It began to attack the foundations of the house.

The time had come to murder the pets.

***

The quaking increased and sent Simon sailing into the air. He landed with a thud beside a limp reverend and a panic-stricken Sasha James. Beneath him, the floorboards buckled.

Using the shelf for support, he pulled himself back to the keyhole only to discover he no longer held the key. *Where had it fallen?* He looked about, knowing that searching would be pointless. Books and debris were everywhere. Finding this needle in the haystack would be nothing short of a miracle.

Another blast from below sent him falling once more. This time, a portion of the floor fell away. He had just enough time to grab hold of the reverend, thus saving him from plummeting down.

He clung upon a ledge which was all that remained of the floor, gripping Xavier tight to him. The room was bathed in a red glow. He looked down into that hole. There was no more basement. Hell had literally broken loose.

The raging demons swirled within the infinite depths. He saw them and shuddered. Among the demons were others as well, tortured souls. Simon recognized one as the chief, but he was not the man he remembered. This creature was emaciated, beaten, covered in sores, and cowering like a bad dog under the scourge of a rolled-up newspaper. There also was Mr. Kahler, looking worse than earlier, if that was possible, as the demons swarmed like flies on his rotten carcass.

Simon looked away, but the image of those beaten slaves remained in his mind. It was an image he knew would never leave him.

Another slam and the remaining floor became less. He knew the house would not stand much longer. They had to get out *now*!

"Look at the light!" Simon heard Sasha's exclamation. He turned and saw the light.

***

Sasha couldn't believe their luck. Legion's tantrum actually broke a hole in the only spot on the house's exterior that had not been reinforced to prevent escape.

Daylight poured in through the crack in the book's shelf. Precariously balanced on the narrow ledge of floor that still existed, she began to kick at the hole, widening it with every strike. Unfortunately, she only got two solid kicks in before the next tremor hit.

Struggling to keep her balance and landing only inches from the drop-off, her eyes darted to the depths where chaos reigned. The demons stared up at her, locking their dead gaze against her living eyes. Seeing her so close to the edge of their world seemed to frenzy them. The swirling increased as they leapt for her like hungry piranhas, missing her by micro-measurements.

She scooted herself flush against the shelf and looked at Simon. He clung to the shelf with one hand. In the other, he held the dead-weight reverend by the shirt.

That last tremor dislodged Xavier, who hung half off the ledge, his legs dangling past the safety of the precipice on which they clung. Below, the demons congregated toward those low-hanging appendages, jumping and snapping their devil's fangs, missing their target only by inches.

***

Legion worked as a team. Some of them pounded the house down. Others used their tactics of terror as a last ditch effort to break the tenacious faith of their pets.

They knew the reverend was beyond their control to possess. They only hoped their little act would convince the other two they were far from safe.

***

Time ran out.

Sasha knew it.

In desperation, she smashed headfirst through the hole created within the bookshelf. The impact pained her, but she had no time to dwell on it. Shaking away the spots dancing before her eyes, she slammed her head into the crack again. Gaining ground, the crack widened. She found herself lodged in the hole like a cork in a bottle. Unfortunately, she had no corkscrew.

The fresh air outside motived her–along with fear of what may be grasping for her feet. She squirmed. She kicked. She grappled. Finally, she prayed and popped free.

She was outside. The air was warm, but she shivered as it touched her sweat-drenched body.

She didn't have a lot of room. The house was behind her and a dense row of shrubs hiding the secret entrance stood before her.

Her instinct told her to run away, but she didn't. Reaching back through the hole, she grabbed the first thing her hands touched. She pulled and the reverend's head emerged.

In the outside light his face looked even paler: the face of a dead man. Simon must have been pushing him from behind because the rest of Xavier slid through the hole in the house.

She laid him in the narrow space between the house and the shrubs. He was as still as a corpse.

She reached back into the hole for a third time and felt Simon's hand but before she could grip him, the demons struck the house with a mighty pounding.

Losing contact with him, she screamed as she stuck her head back through the hole, searching. She saw him bathed in the crimson glow. He was just to her left, clinging to the shelf because there was no floor left upon which to stand.

She looked down and shrieked. There, the demons swirled and roared. "Go ahead and abandon your friend! We will take good care of him!"

She looked back at Simon and noticed he was crying and so was she.

***

Simon considered letting go of the shelf and letting the demons take him. But, then he saw Sasha. She was crying. Somehow her tears motivated him.

He clung to that shelf with renewed vigor as the heat from the abyss penetrated his core, chilling him despite the heat. Still, he refused to look down. He knew what was down there and would not give that horde of demons the satisfaction. Plus looking down invited the temptation to surrender.

Instead, he kept his eyes on Sasha, whose face was haloed by the outside light of the hole. In that light, she looked positively angelic.

He tried to manage a smile. If he was to die, then he wanted her to remember him smiling.

The thought entered his mind: *Why don't the demons simply reach up and pluck me from the shelf.*

"Because you are mine," came the answer. It was that still quiet voice of Jesus once again. *Because you are mine.*

In that moment, everything fell into place. Simon realized the demons weren't taking him because they had no permission to do so. He belonged to one greater. He belonged to God.

Below, the demons taunted him, challenging him to let go and be taken. Like smooth-talking salesmen, they sweetened the deal with promises of treasure and honor and glory if he only let go of the shelf. He was no longer listening to them. He knew he had not followed God perfectly through all of this, but God had not abandoned him.

"Jesus, help me!" he screamed.

Instantly, stillness reigned.

"Jesus, save me," he said again, this time in a whisper.

Something touched his wrist. It was Sasha. She leaned in and grabbed for him.

Logic said her efforts were in vain. He was much bigger than she. There was no way she could pull him out of this mess. Then again, nothing that had happened to him within the last day had been logical.

She held on both of his wrists. Instinctively, he locked his hands on her forearms and leaned toward her. He left the safety of the shelf, feeling like Peter stepping from the boat to be with Jesus on the stormy lake. Only the toes of his shoes remained in contact with the shelf.

"On the count of three, jump to me!" she shouted—although in the unsettling silence—she really didn't need such volume.

"One," she said as he said a final prayer.

"Two," he heard her say as he mentally uttered "amen."

"Three." He closed his eyes, pushed off from the shelf, and put his life in God's hands.

He felt as if he were falling, but then their grip on each other tightened. Sasha's body slide a bit further into the house as she bore his weight, but then it stopped. She must have been able to brace her legs against the outside of the house.

The demons below him remained silent. He refused to look down at them but mentally pictured them churning in a swirling vortex of anger.

He knew God was with them, and there was no need to fear the evil below. Still, fear persisted. He continued to pray. He prayed hard.

***

By all accounts, Sasha should not have been able to keep Simon from falling. That was simple physics. She had learned however God was mighty to save. She knew His strength was saving them now.

Her knees hurt as she braced them against the side of the house and began to pull Simon to her. All the while, she continued to pray.

He neared the hole in the wall and she changed her position, putting her feet where her knees had been and therefore providing greater leverage. She pulled with all of her might and suddenly found herself falling backward upon the dirt.

Had she lost him? This was her first thought as she fell. No, she still had him in her grip. He came flying on top of her, free and clear of the abyss that claimed the house.

***

He rolled off her and thanked God for the miracle that had just occurred. Beside him was the reverend. Simon felt for a pulse. It was weak, but it was there.

Perhaps it was Simon's touch on the reverend's neck; perhaps it was the shrubs poking him. For whatever reason, Xavier opened his eyes and spoke. "It's not over yet."

"What?" Simon asked, but the reverend was once again unresponsive.

Chaos broke loose.

***

Legion raged. It was beyond angry.

Legion failed to obtain pets. It failed to obtain servants. It failed to crush the faith of the faithful. It failed to keep them from escaping the house. It failed!

The demons had not been so furious since Jesus banished them to the abyss. At least then Legion had been given the pleasure of killing a herd of pigs. Now, their pigs ran to safety.

In blind rage, it ripped the home apart, pulling it down with a great crash. It was not the same as destroying souls. It was not as fulfilling as killing pigs, but at least it was destruction.

It pulled with all of its might. It pulled out of desperation in an effort to salvage the day.

***

The house imploded upon itself, sinking into the earth. Outside, Sasha scrambled.

She got to her feet only to fall as the ground beneath her sucked her into the void where the house once stood. She scurried against the current, but within the disorientation of the landslide, she couldn't tell if she was gaining or losing ground.

She tried to scream, but her mouth quickly filled with dirt. Something slammed into her back. It was Simon. She felt his grip tighten in fistfuls of her shirt.

She looked up at him. He had the reverend pinched between his legs. The hand that had not grabbed her was holding onto the shrubs. His grip on those shrubs were precarious at best; the supple, thin branches slipping through his hands, leaves popping free as he slid. The soil continued to drain into the void where the house had once been, and the moving dirt continued to push against them.

She prayed to the Almighty for rescue. There was nothing else she could do.

Demonic voices boomed over the roar of the moving earth. They were laughing, cursing, and blaspheming all at once with their many voices.

In an instant, it all stopped. The demon voices stopped. The earth stilled.

She spit out a lump of mud and looked up at the other two. They were half buried. Simon's shrub-griping hand barely held the end of one young twig. He shook his head and a cloud of dust erupted from his hair. The Reverend remained unmoving.

She looked down at herself laughing and crying all at once. With effort, she broke free from the shallow grave which entombed her and staggered over to the others.

Together, they moved away from the rim of the great sink hole but only made it a few yards before collapsing from exhaustion.

Within the silence a sound emerged, a static-ridden noise. It took a moment to identify it.

Simon grabbed his police radio which had suddenly come back to life.

Sasha didn't realize until that moment she had been holding her breath. With the radio now working, she exhaled.

Finally, it was over. They were safe, and for that, she praised God.

One Year Later

Reverend Xavier Hernandez stood in front of the church and stared out at the full sanctuary massaging his still-healing arm. The doctors restored some strength and mobility but had not been able to fix the deep ache within. Massaging it helped.

Sasha, Simon, and he only referred to what happened to them as *the incident*. Perhaps in the future, they might talk about it more openly but for now they all seemed content to keep it buried.

He looked out the window of the sanctuary where the mobile blood drive truck was parked. He had become a big proponent of blood drives over the last 12 months. Without blood banks, he surely would not have survived that fateful day.

He looked at Simon who stood in front of him. He was so proud of that hero, the one who kept Sasha and himself from sliding into the earth when the demons pulled the house down. Since then, this man had made history as the youngest ever Getreide Police Chief. Even more, he was proud of the direction the man had taken. He had become deeply involved with his faith and started a ministry dedicated to helping victims of bullying and domestic violence.

Finally, the reverend looked at Sasha who stood beside Simon. She had grown in faith as well over the last year, leading Bible studies, studying the scriptures and helping Simon with his ministry by counseling women who had experienced abusive relationships.

He watched as Sasha gazed at Simon. Her expression could only be described as glowing.

He noticed that she started to treat Simon differently shortly after *the incident.* It was the way she would glance at him. Or, sometimes, she would touch Simon's shoulder when speaking with him and Xavier would notice her touch linger.

The reverend shook his head as he thought back on *the incident* that had brought these two together. God truly did work in mysterious ways.

He looked beyond Simon and Sasha glancing out at those who filled the pews. "Dearly beloved, we are gathered today to join in holy matrimony two of my dearest friends, Simon Birch and Sasha James. If there are any persons present who would object to this union, please speak now or forever hold your peace."

Xavier paused.

He could almost hear the many selves of Legion object—almost.

THE END

Acknowledgement

This book would not exist in its present form without help from others. I would like to take a moment and acknowledge these contributors. I've listed them here in no particular order.

I would like to express gratitude to Elizabeth Fortin and her staff at Tell-Tale Publishing for giving me this opportunity. Elizabeth, because of your fine eye for detail, this book really shines.

Many thanks to my agent, Christopher Liverman of Liverman Literary Agency. Your support, guidance, and direction keeps me focused.

Tiffany Harris, thank you for your manuscript analysis. Your grasp of the English language and the finer points of grammar are top notch.

Extra appreciation goes to my wife Katie and my children Zoe, Joshua, Elijah, and Paige. I know it's not easy living with a writer. Thanks for your patience, positive feedback, and constant encouragement. You guys rock.

Hats off to all the readers of fiction. Without you, there is no audience.

Kudos to the many others who inspire me, direct me, or motivate me in any way. There are too many in this list to include by name. Thank you all.

Most of all, I thank God. Your mercy and grace are beyond my understanding. You saved me and made me your child. Thank you Jesus.

About the Author

Shawn D. Brink resides in Eastern Nebraska and has been writing since old enough to hold a pencil. *Pets for Legion* is his fifth novel.

Shawn also has numerous shorter works in various publications and anthologies. When not writing, he spends time with family, church, and enjoys playing guitar.

For a complete list of published works and/or to learn more about Shawn's writing, please see:

https://shawnbrinkauthor.wordpress.com/

Shawn is represented by Liverman Literary Agency.